1

To the most beautiful woman in the world: My wife Theresa

To my beautiful daughters: Fallon and Danica

To my friends: You know who you are

To my parents: Ben and Pat

To my sisters: Rhonda, Lisa, and Sheri

To my in-laws: Bob and Jan

I love you all!

Chapter One

10 Days Before My Wedding Day

The Day Frownie Mae Disappeared

Two weekends before my wedding to Cherrie, I received an email from my friend Mark Smith. On the subject line Mark had typed in all caps: DO NOT OPEN UNTIL YOU HEAR FROM ME. That was an odd request, but I assumed it had to do with my wedding present or something along those lines. I already had a folder saved that I usually send important documents to; so I added Marks email to it. That was Saturday, four days ago. Today is Wednesday.

My cell phone vibrated in my back pocket. I removed it quickly and saw an incoming call from a number I did not recognize. That is not uncommon for me or my partner in crime, Ian Parker, since we are private investigators and have our cell phone numbers listed on our business cards. I touched the green square on the screen that read 'answer'.

"Dalen Reese, the worlds sexiest bald private eye at your service, how can I help you?" I thought I'd start the conversation out on a light note.

 That quickly changed when the woman on the other end of the invisible line spoke. She said, "Dalen, its Mrs. Smith, Mark's mother."

I recognized her voice, as I had spoken to her on many occasions. The Smiths lived in the subdivision behind McCatty Drive, the street I grew up on and where I currently live. Mr. and Mrs. Smith were probably ten years younger than my parents and, at the time, were the only African American family in our neighborhood, even though we lived in a suburb of Detroit. That was in the 1970's and early 1980's.

"Hello Mrs. Smith. How are…" I started to ask her how she was feeling, before she interrupted me.

"Mark is missing!"

I heard what she said, I was just not expecting her to say that. "What?" I said. I guess I was looking for confirmation.

"Mark…Is…Missing!" she said slowly and sternly.

I had heard correctly. I wanted to tell her to slow down, but she had already done that. "Ok," I said, letting her know that we were on the same page. "What exactly do you mean when you say, 'Mark is missing'?"

"Dalen, Honey, you know how Mark came down to Florida to pick me up and bring my back home so as I can attend your wedding to Miss Cherrie?"

"Mmm hmm," I said in agreement, without opening my mouth.

"Well Honey, we stopped at a roadside diner in Ohio, here, to get a bite to eat. We were just about finished when two young fellas, in suits, walked up to our booth and asked if they might have a word with my son. Mark must have recognized them and he asked me if I would mind going to the rest room for a moment while he had a word with the men. Well, Dalen, I knew we were about to hit the road again, so I thought it wasn't the worst idea. I excused myself and went to powder my nose. Now I assumed the gentlemen were fans of Frownie Mae or in the music industry or something like that but now I have the sneaky feeling that they may had been from the wrong side of the law."

"When did Mark go missing?" I asked.

"Dalen, Honey, when I came out of the powder room, Mark was no longer here, in the diner. His car was gone too. The men he was talking with are also gone. That was four hours ago. Now you know as well as I do that Mark would never in a million years leave me alone, at a diner, in Ohio, and not tell me where he was going."

"Mrs. Smith, did you contact the police?" I asked. That sounded like a stupid question, as I was certain she already had.

"I sure did. Two young men from the Ohio State Highway Patrol are here as we speak. Brenda, our waitress was kind enough to call them for me. She has been an angel through this ordeal."

"I assume you have filled them in on everything that has happened. Did they file a report? Have they put out an APB? Did you see what kind of car the two men were driving? I'm assuming you gave the officers the make and model of Mark's car, right?"

"I did, Honey, I did," she said.

I have to admit, for a woman that has been abandoned at a roadside diner, in the middle of nowhere, in B.F. Ohio, Mrs. Smith seemed remarkably calm.

"Mrs. Smith, are you calling me from your cell phone or from the phone at the diner?"

"From my cell phone, Dear," she said.

I pulled the phone away from my ear, put her on speaker, tapped a few times on the phone's screen and added Mrs. Smith to my contact list. "Would you mind handing your phone to one of the officers for a moment? I'd like to ask them a few questions."

She handed the phone to one of the patrol men. I heard a short, distant, and quietly muffled conversation between the two men before a voice spoke clearly into the phone, "This is Senior Patrol Officer Dale Fontana," the voice said. "Is this Mr. Dalen Reese I am speaking with?"

"The one and only," I said.

"How may I help you?" he asked. He sounded a lot like Dick Clark. I wondered if anyone had ever told him that.

I spoke to Senior Patrol Officer Dale Fontana for all of three minutes. He answered every question I had. He was blunt and polite. I jotted down the information on a yellow note pad I keep near the phone on the desk in the office, in the back of The Coffee Cabin.

When our conversation was complete, he handed the phone back to Mrs. Smith. She said, "Dalen, Honey, would you mind if I became an imposition and asked you to come pick me up? It doesn't appear as though my son is coming back to get me." For the first time in our conversation, I heard fear and concern in her voice.

I had brought up the address of the diner on Google Maps, from the laptop on the desk. "Mrs. Smith, I will leave in a few minutes. It looks as though it will take me five hours to get there, though. Is the diner open 24/7? "

"Yes, Honey, it is. Miss Brenda said she will stay with me until you arrive, or until Mark comes back; whichever happens first."

"Ok, Mrs. Smith. I'm on my way. Call me as soon as you hear from Mark. I'll get there as soon as I can." I ended the call without saying 'Good-bye'. I wished I hadn't but I was in I hurry. Now I felt bad, but I was sure she would understand.

I ripped the top page off of the note pad, folded it and placed it in my back pocket. Sweat had bubbled on the top of my head. A knot had tightened in my stomach. Adrenaline was beginning to pump through my veins. The race was on and I loved every minute of it.

Tondalaya, the afternoon shift manager of The Coffee Cabin, was behind the counter. At the moment, there were no customers present. I filled her in on what had just transpired. I called Aunt Lonnie and asked her if she and Uncle Bill could take over for Ian and me at midnight tonight and into tomorrow. Always there when we need them, she said she would. She said Uncle Bill was already taking a nap, so she would ask him to cover Ian's midnight shift. She said she would come in, in the morning, to cover my shift.

I kissed Tondalaya on the cheek, then left. I climbed into my 1999 dark green Jeep Wrangler with a black hard top. Before I left the parking lot, I called Ian and explained everything; at least what I could remember without looking at the yellow sheet of paper in my pocket. I had to swing by my house to grab a few things and told Ian

I would pick him up in 25 minutes. Ian also lives on McCatty Drive, so it wasn't out of my way.

We both live a five minute drive or a fifteen minute walk to The Coffee Cabin. I listen to music as often as I can. I flipped down the passenger sun visor. Strapped to the inside of it is a flat sleeve that holds 15 compact discs. I slipped the first one out with one hand and loaded it into the CD player in my radio console. All of the CD's in the sleeve were compilations I had put together with some of my favorite songs. *"With or Without You"* by U2 began to play.

Though my mind was on my missing friend and the unnatural events that were unfolding, the song brought back a memory.

I remember....

Ian said, "Are you ready for this?"

I was raising my chin so Ian could tie my bowtie for me. We were standing in the groom's room to the right of the altar at the First Presbyterian Church in Pontiac. It was my wedding day. I was about to marry Tara, the love of my life.

A young boy with very blonde hair said, "Dude, he was born ready!" That boy was Ian's nephew, Tommy. He was my ring bearer. He was 4. Everything he said sounded cute. He was always quoting movie and television lines, even when he didn't understand what they meant.

We were each in black tuxes and white dress shirts, with a blood red cummerbund and matching bowties. "Why didn't you get a clip-on tie like me?" Ian asked. "This doesn't look right. I don't know how to tie this stupid thing," he said. "Here, wear mine. I'll go without." He had quit trying to tie my bowtie and was unclipping the one around his neck."

"Keep yours on. I'll tie mine myself," I said. I slid over to a large oval, oak framed mirror that was mounted on the wall. I tied my bowtie the best I could. It looked right, but probably wasn't. It didn't matter. I stood in front of the mirror and starred at myself for a moment. I was about to get married. This was going to be the last time I would see myself as a single man. I looked good in the tux. Hell, every guy who ever donned a tux looked good.

Ian slid behind me. We made eye contact in the mirror. "Again, are you ready for this?" he asked.

"Like little Crash said, 'Dude, I was born ready!'" Crash was Tommy's nickname, because his last name was Crashowski. It fit him, too.

"Where are my shoes?" I asked, looking down at my feet. My black dress socks looked funny on me. They looked like nylons. I hated them, but Tara said I had to wear them. She strongly suggested I not wear my black tube socks with my tux.

"Here they are, man," Tommy said, handing them to me.

I had a bad feeling. I turned them over. My feeling was correct. Ian had used red nail polish to paint the word 'HELP' on the bottom of my left shoe and 'ME' on the bottom of the right. This was done so when Tara and I knelt down at the altar, our guests would get a good chuckle.

"You son-of-a-bitch!" I said. I tried to scrape the words off with my fingernail. It didn't work.

Ian laughed. "You better put them on. The ceremony is about to start." He laughed some more. Tommy laughed with him.

I shook my head as I sat down to put them on. The organist started to play music from inside the sanctuary. Butterflies danced in my stomach.

"It's show time," Ian said.

I stood. I walked over to the heavy wooden door with a tarnished brass handle. I placed my hand on it. I took a long deep breath and said, "Let's do this." I looked at Tommy. "Do you have the ring, little man?" I asked.

Tommy patted the right pocket in his little tuxedo jacket, double checking. He nodded.

I made eye contact with Ian. "I love you!" I said to him.

"Everybody loves me!" he said sarcastically.

"Dick!" I responded under my breath.

We stepped into the sanctuary. Ian received a shock to his hand, from the brass doorknob, as he started to close the door behind him. I laughed. We took our positions in front of our audience, next to the minister. The organist started to play, "You Are So Beautiful," a song originally recorded by Joe Cocker. Anna, our flower girl, started down the aisle dropping red rose pedals on the ground as she walked toward me. She was followed by Miranda, Tara's Maid of Honor. The organist switched tunes. She started playing "Here Comes the Bride"; at least that's what I assume it is called. Everyone in the church stood and turned around to watch my bride walk down the aisle. She was being escorted by her Uncle James. Tara was young when she lost her father. He was a cop that died in the line of duty. Tara looked more beautiful than any woman I had ever seen, at any moment, in my entire life. My butterflies disappeared. A calm feeling traveled through my body. Yes, I was ready to do this.

After the wedding was complete and the photos were taken, our limo ride to the reception was through and our exquisite dinner was consumed, Tara and I had heard a wonderful toast from both Ian and Miranda. I felt relieved when I finally had my chance to dance with my new wife.

We were introduced by the DJ for hire. Our song was supposed to be a song by Tim McGraw and Faith Hill, but our DJ started to play "With or Without You" by U2 instead. I thought it might have been a mistake. It wasn't. Tara had requested the change without my knowledge.

I took her hand and led her to the dance floor. We started to dance to the beautiful ballad. I dance with two left feet, but I did the best I could.

"This isn't Tim McGraw," I said softly into her ear.

"No, it is not. I asked him to play this instead. I hope you don't mind, Dalen," she said looking into my eyes.

"Not at all," I said. "I love this song."

"Dalen," Tara said. "Do you remember the promise we made to each other when we first started dating?"

"Yes. No lies. No secrets. No regrets. That one?" I asked, wondering why she was bringing it up now as I was trying not to look like a fool in front of all of our guests.

Tara nodded her beautiful little head in agreement. Our eyes were still locked. "I asked the DJ to play this song because I have something to tell you."

Shit, I did not have a good feeling about that statement.

"No secrets. No lies. No regrets," she said. "I do not want to start our marriage off with any secrets. I waited until after the ceremony to tell you. I didn't want to ruin that too."

I interrupted her. "Then don't tell me!" I said.

"Babe, I have cancer." Tears had filled her eyes. She was trying too hard not to blink.

I stopped dancing. A sudden lump appeared in my throat. It made it hard for me to swallow. Tears filled my eyes as well. I didn't try to hold them back. One blink was all it took for mine to run in a steady stream down my cheeks. My bottom lip was quivering. Tara had yet to blink. She was being strong.

In the background, someone started tapping on their glass with their silverware. More people followed suit. I took as deep of a breath as I could. Without breaking eye contact with me, Tara Reese rose up on her toes and placed a kiss on my lips. When she was finished and the applause had died down a bit, she buried her face into chest. She wept. Neither of us moved. Our DJ introduced the Best Man and the Maid of Honor and asked them to join Tara and myself on the dance floor. They did; more applause.

"What kind?" I asked Tara as we started to sway again.

"Breast," she said as a matter of fact, "breast cancer!"

Trying to sound positive and lighten to mood in front of our guests, I said, "They have made excellent strides in research and most women survive..."

Tara stopped me from continuing by placing her index finger on my lips. She shook her head, ever so slightly. "We'll talk about it later. For now, just keep your head up. I'll be fine. Let's enjoy the rest of the night." She stopped dancing and walked over to Miranda, whom she tapped on the shoulder. "May I cut in?" she asked, grabbing Ian's hand.

I followed Tara's lead. I took Miranda's hand and danced as well as I could with her. My wife danced with my best friend. Many other couples joined us on the dance floor.

"She told you?" Miranda asked me.

"She did!" I said.

"I begged her to wait until tonight, after this reception," she said.

"No secrets. No lies. No regrets," Miranda and I said in unison. Then we both laughed.

By the time U2 had finished and a song by Johnny Mathis had started playing, I had auto piloted myself home. I turned into our driveway and parked the car. I got out and went inside. Cherrie had been sitting at our kitchen table. She stood up when I walked in. I walked over to her, bent down and gave her a kiss on her cherry red lips. She gently took her thumb and wiped away a few tears that were resting on my cheeks.

"Tara knows you miss her," Cherrie said.

I took a deep breath and let it out slowly. "I know."

"Why are you home so soon? I wasn't expecting you until dinner time," Cherrie said.

"I received a phone call from Mrs. Smith; Mark's mom." I spent the next few minutes filling her in on what my plan was.

"Do you and Ian need a bag of snacks packed? I'm going to fill the cooler with ice, pop, and a few samiches," Cherrie said. I knew she meant sandwiches, she just never said it correctly. I tried to correct her once. It led to an argument that could have been avoided. I didn't correct her this time either. She continued, "Would you like meat and cheese or PB&J's?"

"Would you make four of each, please?" I asked as I headed to my bedroom to fill my duffel bag with a few things I might need for our journey. I packed a dark blue Hoodie with the old English D on the chest, a bottle of Tums, my prescription medicines, as well as Advil, and my toothbrush and toothpaste. I tossed in a clean pair of socks and a change of boxers. I laid my Wayne State University tee shirt on the top of the bag and retrieved my pistol and a small box of ammo from my nightstand. I wrapped them with my shirt and placed them in the duffel bag before I zipped it shut. I unplugged my phone charger from the wall and placed it in a side pocket. I went into the bathroom to take care of some personal business before our long drive. I carried my duffle bag to the kitchen and helped Cherrie clean up the tiny mess she had made.

The cooler was filled and was sitting by the back door.

"You better get moving. You don't want to keep Mrs. Smith waiting any longer than she has to," Cherrie said. She gave me another kiss, told me she loved me and watched me load my things into my Jeep and drive away.

I picked Ian up; he had been waiting outside in his driveway with a back pack. We hadn't been gone 15 minutes when Ian said, through a mouthful of food, "Is Mrs. Smith going to sit in the back seat with the cooler?"

It hadn't occurred to me that it might be difficult to fit three grown adults into my old Jeep Wrangler.

"Ummm, no?" I said, thinking about how it was going to work. "You can sit in back!" I said as a matter of fact.

"Yeah, right! All 6'4"of me is going to cram into the back seat of this tiny Jeep. Yeah, that ain't gonna happen!" Ian said, hoping he was convincing.

"Well, you can't drive a stick. I can. I'm not asking Mrs. Smith to drive, even if she can drive this Jeep. So unless you want me to turn around and we drive that beat up jalopy you have, you'll be straddling that cooler back there," I said. Ian drives a Dodge Avenger. It's not as old as my Jeep but it has been in a few wrecks. At least it runs. He can afford to buy a new car. I can too. But it's nice not having to pay a car payment. We have a friend that is an auto mechanic and keeps our cars running smoothly. We give him free coffee, daily. It's an even trade.

"I guess I'll just have to hang my feet out the driver's side window," Ian said laughing.

"The hell you will," I said.

"We could borrow Cherrie's Liberty. Do you think she'd let us?" he asked hopeful.

"I'm not asking her," I said. "You'll be fine back there. I'm sure of it. Besides, it'll only be a five hour drive back home." I started laughing.

Ian mumbled something under his breath. I laughed harder.

Chapter Two

We had been on the road nearly an hour. Ian had polished off his four sandwiches and asked if he could have my fourth as well. I was still on my third. "Go ahead," I said. I had already eaten one with ham and Swiss cheese, another with turkey and cheddar, and I was in the process of eating, what Cherrie called her 'sweet treat samich' which consisted of crunchy peanut butter with orange marmalade and fresh blueberries, all on two slices of her homemade banana bread. I hadn't gotten to my strawberry jam and Nutella sandwich, which Ian was currently biting into.

With a mouthful of food he said, "So, what do we know so far?" If there had been a woman present, Ian would have covered his mouth with his hand as he spoke while chewing. There wasn't. He didn't.

"Well, Mark left his mother at the diner in Ohio. Before that, two men in suits approached Mark while he and his mother were finishing their lunch. Mrs. Smith assumed Mark knew them by the way he acted when they asked if they could talk to him in private.

Mrs. Smith excused herself, at Mark's request, and went to the Powder Room; her words, not mine. When she returned, Mark was not at the table. She assumed he was outside talking to the men. She sat back down in their booth and waited for him to return. After approximately 10 minutes, she went to the parking lot and noticed his car was gone. She said she went back inside and tried to call him. She said the phone rang a few times before it went to voicemail. She patiently waited a short time before trying his phone again; same thing, voicemail. Her waitress, what the hell was her name?"

"I don't know," Ian said.

"That was a rhetorical question," I said. Ian knew it was. "Uummm…Brenda. Her waitress, Brenda, called the police. I'm sorry; I mean Brenda called the Ohio State Highway Patrol to report Mark missing. When the State Patrolman arrived, they interviewed Mrs. Smith. I spoke to a Dick Clark sounding guy named Senior Patrol Officer Dale Fontana."

"Dale Fontana?" Ian asked. "He sounds like he should have been a singer on American Bandstand in the 1960's. Dale Fontana! Ha! What kind of stupid name is that?"

"Ohhh kaaay," I said. "Anyway, Officer Fontana said he would put out an APB on Mark's car. Mrs. Smith did not see what kind of vehicle the other men were driving. Fontana also stated that a missing persons report has been filed on Mark."

"Did Mark have his Chrysler 300, the black one?" Ian asked me.

"He did," I said.

"Did Mrs. Smith happen to mention to the police that Mark is Frownie Mae?"

"I doubt it. I don't think she would have done that. But she didn't say so and Officer Fontana didn't mention it either," I said.

I don't know how Ian put away so much food, but he did. He had already finished eating five sandwiches. He dug through the cooler and pulled out an orange Faygo pop can. He popped the tab and handed the can to me. I thanked him before I took a couple of long swigs. He found a Rock & Rye, popped that tab, and drank half of the can in 10 seconds. Within one minute he would let out a lengthy belch. He was proud of it, too.

"Dale Fontana!" Ian said, shaking his head and laughing.

"Senior Patrol Officer Dale Fontana," I said.

"Hey, let me ask you a stupid question," Ian said. "Did you try to call Mark; I mean, after you spoke to his mother?"

Ok. That question hit me like slap across my face. How had I not thought to call Mark? I looked at Ian as he finished off his can of pop. "What do you think?" I asked sarcastically.

"Did it go straight to voicemail?"

I didn't answer. Instead, I took my cell from the back pocket of my jeans, held it above the steering wheel so I could see it and the road at the same time and I located Mark's number in my contacts.

Ian laughed and said, "The world's greatest bald detective strikes again. How could you forget the most basic rule in searching for a lost soul? The first rule from Detective Class 101 is; call the missing person. If they answer the phone, ask them where they are!"

"Shut up," I said. I turned down the radio so I could hear Mark better if he answered the phone. It went directly to voicemail. I didn't think it would do any good to leave a message. I was sure he would see my name on his missed calls list. I left one anyhow. "Mark, it's Dalen. Call me!"

"Good work," Ian said. "Where would you be without me? That's why we make a great detective team. I do the thinking, you make the calls."

"We are not detectives, Ian. We are Private Investigators," I said.

"Well, I like saying I'm a Private Detective. It sounds more rugged, more professional," he said.

I turned the music back up.

"Ian, a few days ago Mark sent me an email. On the subject line he typed, 'DO NOT OPEN UNTIL YOU HEAR FROM ME.'"

"Did you open it?" Ian asked.

"No," I said. "I saved it to a file in my email."

I still had my phone in my hand. Ian grabbed it from me before I could stop him.

"Is it in Yahoo mail or your Gmail?" he said looking at my screen.

I tried to grab my phone from him. He pulled it away from me.

"Don't open it!" I said, referring to the file Mark had sent me. I was serious.

Ian didn't care. He tapped the Yahoo mail icon on my phone. He clicked on the folders file. At the top of the list was the email from Mark Smith.

I reached for my phone again. I steered the car across the center lane nearly clipping an oncoming car. I grabbed the steering wheel with both hands and corrected my swerve. "Give me my damn phone!" I shouted.

Ian tossed my phone at my lap. It bounced off my leg and fell onto floor near my left foot. I left it there. It was safer where it was.

"Why won't you check the email?" Ian asked.

"Mark asked me not to," I said. It didn't sound like a valid excuse when I said it out loud. "Let's talk this through. Mark sends me an email and instructs me not to open it until I hear from him. Why? I just assumed it was note or something that he didn't want me to see until after my wedding. I don't know. I thought it could have been a receipt for a wedding gift or something. I didn't think it was a big deal, at the time."

Ian said, "Well, there is only one way to find out."

Together Ian and I said, "Open the email!"

Ian said, "It sounds like a no brainer to me."

"No," I said. "Mark asked me not to. I don't feel right about it. And besides, he sent it to me days ago. If it has anything to do with his disappearance, it would mean Mark knew he might be taken. Would he have put his mother in harms ways if he had thought that? Come on now, how does that make sense?"

"Maybe he thought his life could be in danger," Ian said. "Maybe that's why he sent you this email. How about this; let me open the email. If it pertains to your wedding, I won't let you see it. But, if it is something pertaining to his disappearance, I'll share it with you."

I didn't say anything for a few moments. I leaned down to pick the phone up from the floor of the car. I managed to keep the car in one single lane. I handed the phone to Ian. As Ian looked up the file, I asked, "If they were driving up from Florida, why were they stopped at a diner in the south east corner of Ohio? Wouldn't they have just stayed on I-75? I would have. I'll have to remember to ask Mrs. Smith."

"Son-of-a-bitch!" Ian said staring at my phone. "Son! Of! A! Bitch!"

"What? What is it?" I said, taking my eyes off the road, trying to get a look at my phone's screen. Ian held the phone so I could see it.

"Son-of-a-bitch is right!" I agreed. "Who the hell is that? Are you sure that is the right file; that's the file from Mark Smith?"

"Are you telling me that you have other pictures like this saved in other folders in your email?" Ian asked jokingly.

"Believe me; I don't," I said. "I'm just asking if you are sure that that file is from Mark."

"Yeah, it is," Ian said. "I want to know who these pictures are of."

I had flipped my blinker on and pulled over to the shoulder of the road. I turned the car off and activated my hazard flashers. "Let me see them," I said. Ian handed me my phone.

I scrolled through the photos attached to the file Mark didn't want me to open until he told me to. There were 15 pictures in all. There were no dates listed on any of them. There was no way to tell how old the photos were. What I could see, in all 15 pictures were two men; one black and one white. Both men were scantily dressed. What little clothing they had on appeared to be made of black leather. The white male had dark hair, slicked straight back with some kind of grease, though it could have just been wet. That was a possibility too. He had on a studded leather vest that exposed his hairy chest. More disturbing to me was the crotch less chaps he was wearing. He was well endowed and standing at attention in all of the photos. In 14 of the photos, the black male did not show his face, but exposed his naked rear. He was not wearing any clothes but did have a black leather biker cap on his head. The one photograph that did show his face was a bit too blurry to identify him. I could tell that both men were physically fit and appeared to work out regularly. Their bodies were well sculpted.

I used my fingers to enlarge the image and stopped when the white man's face was as large as the screen on my phone. I had never seen the man before. I had no idea who he was. "You don't recognize this guy?" I asked handing the phone back to Ian. I started the car and merged into the light traffic.

"I don't know who he is," Ian said. "I don't recognize the black male either, but with him there is very little to go on. No pun intended." Ian flipped through the pictures for another minute before closing the file. He handed me my phone. "The black man looks like he might shave his head. Wait a second!" Ian said enthusiastically. "Give me the phone back."

I did. He opened the file again and scrolled through the pictures. He stopped on one in particular. He zoomed in on the lower left hand corner of it. "There!" he said. "Look at that! What is that?"

I tried to see what he was showing me. Before I had any clue what it was, Ian shouted, "It's a finger!"

"OK. So there is a finger in the picture. That happens all the time," I said.

"Yeah. Yeah. But it isn't the finger of either man in the other pictures. They are both too far away from the shot. This finger belongs to a third person. A third person took these pictures!" Ian was clearly excited about this revelation.

"OK, Colombo," I said. "Can you identify the person the finger belongs to?" I laughed.

"No. But we know there are at least three people in the room. That's something," Ian said.

He was right. We now know there were three people in the room. Two of them were nearly naked. It is safe to assume that some kinky sex stuff was going on while the pictures were being taken. We know Mark Smith, aka Industrial Rapper Frownie Mae, picked his mother up in Florida and abandoned her at a diner in Ohio after two white men in suits asked him if they could have a word with him in private. The police had been contacted and Ian and I were on our way to Ohio to pick Mrs. Smith up and bring her back to Michigan.

I grabbed my phone again and called Mark. It went to voicemail. I ended the call.

"Can you pull over at the next rest area?" Ian asked. "I need to sit down for a few minutes, if you know what I mean."

Fifteen minutes later, I pulled into a rest stop. I had barely pulled the parking brake when Ian opened his car door and bolted to the building. "You probably shouldn't have eaten my last sandwich," I said to him, knowing he couldn't hear me. "It serves you right."

I walked to the rest room as well. When I was finished, I paid for a small cup of black coffee from a vending machine. I had finished drinking it before Ian exited the men's room. He dropped a handful of loose change into the candy machine and chose a couple of candy bars and a bag of generic potato chips. I just shook my head in disbelief as he unwrapped the first candy bar; a Twix. I paid for a second cup of coffee and we were on the road in no time. It was difficult steering the car and shifting it while holding my coffee without spilling it. I somehow managed.

When we were back on the road, I set the cruise control at 73. I switched the CD and turned the volume up when *"Highway to Hell"* began to play. Ian joined me in singing horribly and loudly. *"Stairway to Heaven"* came on next.

Ian asked, "Why is there a highway to Hell and only a Stairway to Heaven? Shouldn't it be the other way around?"

"Man, that question is way too complicated for me to consider. But now I actually have a vision of cars being driven to Hell by those entering as opposed to them taking the elevator I used to envision as a child," I said.

I joined Robert Plant singing *"Stairway."* Ian did not. Instead, he grabbed his backpack from the back seat. He removed a notebook and a pen, zipped the bag closed and returned it to the back seat. He slouched in his seat so his shins were resting on the dashboard. He opened the book to a blank page and began writing.

"What are you starting?" I asked.

"I'm going to write about our journey in finding Mark. I think I'll call it *Searching For Frownie Mae*. Though I guess that depends on the outcome. Right now, it's called *Searching For Mark Smith* but I like the other title better. I can't use Frownie Mae in the title unless it has a tragic outcome. I certainty do not want that to happen," Ian said. "I can't reveal his identity."

"How are you going to start it?" I asked. "You should start it with my phone call from Mrs. Smith."

"Sure," Ian said, "I'll just make you the center of attention. I'll write this all about you."

"That's not what I'm saying," I said.

Ian didn't respond. Instead, he let his pen do his talking for him. He wrote at a frantic pace. I guess he wanted to get his thoughts down before they disappeared.

When Led Zeppelin was finished with their anthem, a ballad from Air Supply started. "Every Woman in the World" brought up another memory.

I remember....

Tara's Doctor walked into the examination room. She closed the door behind her. Tara was sitting on the examination table. The bottom of her backless gown was tucked under her thighs. The

white roll of paper that covered the table crinkled under her as she
moved.

"Every Woman in the World" by Air Supply was playing through a
little round speaker mounted in the ceiling. A painting of a waterfall
attempted to decorate the drab cream colored walls. It was joined
by a few diagrams of the human body. I sat on a rollaway stool next
to Tara. I was holding her hand.

 Tara had been through an extremely trying year. After our wedding
and honeymoon, she started Chemotherapy and Radiation to battle
her cancer. Many days and nights were spent with her feeling sick to
her stomach. For too many days, Tara was in more pain that I could
ever imagine. The Chemo had played a temporary but nasty trick on
her nervous system. It attacked her hands and her feet. I wanted to
suffer the pain for her. If only I could have. And much to her dismay,
she had to deal with the loss of her hair; not only from her head,
which fell out in clumps, but also the hair from her eyebrows, arms
and the rest of her body. To her delight, it was all growing back. She
had been cancer free for six months now. We were in for her second
follow up exam.

"Mr. Reese," the doctor said. "It's nice to see you. How have you
been?"

"Give us more good news, Doc, and I'll tell you I'm great," I said.

She patted Tara's leg with three pats. "Tara," she began, "I have
some good news and some unexpected news. Which would you like
first?"

"Is the unexpected news also good news?" I asked.

"That depends on whether or not you were planning on having a child," she said, trying hard to hold back her excitement.

"What the...?" I started to say, before Tara demanded I not finish my thought by shouting my name and cutting me off.

The doctor laughed.

"Are you serious Doctor Manning?" Tara asked. She too, could hardly contain her excitement. She hopped off of table and spun around to face me. I stood up to catch her, in case she slipped on her stocking covered feet. She threw her arms around my neck and gave me a passionate kiss. I think she had forgotten the doctor was in the room.

A long moment had passed when Doctor Manning cleared her throat. "So, the good news is," she paused for a moment. When she had both of our attention, she continued, "You are officially six months cancer free." However, due to your previous predicament; we are going to keep a very close eye on you during your pregnancy."

The doctor and Tara continued to have a conversation, but my mind had wandered off to the impending birth of our child.

That night, after a celebratory dinner in front of two flickering candles, Tara led me to the bedroom of our two story condominium. She had a soft spot for Bryan Adams. She had all of his records. She chose his greatest hits, removed it from the paper sleeve, and placed it on the turntable which was on my dresser, lifted the needle's arm and gently placed it on the spinning vinyl. Through the quiet popping sound, Bryan began to serenade us.

Tara sat me on the edge of our bed and removed my shirt and then my blue jeans. She slipped her shirt over her head, unhooked her bra and let it drop to the floor. She slid out of her jeans and climbed on top of me, placing a pillow under my head. She placed a passionate kiss on my lips, before moving to my neck, my chest, and then further down my body. That was the beginning of one of the most enjoyable evenings of my entire life.

When the morning arrived, I made us breakfast. We had a discussion about possible names for our child.

"I was thinking if it's a boy," Tara said after she sipped some hot coffee, "we could name him after you. We could call him D.J. when he's young; ya know, Dalen Junior. What do you think?"

I didn't like the idea. "Possibly," I said. "I kinda wanted to name him after Edgar Allan Poe."

"Edgar or Allan?" Tara asked. "I really don't like either of them for our son."

"No," I said. "I was thinking of naming him Poe."

"Poe?" Tara asked. "Just...Poe?"

"Poe Edgar Allan Reese," I said as a matter of fact.

"But, Poe? You really want to name him Poe? Poe Reese?" she said with a wrinkled nose and a turned up lip. "Really?"

"I like it," I said.

"It sounds like a character from 'To Kill a Mockingbird' or an Alfred Hitchcock movie or something," Tara said. "Quick, someone call the

Poe Reese! I can't do that to him." She started laughing. "It's too easy for others to make fun of him."

"OK. It's obvious you don't like that choice. So, how about naming him Vincent?" I asked.

"After Vincent Price, I assume," she said.

"Yes." I drank some hot coffee and then stuffed a forkful of waffles into my mouth. I pushed them to my cheek and said, "We could call him Vin. Vin Reese."

Tara asked, "Why do you insist on our boy having a first name that only has 3 letters in it?"

I laughed. "That was not intentional. What are you thinking about a name for our daughter?"

"Well, sticking with your obsessive theme of Edgar and Vincent, I was thinking we could name her Raven," she said with a smile.

A chill and goose bumps ran along my arms. "I love it." I leaned over the kitchen table and gave her a kiss on her maple syrup tasting lips. "Raven, I just love it!"

Without my noticing, Ian had stopped writing and was talking on his cell. I assumed he was speaking to Nixie, his girlfriend of 4 plus years. There was a long minute where he didn't say a word to her. I assumed he was just listening to her talk. She loved to talk. He loved it when she did. When he finally did have something to say he said, "Today? You just sent it back today?"

As he listened to her talk, he kept nodding his head. A minute more went by before he said, "Ok. I love you." He pulled his cell away from his ear. He tapped the screen and ended the call.

"Do you know the novel I have been writing; The Coffee Cabin?" he asked me.

I nodded.

"Do you know how I didn't know exactly how to end it? Well, now I have the ending. It's different than I thought it would be but, I do have an ending for it."

I realized that his girlfriend Nixie, whom has been living in New Orleans for the past year as an art instructor at a community college, broke off their engagement.

"She just mailed her engagement ring back to me this morning," Ian said. "She sent it Fed Ex. She bought extra insurance, as if that makes it better."

I felt bad for him. He loved Nixie. I know Nixie loved him. She had taken the teaching job a year ago. Ian had only been down to see her once. He spent a week with her. That's when he proposed. Skyping everyday online was the only thing they had going for them. He wasn't going to move down to Louisiana and he couldn't bring himself to ask her to quit the job she loved and return to Michigan. They both knew the end was inevitable. The only thing left to figure out is who was actually going to end it.

"I'm sorry, Ian," I said. I didn't know what else to say. I knew he wasn't looking for advice. I didn't have anything to offer him either; at least nothing that wasn't cliché.

We sat in silence for the rest of the ride. At 9:30 in the evening, I pulled the Jeep into the parking lot of the diner. It was already dark outside. The diner was well lit inside. I could see Mrs. Smith sitting in a booth near the window. A beautiful blonde woman was sitting across the table from her. I assumed it was Brenda, the waitress. The parking lot had 3 cars in it. None of them were a black Chrysler 300. None of them belonged to Mark Smith.

Chapter Three

"Are you OK?" I asked Ian.

He nodded his head without making eye contact with me. He opened his car door and said, "Let's go get Mrs. Smith." In typical Ian fashion, he kept his feelings bottled up. I couldn't blame him. I do not like to share my feelings either. Ian knows that if he needs an ear, he's got mine.

I climbed out of the Jeep and closed the door. I met Ian in front of the door to the diner. I grabbed his elbow. He stopped. I wanted to let him know I was there for him. I knew he was hurting. His silence spoke loud. He looked into my eyes and nodded his head once. I knew he would be ok. It would take some time but he would be alright.

I nodded once too.

"I'm good," Ian said, before I could say anything. "I'm good." With that, he opened the single glass door to the diner and walked in.

I took a deep breath and followed him.

Mrs. Smith saw us enter. She slid out of the booth and approached Ian with open arms. She gave him a hug and then a kiss on his cheek before she greeted me the same way.

"It's so lovely to see you both. You two must be famished. Let me buy you dinner," she said.

I started to say, "No thank you," before Ian spoke up louder saying, "I'd love a piece of apple pie."

Mrs. Smith introduced us to her friend Brenda, the waitress. Brenda said it was a pleasure to meet us before excusing herself to get each of us a piece of apple pie, that Mrs. Smith had insisted I have.

Ian and I shared a bench and sat across from Mark's mother. She looked incredibly young and fit for a woman in her late sixties. Like most women, she never left her house without a bit of makeup on and her hair was always neat. It was slightly gray in one patch near her right temple. She had aged well.

While we waited for our apple pie slices to arrive, Mrs. Smith looked around the diner as if to make sure there weren't any eyes on us. When she felt safe, she reached into her purse and grabbed an iPad Mini. She pulled it out and slid it across the table to me.

"Mark left his computer screen on this table. He had hid it under this paper placemat," she said, lifting the corner of the one in front of her. "I'm pretty sure he wanted me to find it. But I still don't know why he left without saying a word. But there it is. Maybe you can find him by something he wrote on that screen."

I thanked her. I turned the screen on. It took a moment to light up. When it did, it asked for a user name and a password. I tried MarkSmith@yahoo.com. For the password I tried to input Frownie

Mae. I was unsuccessful. I tried a few variations of each, again, but to no avail.

"Mrs. Smith, would you happen to know Mark's ID and password?" I asked, assuming she did not know. I was correct. She did not.

Our slices of pie arrived. Brenda placed our plates in front of each of us. She had brought one for herself. She sat next to Mrs. Smith.

"Mrs. Smith, I took the initiative and assumed you would like a slice of cheddar cheese on yours. Was I correct?" Brenda asked. "Mrs. Smith told me earlier tonight that that is the best way to eat apple pie," Brenda said to Ian and me.

Our pies were just topped with the traditional spoonful of Cool-Whip.

"Dig in, boys," Mrs. Smith said.

I placed the iPad Mini on the seat between Ian and myself. We ate our pie. It was delicious.

"Mrs. Smith," I said, when our plates were cleared, "did Mark use this at all over the past two days?" I was referring to the iPad Mini tablet, as Ian was trying to unlock it.

"I never saw him use it. I knew he had it, but he wasn't using it when he was with me," she said, as a matter of fact.

Ian kept trying different combinations of words, names, and numbers with addresses. Nothing worked. He turned it off.

"Why did you and Mark stop here? Had you been here before?" I asked Mrs. Smith.

"No Dear. We had never been here before. We were hungry. It looked like a nice clean place to eat. Mark found it. I think there was a road sign for it a few miles back, off of the express way," Mrs. Smith said as she blotted her lips with the corner of a paper napkin.

Ian asked, "How did you both end in the south east corner of Ohio? I mean, if you were coming from Florida, why wouldn't you have come up I-75?"

"We spent last night at my Cousin Carol's house. She lives in West Virginia. We left before noon, this morning. I have no idea what roads we took to get there or here. Mark drove. I just put my faith in him."

"Well, that answers that question," Ian said. "Thanks for suggesting the pie. It was fantastic. Dalen slide out, I've got to hit the head before we leave."

I stood. Ian inched his way out of the booth and headed for the rest room.

"Excuse me Mrs. Smith, I'd like to have a word with Brenda before she leaves," I said.

I walked up to the counter where Brenda was pounding a pack of smokes with the palm of her hand.

"The pie here is wonderful," I said as I dug a twenty dollar bill out of my wallet. I handed it to Brenda. "Keep the change."

She punched some keys on the cash register and slipped the twenty into the slot with the other Jacksons. She removed a five spot and five singles from the drawer and placed them on the counter in front of me. I slid them back at her. She stuffed them in her jeans pocket. "Thanks."

"Do you mind if I ask you a few questions?"

"No, go ahead," she said.

"Were there any other customers in here when Mark disappeared; any regular customers that might have seen what transpired in the parking lot when Mark and the men from the other car drove off?" I asked.

"Let me think. Wanda was in that booth with Mandy. But they would have had their backs to the window. They were sharing a seat and looking at some bridal magazines. Mrs. Smith tells me you're the one that is taking the plunge next week. How nice for you. I was married once. It didn't work out. My ex..."

"Brenda," I said, trying not to be rude, "was there anyone else that you can remember?"

"Oh, I'm sorry Sugar," she said, blushing. "Umm, let me think some more." A moment passed. She had been pointing at the booths with her pen, talking to herself. "Miss Jackson was in booth number three, right there." She pointed with the pen again then walked to the booth and stood behind it. She leaned over the back of the backrest to get a better perspective of the parking lot. "Yeah, right here. Miss Jackson was right here. She would have been able to see what was going on."

Ian had joined Mrs. Smith in the booth. He nodded at me as if to tell me he was ready to go. I raised my index finger, suggesting we would leave in a minute.

I removed a business card from my wallet and handed it to Brenda. "The next time she comes in, could you please ask her to call me. I just have a few questions for her." Brenda took the card. "Did you happen to see or recognize the two men that came in to speak to Mark Smith?"

"No Sugar, I did not. They have never been in here before," she said.

"Did you wait on them? Did they order anything? Did they sit down? Did you actually hear them speak to Mark? Would you recognize them if they came in here again?" I asked.

"You already asked me that last question a moment ago. But my answer again is, 'No.' No to each of your other questions too, except 'Yes,' I will give Miss Jackson your card and ask her to call you the next time she comes in here. That should be on Friday for lunch. Miss Jackson always comes in on Friday and orders the fish and chips special."

I raised my hand to politely stop her from carrying on for another few minutes. She blushed again before apologizing. "We really need to get Mrs. Smith back to Detroit. It's been a long day for her and we have a long drive home. Thank you for taking such good care of her today. You are a wonderful, wonderful person. Please call me if you can think of anything else that might be helpful in finding Mrs. Smith's son. I know she is worried sick. She sure puts on a good front, though. Again, thank you."

I walked back to the table. "Come on Mrs. Smith; let's get you back to Detroit."

She and Ian stood. I helped her on with her coat. "You'll find my boy. I know you will." She grabbed my hand and patted it. "Bless you boys."

We said our final thank you and goodbyes to Brenda and walked to the Jeep. I opened the passenger door and helped Mrs. Smith climb into the front seat. I even fastened her seatbelt for her. I walked around to the driver's side and saw Ian standing beside the opened door. He just shook his head and said something under his breath before leaning my seat forward. He squeezed his large frame into the tiny back seat. When he was as comfortable as he could possibly be, he showed me his middle finger and shook his very red face some more. His legs were stretched to the passenger side floor mat. His back was resting on the small side window beside me. His head was tilted slightly to his left. I laughed then climbed into the front seat and started the engine. We were on the road and headed up north; driving into the nighttime sky.

"Mrs. Smith," I said, "did Mark make any phone calls on your phone over the past couple of days?"

"No. I don't believe he did. He did however receive a call yesterday afternoon when we were at Carol's house. He took the call onto the porch, for privacy. I didn't ask who it was. It was none of my business. If Mark wanted me to know who it was, he would have told me." Mrs. Smith looked puzzled. "Maybe I should have asked him. But I try not to live my life in hindsight. I'm sorry Dear, that's all I can remember about Mark's phone calls."

"That's fine." I reached over and patted her leg a few times. "We'll find him Mrs. Smith. I give you my word. We'll find him." I looked into the rear view mirror, Ian was either fast asleep or having been folded into a shoebox had cut off the blood running to his head and he had passed out.

"I know Dalen," she said. "I know you will dear. And thank you for rescuing me. I'm very sorry I've been an imposition."

"Please Mrs. Smith. You are not an imposition and we are happy to help. It's a long ride back and although this is not a Cadillac, why don't you try to get comfortable and catch some shut eye?"

Chapter Four

Before she could answer, my cell phone began to play 'Play that Funky Music White Boy', my ringtone. I removed the phone from my back pocket. I swiped my finger across the green phone symbol and answered it.

"Dalen Reese here; the world's sexiest bald private eye. To whom am I speaking?"

"Reese, its Macy."

"Detective Macy, to what do I owe this pleasure?" I said.

"It's Lieutenant Macy, now," she said.

"Oh, congratulations," I said. "I hadn't heard."

"It's neither here nor there. Do you have a minute?" She didn't wait for me to respond. "Robert Samuel Johnson is out!"

I felt my blood rush to my head. Sweat instantly bubbled on my bald scalp. A knot appeared in the middle of my back. The very thought of Robert Samuel Johnson upset my stomach, but to hear

Macy say those words, really pissed me off. Robert Johnson was The Trench Coat Rapist. He had terrorized the city of Detroit almost five years ago.

 He had raped many women including my daughter Olivia. When he was in the process of raping and nearly beating her to death, I interrupted him. We fought in a torrential rain storm. He had escaped from me. He stalked me and my family for the next several months before, as luck would have it, I was lucky enough to prevent him from attacking another victim. I had chased him through the streets of the city, before I nearly killed him myself. The police prevented me for doing so, which actually made me a local hero.

Johnson was sentenced to eleven years in Jackson State Penitentiary. He was only convicted of one rape, Olivia's. His lawyers managed to successfully defend him against every other count of rape or attempted rape.

"What the hell are you talking about; he's out?" I asked. My voiced cracked as I spoke.

"It appears he was released with time off and money," Lieutenant Macy said.

"What does that mean?" I asked. I had raised my voice. Ian woke up. He nearly hit his head on the ceiling of the cab of the Jeep. We made eye contact in the rear view mirror.

"According to the memo I have in front of me," she said, "it means the time he had served in jail while the court proceedings were taking place, count toward his time served. He must have had excellent behavior in Jackson, because he was up for his first parole hearing last week. Now I can only assume that the judge, the warden, and /or the parole board were also paid some serious cash to approve his release. It is not unheard of. But that is beside the point. I'm calling you to let you know he was released and is now a free man. His time has been served. However, with the animosity I believe he has toward you, I wanted to give you a heads up. We both know what he is capable of. I do not for a single second believe that he has been rehabilitated."

I didn't care how he got out. All I cared about is that he was out. The man that nearly killed my daughter was a free man. I punched the steering wheel of the Jeep. The horn honked. I didn't care. I hit it again. Another honk! And again and again and again. Honk! Honk! Honk! I actually hurt my knuckle the last time I hit it, so I stopped. I removed the phone from my ear and swiped the red phone symbol to end the call. I rolled my window down, manually, as fast as I could. The cold air slapped me in my face. I pulled the car over to the shoulder of the road. I jumped out and began walking in a small circle, in front of the car. I started screaming a string of profanities at the top of my lungs.

I hadn't noticed that Ian had climbed out of the back seat. He approached me from behind and wrapped his arms around my waist. My arms were snug against my sides, tightly in his grip.

"Stop!" Ian said in a calming voice. "Stop!"

I let out one more loud scream; a roar if you will. I actually hurt my vocal chords with that one.

"Stop," Ian said, practically whispering in my ear.

I heard him. I took a very deep breath. The cool evening air felt nice on my throat. I took a second breath and looked Ian in his eyes. "That son-of-a-bitch is out," I said. "They released him today. He is a free man."

I made eye contact with Mrs. Smith. Her face was dimly lit by the interior lights of the dashboard. I had forgotten for a moment that she was in the car. "Let's go," I said to Ian.

I waited for him to climb his tall frame into the tiny back seat. When he was in, I returned my seat to the driving position and I climbed in as well. I shifted the car as I reentered the highway.

Mrs. Smith hadn't said a word. I'm quite sure she didn't want to be nosey.

"Mrs. Smith," I said.

"Yes dear," she responded, turning her head to look at me as she spoke. She had her hands folded neatly in her lap.

"I apologize for my behavior back there," I said.

"There is no need to, sweetheart. You were just expressing your feelings," she said politely.

"Detective Macy... I mean Lieutenant Macy just informed me that Robert Samuel Johnson has been released from prison. I just realized that I hung up on her. Maybe I should call her back," I said.

From the backseat, Ian said, "You don't really hang up a cell phone, Dalen, you more of less just end the call. I believe you can only hang up a land line phone where you have two separate pieces that..."

I shot him the nastiest look I could make, in the rear view mirror. He stopped talking immediately.

"Dear," Mrs. Smith said. "Try not to let your imagination take control of your life. You do not know what Mr. Johnson is going to do. His attentions have not been made clear. It is very possible that he is in fact rehabilitated. He may not even attempt to contact you. The best thing you can do is not worry about what might happen. Do not assume that he is out to get you. Just worry about what happens as it happens. Do not question the future before it arrives and, as hard as it might be, do not live in the past. I am not suggesting you forgive or forget what he did but rather hold your final judgment until the end. Things may play out just fine."

I listened to what she had said. I took a deep breath and slowly exhaled. Mrs. Smith made sense. I thanked her. She had managed to help me relax. And I knew she was correct. She gently patted my thigh. I smiled at her. She returned her attention to the road ahead of us.

Ian had fallen back to sleep. I had a lot to think about. I had my upcoming nuptials, my dear friend Mark Smith was missing, and now the man that raped my daughter was no longer incarcerated. Mrs. Smith sat silently.

"Do you mind if I turn the radio up?" I asked.

Mrs. Smith did not respond. Instead, she used her left hand and turned the dial up herself. I smiled.

"I love this song," she said as a matter of fact. "Though Michael Bolton is no Otis Redding."

The song that was playing was *Sitting on the Dock of the Bay*.

I started to remember…

"Dalen, do you want a hotdog or pizza?" Tara asked me as we stood at the concession stand and looked up at the menu over head. We were at the Palace of Auburn Hills, in Michigan. It was New Years Eve. I had bought Tara concerts tickets to see Michael Bolton so we could ring in the New Year together.

Tara looked amazing that night. She always looked beautiful, but when she did herself up, man, she really looked good. She had purchased a royal blue sparkly dress. It stopped just a few inches above her knees. It was a low cut dress with spaghetti straps. She had a white knitted shawl over her shoulders. She wore blue shoes that matched her dress. Her long blonde hair was pulled up in the back and tied at the top of her head with a blue ribbon. She smelled of lavender.

I looked over at her and said, "I can go for a few hot dogs."

Tara told the young lady working at the concession stand that we would like to have four hotdogs and two draft beers. Three of the dogs were for me. We took our food and drinks to our seats. They were eight rows up and on the side of the stage. They were very good seats.

Tara was excited to see the man of her dreams in concert. I was sure most of the men attending the concert that night had an ulterior motive. I assumed they were all hoping his baritone voice was going to turn their dates on so they might reap the reward later that night.

Our hotdogs were not yet warm and the beers were not yet cold. Cold dogs and warm beer were not my idea of a decent meal; still I managed to make them all disappear. Tara did not finish her beer. I drank it for her.

A half hour had passed since we had finished our dinner. The start of the concert was still an hour away. The arena was beginning to fill with nicely dressed women. They were all with men that looked like they didn't really want to be there.

I began to feel flush. It was really getting hot in The Palace. I took my sport coat off and rolled up my shirt sleeves. It didn't help, much. "I think I'm getting sick," I said to Tara.

"If you didn't want to come, why did you buy the tickets? I'm going to sleep with you anyway," Tara said, laughing.

I grabbed her right hand and placed it on my clammy forehead. Her cool hand felt nice.

"Let's get you some fresh air," she said. "Leave your coat on the chair. It'll be fine." She took my hand and led me up the stairs, like a little boy following his mother. We arrived at the top step, in the corridor, when I felt my stomach launch my dinner into my throat. I quickly covered my mouth with my free hand. I managed to keep my dinner from coming out.

"I've got to get in there," I said to Tara, as I pointed to the men's room. I sprinted. I found an open stall, dropped to my knees and tossed all my dinner and the warm beers into the bowl. It burned my throat. My bald head broke into a cold sweat. I had chills. I didn't feel much better. Just as quickly, I realized I needed to sit down to accommodate my queasy stomach's impulses. I lined the seat with toilet paper; long strips of double folded toilet paper. I am a bit of a germaphobe. When I was finished with my personal business, I pulled my trousers up, buckled my belt and went to wash my hands and face with cold water. I began to feel more normal. My skin began to cool down.

I walked back into the corridor and looked for my bride. I didn't see her. I went to the top steps and looked down at our seats. They were empty. I assumed she was in the ladies room. I leaned up against a cement pillar. I folded my arms and watched the passersby. There were a lot of scantily clad dressed women with big hair and men with mullets and sport coats. I took a Swisher Sweet cherry cigar from a pack in my pocket. I lit it with my Bic lighter. Smoking was still allowed in the corridors back then, but not in the seats. I began to pace as I waited for Tara to exit the restroom. I walked from one section of the stands to the next and back again. I checked my watch.

More and more women entered the restroom. Fewer and fewer women came out. I paced some more; back and forth, back and forth. I was trying to look as tough and as cool as I could at a Michael Bolton concert. I finished my cigar and disposed of it in the proper receptacle. Finally, Tara emerged, looking even more beautiful. I never knew how that was possible, but she always managed to accomplish it.

"Are you feeling better?" she asked.

"I am," I said. I took her hand and led her behind me, down the steps toward our seats. She let go of my hand after we went down a couple of steps. I thought nothing of it. I just assumed she was following me. I continued down the stairs.

"Dalen!" Tara said from rows and rows above me. I turned around.

"Come here!" she said in a stern voice.

I was one row from our seats. I assumed she wanted to be escorted down the rest of the way. I thought, "Well, you should not have let go of my hand." I didn't want to walk back up the forty or so steps, so I just said, "What?" I was slightly perturbed.

"Dalen, get up here!" she said. She pointed to the step directly in front of her. "Now!"

People were looking from her to me and back to her. I was embarrassed.

"Just come down here," I said and I started to walk down the row to my seat.

"Dalen!" Tara said again. I looked back up at her. She was shaking her head, frustrated, yet somewhat amused. I watched her as she marched down the steps with a purpose. Even mad, she looked amazing.

Tara reached our row and walked to my side. "Turn around!" she said to me.

"What? Why?" I asked, very confused.

Tara placed a hand on each of my shoulders and spun me around so my back was facing her. She swiped her hand at my waist and grabbed a long tail of toilet paper from my waistband. It had been flying like a kite tail behind me everywhere I paced or walked, for the last ten minutes. She held it out, in front of my face and said, "It's really hard for a man to look cool at a Michael Bolton concert. It's even harder for him to look cool at a Michael Bolton concert with a roll of toilet paper flying from his ass!"

There was laughter from the audience in our section. Then there was applause. I took the TP from her and used it to wipe the sweat off my head before I sat down.

We made two pit stops on the way back to Detroit. I bought a cup of black coffee at each one. I listened to the third period of the Red Wings and Maple Leafs game. Ken Kal and Paul Woods had the call. The Wings won the game in regulation: 3-2.

Mrs. Smith said, "Dalen, you must be excited about your wedding."

I wanted to smile and tell her everything about it. I wanted to explain what Cherrie's dress looked like and the changes we had made to The Coffee Cabin, where we're having the wedding and the reception. I wanted to tell her about the guest list and anything else I could think of. Instead, I maintained my composure and with a relativity straight face I said, "Yes. I'm stoked."

"Stoked?" she asked with a puzzled look on her face.

"Yeah, stoked! It means happy or excited. I guess I picked that phrase up from Crash." Crash is Ian's nephew. He spends a lot of time at the Coffee Cabin and occasionally helps Ian and me out with our P.I. work.

"Didn't Tommy get married to Emma last year?" Mrs. Smith asked.

"Hemma," I said. "Her name is Hemma; with an H. But yes, they married last summer. Tommy, or 'Crash' as he still likes to be called, is actually Cherrie's camera man and producer. You do know that Cherrie has that show on the Food Network, right? It's called Very Cherrie. They film it right here in Detroit." Technically, we weren't in Detroit yet. We were on our way and getting closer. But, she knew what I meant.

"It's a very good show. I record every episode and watch it after Wheel of Fortune is finished. She is so darn cute," Mrs. Smith said.

"I know, right?" I said. I was beaming with a bright smile as I spoke. "Hemma passed the bar last year, a month before they got married." I had returned the conversation to Tommy and Hemma. "Hemma is working with Walt Perkins. He left Johnson, Smith, Urban, and Yablonski."

"Attorneys at law," she sang, on cue. It's what you do whenever you hear the names Johnson, Smith, Urban, and Yablonski. Their radio jingle has been played on the radio and television for more than 30 years.

I nodded. "Right. Anyhow, Hemma is working with Walt Perkins. They have a pretty nice divorce firm in Rochester."

"Now, is Hemma," she said with emphasis on the H, "the waitress that used to dance on the tables at the coffee house?"

I laughed in remembrance. "She is. Walt's wife, Tondalaya is still the manager at The Coffee Cabin. It's like we are all just one big happy family. You could play 6 Degrees of Dalen Reese with us."

"Pardon me?" Mrs. Smith said, confused.

"Nothing," I said. "It's just a game normally used with Kevin Bacon." I was pretty sure I had lost her so I just carried on with our Michigan updates. "Last summer, we had 3 weddings. Tommy and Hemma married first, Sharona and Ricky married next. Sharona is the other blonde waitress. And Ian's ex, Rita, finally married Bob, after a long engagement."

"Bob is the rich car dealership guy, correct? He's the guy with the commercials on local TV too. The last time I stayed up here for a week, it seemed like every time advertisements were on TV, it was either his ad or Johnson, Smith, Urban, and Yablonski ..."

Together we sang, "Attorneys at laaaaaw!" just like in the jingle. Then we laughed.

After the smiles faded, Mrs. Smith asked, "Dalen, is Robert Samuel Johnson any relation to the Johnson from the law firm?"

"He is indeed. He is the son-in-law of the Johnson from the law firm. I'll bet that the Papa-in-law actually had a hand in Robert's early release," I said. A knot re-appeared in the middle of my back as I said that. It hurt like hell. "Can we change the subject?"

Mrs. Smith simply said, "I'm sorry." She returned her hands to her lap. Her fingers were laced. She stared straight ahead.

The street lights passed by at an alarming rate. They actually looked like strobe lights blinking inside the car. I slowed the car down. The lights blinked slower. We passed the Detroit Zoo water tower on Woodward Ave. We would be home soon.

She smiled. She was a very beautiful woman. I just reached over and patted her forearm. Within minutes, I dropped Mrs. Smith off at her friend's house, a block away from Ian's.

"Mrs. Smith," I said, as I helped her climb out of the Jeep, "do you think Mark knew the two men he left with? I mean, what was his initial reaction when he saw them walk through the door of the diner? Did he say anything to you before they reached your booth?"

"I thought I saw Mark blink pretty fast, a few times, almost as if he were trying to focus on something or someone. It was almost as if he truly couldn't believe his eyes were seeing what he was actually seeing. But he has always been one to keep his composure," Mrs. Smith said. "It all happened pretty quickly. I may just be reaching for straws. I cannot be certain he did that, and my recollection is only in hindsight. Maybe I am just imagining his reaction. But, no, Mark didn't say anything before the gentlemen arrived at our tableside and yes I do believe he knew the two men."

"They are not gentlemen, Mrs. Smith. They kidnapped your son," I said. I closed the door behind her and retrieved her bag from the small trunk of my car. I gave her a kiss on her cheek and waited until she was in her friend's house before I took Ian home.

It was nearly three o'clock in the very early morning before I climbed into bed, next to Cherrie. I kissed her on her forehead and whispered, "I love you," into her ear. I was exhausted. I covered her up with the blanket and within a few minutes I fell asleep next to the woman I love.

Chapter Five

9 Days Before My Wedding

Day 2 of Frownie Mae's Disappearance

I woke up and called Aunt Lonnie. I asked her if she and Uncle Bill could cover more of my and Ian's shifts. They cover a lot of days for the two of us, as our private investigative agency seems to take us away from The Coffee Cabin more and more often. They are great people and love helping us out as much as they actually love working there.

I woke Cherrie up with a kiss on her neck. "Come back to bed for a bit," she said.

"I'm not tired. I have a lot of things I need to do," I said as I kissed the other side of her neck.

She wrapped her arms around my waist and pulled me on top of her. "They can wait, I can't," she said as she slipped my boxers down my legs.

When we had finished messing up the sheets, I climbed into the shower. I washed and then shaved my head. I dried off before dressing myself in my jeans, my best Tigers T-shirt and my favorite blue Tigers hoodie. I looked at myself in the mirror above Cherrie's dresser. My beard was more grey than brown. I had bags under my eyes that, when I didn't wear my glasses, made me look like I hadn't slept in months. Aging has not been kind to me.

Cherrie walked up behind me and straightened out the hood on my jacket. "You look so sexy with your head so shiny and smooth." She ran her hand over my scalp.

"I'm thinking of shaving my beard off before the wedding," I said to her reflection in the mirror.

"I won't love you any less," she said. With that, she turned and walked out of the bedroom.

I wasn't sure if that was a, "do it" or "not" from her.

I walked into the kitchen where she had just finished pouring me a hot cup of coffee. She handed it to me. "Is this payment for a job well done," I asked.

"No, that deserves a full pot." She smiled.

I bent down and gave her a kiss on the top of her head.

"Is that my payment?" she asked.

I smiled. "No." I planted a kiss on her lips. I lifted her up and placed her on the kitchen counter. I kissed her some more.

Not wanting to dampen the mood, but feeling like I had to, I said, "Johnson is out."

Her smile slowly disappeared. She knew exactly what I meant. I didn't have to explain who Johnson was or what he was out of.

"Are you fucking kidding me?" she whispered.

I stared at her and shook my head. My heart began racing, again.

"Does Olivia know?" Cherrie asked.

"I'm assuming Macy called her. I didn't think to call her last night. How the hell could I not have thought to call her? She needs to know. I should have called her last night. What kind of father am I?" Now I was mad at myself. I removed my cell from my back pocket. "I'll call her now." I took a sip of coffee. It warmed my insides.

I found Olivia's number in my contact's list. I tapped the green phone symbol. It rang twice before going to voice mail. I left a message, after I was instructed to. "It's Dalen, er, ah, Dad. Call me please." I ended the call.

"Smooth," Cherrie said. "Er, ah."

Thirty seconds went by when my cell rang. The screen lit up with a picture of Olivia.

"Hi Honey," I said, when I answered. "Do you have a minute?"

"Dad, Lieutenant Macy called me last night. He's out!" she said. There was a sound of fear in her voice.

"I know. She called me, too. But, Livy, listen. I promise you, I will not let him come near you," I said as a matter of fact. I tried to sound confident. Inside, though, I had as much fear as she did.

"Lieutenant Macy said that she would have me covered. Those were her words, not mine. But what she meant was that she, or Detective Larkin, or any other of her police friends would be watching out for me. She said that someone would be covering me at every hour, day and night. She assured me that I did not have to worry. She said that just because I don't see one of them, it doesn't mean that they are not around. She made me that promise. And Dad, I believe her."

Macy hadn't filled me in on any of that, but I really didn't give her a chance.

"That's comforting," I said. And it was. I felt a small bit of relief. "Is someone watching you now?"

"I'm looking out my window now. I don't see anyone outside. But, that's the point, I assume, not to see them," Olivia said.

"Ok. I agree. If Macy says someone is covering you, then someone is. So, what are your plans today?" I asked.

"Dad, I'm not going to report my schedule to you every day. You do not need to worry about me. Don't become obsessed with this. Please, live your life. Everything will be alright. You are getting married in a week. That's what you need to be worried about. Oh, and Cherrie said that Mark Smith is missing. Tell me about that."

"Ha, I see what you are doing. I'd love to tell you about it but I don't have time to. I need to get to work on that." She was right. I didn't need to worry about her. "I've got to let you go," I said. "I love you, Honey. Call me if you need me."

"I love you, too. Go find Frownie Mae," she said.

I ended the call.

Cherrie asked, "Is she ok?"

"She is. Macy has eyes on her 24/7. Hey, let me ask you. Do you know how to get into a tablet if you do not know the password?" I said.

"Can I break into it? Did you forget your password again?" Cherrie asked, laughing.

"It's Mark's. He left it at the restaurant. Mrs. Smith gave it to me. She believes Mark left it behind for Ian and me to get into. We tried to unlock the password and ID and stuff, but can't. Can you?" Cherrie is much better with computers than I am.

"No. You should ask Raven. Maybe she knows how to or knows someone that can," Cherrie said.

"Good idea. Hey, do you know who this is?" I asked, flipping through my cell phone to show her the pictures Mark had emailed me. I found them and handed her the phone. "Scroll to the left to see more."

She did. "I've seen this guy before." She was pointing to the white man in the pictures. "I can't think where from, though." She scrolled left again and again until she had viewed them all. "It'll come to me."

"Mark didn't want me to open the file until I heard from him. Obviously, I have not heard from him. Ian opened them. I do not know if they have any connection to his disappearance or not, but I'd love to find out. I will find out. I will find Mark. But first I need to unlock his tablet. I've got to go. I love you." I gave her a kiss. "Do you want to meet for dinner?"

"I do. Call me later, ok? I love you too," she said.

I gave her another kiss and headed for my Jeep. I made sure I still had the tablet with me. I headed to The Coffee Cabin. Raven was working the morning shift. If she couldn't help me, she could direct me to someone that could. I almost made it off of McCatty Drive before Mrs. O'Flannigin flagged me down from the bottom of her driveway.

I thought about not stopping. I thought I could just wave and drive by. But I didn't. Instead, I rolled my window down. It was colder outside than I thought. Mrs. O'Flannigin was standing in her pink robe and matching Deerfoam slippers. She was holding a copy of the Detroit News under her arm.

"Good Morning Mrs. O'Flannigin," I said forcing the biggest smile I could muster. She looked older than her 90 years of age.

"Dalen, will you do me a huge favor?" she asked.

I have been doing her huge favors since I was in diapers. "What can I help you with?" I asked.

"Would you bring that red headed boy over and move my couch for me?" she said without her false teeth in her mouth.

"Sure. We'd be happy to help you out. Just give me a couple of days, ok?" I said hoping that would be the end of our conversation. It wasn't.

"I just can't move the couch like I used to be able to," she said.

"OK. We'll come over in a couple of days. But right now, Mrs. O'Flannigin, I really need to get moving." I started to roll up my window.

"Dalen," she said.

"Gotta go," I said. "Sorry. I just have…" I finished rolling up my window and shifted from neutral to first gear. I was off. She stood in her driveway still talking to me, as I turned onto the main road. I figured that she wouldn't hold it against me, if she even remembered that I had driven off in the middle of her conversation.

I made my way to The Coffee Cabin within five minutes. I parked in the back. Melvin, a homeless man, was sitting outside of the building with his back up against the wall. He was drinking a warm cup of coffee. Steam was rising from the Styrofoam cup. I knew his coffee had two creamers and four teaspoons of sugar in it.

"Good morning Melvin," I said as I passed by him.

He nodded and raised his cup at me.

I walked through the back door and went into my office. I sat at the desk Ian and I shared. I looked up at a poster I had recently hung up. It was of Paul Newman as Cool Hand Luke. "Good Morning Luke. Do you know how to unlock a tablet without the password?" I waited for a response. He just stared at me with those ice blue eyes of his. "That's ok. I'll get Raven to help me," I said to him.

"Help you with what?" Raven asked as she stood in the doorway to the office. She looked so much like her mother. The older Raven got, the more she sounded like her too. Raven was a beautiful young woman now. She was no bigger than 5'1" and might have weighed a hundred pounds, soaking wet. Her hair was its natural light brown color for once.

"Mark left his tablet for me. At least Mrs. Smith believes he did that. The only thing is, Ian nor I can unlock it without his password. Can you?" I asked her.

"No, but Colton Lewis can," Raven said as a matter of fact. "He can hack anything." She was searching her phone for his number. "Hang on," she said to me, holding up one finger.

"Colton, my father needs your expertise. Are you busy?" She waited for a moment before saying, "Cool. Thanks." She ended her phone call. "He'll be here in five minutes."

"Damn," I said, amazed at how quickly she had handled Colton. "Really?" I asked, still in amazement.

"Just go get a cup of coffee. He's on his way." She smiled and left the office.

I went into the lobby and said good morning to Aunt Lonnie. I gave her a kiss on her cheek. I poured myself a hot cup of Joe. I took a seat on the barstool nearest the end of the counter. I watched the end of an episode of Good Times, which was playing on all four television screens. There was one mounted in each corner of the walls, near the ceiling. Jimmy Walker was in rare form. "Dyn-o-mite!" I laughed. He got me every time.

I was sipping my coffee. It was still very hot. Colton Lewis slid onto the barstool next to me. He sat his laptop on the counter in front of him. He opened it up and started typing.

"Good morning Colton," I said without taking my eyes off of the TV.

"Good morning, Sir," he said. Type. Type. Type. "Is this the tablet I'm taking care of for you?" He grabbed it from in front of me before I could answer. He plugged a cord into the port and ran it to his laptop. Type. Type. Type. "Do you want me to reset all the passwords to something or would you prefer to have them bypassed?" Type. Type. Type.

"Bypass them all, please," I said.

Good Times segued into *What's Happening!!* with Raj, Dwayne, Rerun, Dee, and Shirley. "Oooo, I'm going to tell Mama!" I could have watched this channel all day. I knew *Sanford and Son* was coming up next.

Type. Type. Type. "Ok, you're all set," Colton said. He unplugged the cord from both ports and stuffed it into his coat pocket.

"You're all done?" I asked. "That was fast."

"I aim to please," Colton said. He slid Mark's tablet back in front of me. He restarted it. "When it turns itself back on, you'll be able to get onto every app, email address, and website that is on it."

"What do I owe you?" I asked Colton.

"I didn't do this for you. I did it for Raven. Just tell her I aim to please." With that, Colton stood up, swiped his laptop from the counter, slipped it under his arm and walked over to Raven. He said something to her. I couldn't hear what he said. Then he left.

Raven walked up to me and kissed me on my cheek. "You owe me, big time," she said. "He's taking me out to lunch today. I hope it was worth it."

"Me too," I said. I took my phone from my pocket and opened the pictures from Mark's email. "Do you know either of these two men?" I handed her my phone. "There are more, if you swipe left."

She did. "The white guy looks like Ralph Dixon." She said it like she knew him personally.

"Who the hell is Ralph Dixon?" I asked.

"Ummm, he's Michigan's Lieutenant Governor!" she said with a "Duh" type of attitude, as if everyone was supposed to know that.

"Ok," I said. "I don't even know what a Lieutenant Governor is." I didn't either. I just took a stab in the dark. It was kind of a common sense stab, though. "Is that like the vice Governor?"

"Yes," she said. "But, if it is not Ralph Dixon, it sure looks like him."

"Thanks Honey," I said. I gave her a kiss on her cheek. "Have fun at lunch."

Raven punched me in my stomach. I laughed.

I got off the stool and headed to the restroom. As I did, Ian walked in through the front door.

"Sup?" I said to him, as I entered the bathroom.

"Sup?" he responded.

"Holy shit!" I said when I looked at a mess someone had left on the back of the toilet bowl. "Ian, come here!"

He slid next to me, inside the tiny restroom. We stood side by side, looking down at the mess.

"Picasso left us some artwork," Ian said without moving.

"That he did," I said. "That he did."

"You gonna clean it?" Ian asked me, without moving.

I didn't move either. I just stared at the artwork that was stuck inches above the water. "No. You can do it."

Ian said, "I don't want to. You don't want to. One of us should probably clean it."

"Yup," I agreed.

We stood still, starring down into the bowl. It was really nasty. "We could flip a coin," I suggested.

"Are you going to use your two headed coin?" Ian asked me.

"Probably," I said.

He said, "Then, no. How about we play Rock, Paper, Scissors?"

"Too juvenile. How about Ink-a-dink?" I suggested.

"That's even more juvenile," Ian said. "The name alone is ridiculous. We could arm wrestle, loser cleans this mess," he said still staring at it.

"No," I said. "I've got tennis elbow. How about we both run the length of the parking lot, one side to the other and back? Loser cleans the bowl."

"No. I don't have my running shoes on," Ian said. "We could race; my wheels against yours. We can start in the parking lot, drive to Pontiac, around the Woodward Loop and back."

I was actually considering it when Aunt Lonnie stepped in the bathroom doorway. "What are you two amigos up to?"

Without turning around or taking our eyes off of the disaster in the bowl, Ian said, "There is a mess on the wall of the toilet. We are trying to decide which one of us is going to clean it."

"It won't be easy," I said. "It looks pretty bad."

"Did either of you try flushing the water?" she asked.

"No," we said in unison. I stepped one foot forward, reached down and flushed the toilet. It didn't help.

Aunt Lonnie left.

"We could text Big at the same time. The person he texts back first, doesn't have to clean it," I said.

"No," Ian said. He still hadn't moved a muscle. "You have a newer phone than I do."

It wasn't logical, but I didn't argue with him. I thought some more. "We could..."

Aunt Lonnie interrupted me. She pushed me to the wall in the restroom, and squeezed her little frame between Ian and me. She had a carafe of steaming hot water. She poured it on the thick mess in the bowl. She grabbed the toilet bowl brush from under the sink. She wiped the bowl clean in seconds and flushed the water. She squeezed between us and left the restroom without saying a word.

"Or, we could ask Aunt Lonnie to clean it for us," I said.

Chapter Six

I took Mark's tablet to the office. It's located in the back room of The Coffee Cabin. Ian followed me. I sat on the couch which is an old 1957 Chevy's back seat. It was converted into a couch by a friend of mine. Ian sat next to me so we could look through the tablet together.

I started scrolling through the apps. Ian, being the most inpatient person I know, grabbed the tablet from on my lap and opened the photo app without saying a word. He tapped the screen, swiped his finger across the screen, turned the tablet from vertical to horizontal and back a few times, before finally saying, "Here! Here are the pictures Mark sent you."

"Do you realize that, so far, you have managed to get us nowhere, no further in this investigation? All you have managed to do is show me some pictures I already have," I said.

"Well, let's keep looking through the photos. Maybe there are more than the dozen he already sent," Ian said.

We spent the next half an hour or so going through the tablet, opening, surfing, and closing every app on the tablet. "So far we have come up empty," I said.

"Why did he leave this thing for us if there isn't anything on it to help us find him?" Ian asked.

I had emptied my coffee cup. Ian's was empty as well. I stood, picked up both cups and went to the lobby to fill them from a fresh brewed pot. There were about 20 customers occupying the booths as well as the sofa area near the front of the store. The fireplace was burning. It is late March and still pretty cold outside for Michigan. Snow was projected to fall the weekend of my wedding. But, being Michigan, that could change. I hope it does. The temperature today is expected to reach a high of 37. My hoodie kept me warm. Ian was wearing an orange and blue flannel over a navy blue T-shirt to keep himself warm.

I took the filled mugs back to the office.

I handed Ian his coffee. "I think I have something," he said. "Here, in his email, is a short letter that Mark sent the same day he sent you the pictures. It's addressed to a Vicacovi@gmail.com. It simply says, 'Just in case... D. Reese.' It's followed by your phone number. Do you know what or who Vicacovi is?"

I didn't have any idea. "Hang on," I said and I went to ask Raven if she knew.

"Raven, can I have a word with you, when you have a minute?" I whispered to her as she was refilling a cup for a friend of hers.

"Sure Daddy. Hang on a minute," she said with a smile.

I walked to the last stool at the counter and had a seat. Raven went behind the bar and returned the carafe to the warmer before saying, "What's up?"

I patted the stool to my right. She walked around the bar and had a seat next to me. She lowered her voice, "What's up?"

"Ian found an email in Mark's history that was sent to a Vicacovi. He said to contact me, just in case. Have you ever heard of a Vicacovi? Is it a person or a company? Do you have any idea?"

Raven repeated the word a few times. Suddenly a light went off in her head. A metaphoric bell had been rung. "Covi is short for Colavino, I think. Oh, oh, oh, and I'll bet Vica is short for Victoria." Raven was getting excited.

"Sssshhhh!" I said, quietly holding my finger up to my mouth.

"Oh, sorry," Raven said. "I'll bet it is, though. It's gotta be."

Raven sat on the stool next to me with a big smile on her face. She surly had her mother's smile. It was beautiful.

"Ok. So who is Victoria Colavino?" I asked. I literally thought I had no clue.

"Daddy," she said. "Think about it. Colavino. You should know better than anyone I know, who she is."

I just wanted her to tell me, but I played along. I repeated the name a few times. Suddenly, my light bulb went off, as well. "Colavino. Isn't she the reporter that covered the Finlandia University story?"

"She's got to be. It's the only thing that makes sense," Raven said. She was proud.

I had a lot of questions racing through my head. I leaned forward and kissed her on her cheek. "Thanks. Just keep this between us, ok?" I said. She knew "us" included Ian and Cherrie too.

"Sure." She jubilantly jumped down from the stool.

I returned to the office.

"Do you know who Victoria Colavino is?" Ian asked as I walked through the door. He had also figured it out.

"Yes I do. You and Raven must have figured it out at the same time," I said. "How the hell did he figure that out?" I asked myself.

Ian started laughing. "I wish I could take credit for it, but Raven just texted me the name. But you should have seen the look on your face. Who is she, anyway?"

"She's the reporter that covered the story at Finlandia University," I said.

"Oh, that's right," Ian said. "She's the hot brunette that sounds like she's from Minnesota."

"Right," I agreed. "I wonder why Mark would involve her in whatever it is he's wrapped up in."

"I don't know. Let's find out. I'll give her a call," Ian said with a sly look on his freckled face.

"Do you have her number?" I asked.

"Just give me a minute. I'll get it," he said.

He was searching the web for her digits. A few minutes went by. I sat on the edge of our desk and sipped my coffee. Ian picked up his cell phone and began tapping numbers.

He cleared his throat. "May I please speak with Miss Colavino?" he asked the person on the other end of the nonexistent phone line. He paused for a moment before saying, "Please hold for Dalen Reese."

I shot him a confused look as he tried to hand me his phone. I spread my hands, with my palms up. "What the hell?" I mouthed to him without actually saying the words out loud. I shook my head and grabbed his phone. "Asshole!" I mouthed.

"Hello. Is this Miss Colavino?" I asked.

"It is." She asked, "May I ask whose calling?" even though Ian had just told her.

"This is Dalen Reese. Is this a good time to talk?"

"I'm sorry. No it is not. I'll call you when it is," she said. Then in a whisper she said, "If this is about Mark, hang up now, without saying another word."

I pulled the phone away from my ear and touched the red End Call icon on the screen. I found her phone number on the recently called list and selected the text icon on the screen. I texted in all caps, "THIS NUMBER IS IAN PARKER'S. MARK GAVE YOU MINE IN AN EMAIL. CALL MY NUMBER WHEN YOU CAN TALK." I hit send. I gave Ian back his phone.

"It's not a good time to talk, she said. She also said, 'If this is about Mark, hang up now, without saying another word.' So I did," I said.

"She obviously knows who I am. I'm not sure if she knows that Mark is missing, though."

I grabbed my phone and called Mrs. Smith.

"Hello Dalen. How are you doing this morning?" she said. She sounded pretty chipper. I know one thing for sure, if Raven or Olivia went missing, I wouldn't be so calm and collected.

I filled her in on what had transpired since I dropped her off last night.

"I know you'll find him, Dalen. I have every bit of faith in you and Ian," Mrs. Smith said.

"Ok. Mrs. Smith. I'll keep you updated. Try to have a good day. Take care," I said. I ended the call.

I put the phone back in my pocket. Just as I did, my ringtone started to play. I answered the phone. "You've got Dalen Reese. Detroit's toughest and best looking Private Eye."

"Mr. Reese," the voice said from inside my phone. "This is Senior Patrol Officer Dale Fontana."

"Do you ever get tired of saying that? I know who you are. You sound like Dick Clark. You can just say, 'This is Dale.' I'll know who you are," I said. I had cut him off. I paused so he could finish talking.

He ignored my interruption. "We found Mr. Smith's vehicle. It was located three and a half miles from the diner. It has been stripped, completely."

"What do you mean completely?" I asked.

"There isn't anything left but the frame. No tires, seats, electronics. The ceiling carpet is removed. The carpet on the floor has been removed. The doors are gone. The windows are busted clean out. There aren't any screws or nuts or bolts or wires. When I say that there isn't anything left but the frame, that's what I mean, except, the dash is still there. Nothing is attached to the dash except the VIN plate. That is how we were able to identify the vehicle. I'm only assuming here, but that's probably what the strippers wanted us to find."

"Stupid question, but were you able to get any prints?" I asked. "I'm just curious."

"Here's another thing, Mr. Reese. We will not be able to fingerprint the vehicle. Whoever stripped it, painted every inch of the frame, from top to bottom, with petroleum jelly," he said. He waited for my response.

"You're kidding me, right?" I was pretty sure Dick Clark didn't joke about anything, ever. "What do you mean, exactly," I asked.

"I'll send you the photos. Do you want them sent to your email or your phone through your text messages?" Dick asked me. I swear, if you could hear this fella, you'd say he sounded exactly like Dick Clark, too.

"Text them to me, please."

"They will be sent shortly," Senior Patrol Officer Dale Fontana said. "Will you be returning to Ohio anytime soon? I am only asking because, I would like nothing more than to find your friend, Mark Smith. I have enough cases on my plate right now. I don't need the extra work. But, you must know, just because I have a full load, doesn't mean I am not putting all my effort into finding him. If you happen to solve this case before I do, it'll be very beneficial to me."

"I'm not sure where the investigation will lead. But, if something comes up and we have to travel to your neck of the woods, would you like me to give you a heads up?" I asked.

"Yes please. I'll send the photos to your phone now," he said. He ended the call. Within a minute, 15 text messages started rolling through. My phone lit up like a strobe light.

The pictures were not very helpful. As Fontana had said, the entire frame had been painted with Vaseline. The close ups showed paint brush strokes in the yellow jelly. You could not have lifted a fingerprint from any place on any part of the frame of the car. It was strange. I wonder why the strippers didn't just wipe the frame down. You can smear a fingerprint easily with a cloth. This Vaseline job must have taken hours, unless there were many painters, which I guess there could have been. I saved each of the photos to the SIM card in my phone.

I had showed Ian each of the pictures. He agreed; they were not helpful.

There wasn't much I could do as I waited for Miss Colavino to return my call. I grabbed Mark's tablet and a cup of coffee to go. I went to sit in my Jeep so I could listen to music, be by myself, and try to figure out where we should go next. I had to find Mark. The longer he was missing, the bigger the odds become of us not finding him.

I sipped my coffee, I scanned through Mark's tablet, and I listened to a CD while I tried to piece things together.

As I sat there, alone, I began to watch Raven, through the windows, win the hearts of her customers. I started to remember the days before last Thanksgiving when I received a phone call from her. She was a freshman in college at Finlandia University in the Upper Peninsula.

I remember:

My cell phone vibrated in my back pocket. I retrieved it, saw Raven's photo light up the screen, and then I swiped my finger across it to answer the call.

"Hello Raven. How are you Honey?" I said into my cell phone, as I raised it up to my ear.

"Daddy... He's got a gun," Raven whispered into her phone.

I couldn't hardly understand her, let alone hear her. "What?" I asked. "Did you say someone has a gun?"
I was taken back but I was also in disbelief; mostly because I didn't actually think I heard my daughter say what I thought I heard her say.

She spoke louder, but not much louder, "He has a gun, Daddy. He has a gun!"

I understood her that time. "Who," I said, "who has a gun?" As I spoke, sweat instantly bubbled on my bald head. Adrenaline ran through my veins like the water from a burst dam.

Before Raven could answer, I heard two pops. They were faint but I knew what they were.

"Oh, my God! Oh, my God! Oh, my God!" Raven cried.

That time, I understood her perfectly. We spoke at the same time.

"Where are you?" I asked her at the same time she said, "Holy shit!" I could hear the fear in her voice.

"Try to calm down and tell me exactly what's happening," I said, as calmly as I could. I wasn't, but I needed to sound as though I was.

Raven was breathing heavily through the wireless phone line. "There is a guy, or maybe two, or three, I don't know, but someone on our floor has a gun and he is shooting it. I'm scared to death, Daddy. People are running down the hall screaming their heads off. I don't know what's going on. I don't know, Daddy. But..."

There was more gunfire. I could hear at least three more shots, maybe four. With the screaming surrounding the pops, or bangs, it was hard for me to be sure.

"Raven, are you in your room?"

Through tears and fear, Raven said, "Yeah, I'm in my room."

"Are you alone?" I asked.

Raven muffled her scream. My heart sank into my stomach.

"Raven, are you alone?" I slowly repeated.

"Yes," she said, "Myah went out to dinner an hour ago. I don't know where she is." Myah was Raven's roommate.

"Ok, good!" I said.

I was throwing a change of clean clothes into my gym bag.

Cherrie entered the bedroom to see what the all of the commotion was all about. I turned around to look at her. She could see the fear on my face. She gasped! "What's wrong?"

"Raven," I said, "Make sure your door is locked. If you can, drag your dresser over to the door to block it. Can you do that?"

"Yes, but it'll make a lot of noise on the floor. I don't want to draw attention to myself," she said softly.

"Take your time moving it, rock it or walk it slowly. Do you understand?" I asked.

"I do, Daddy. I'll try," Raven said, sounding somewhat calm.

I didn't hear any noise in the background. I felt a little relief. "Honey," I said, "put your phone on vibrate, make sure the volume is turned off and lay the phone on the bed. I'll call you back in 5 minutes. I'm leaving now. I'm on my way. I'll get there as fast as I can. I love you."

"Hurry, Daddy, hurry!" Raven cried.

Again, I heard...Pop! Pop! Pop! And the line went silent.

"What's happening?" Cherrie asked. "Is she ok?"

"She is, at the moment, yes. Apparently there is at least one male on her floor with a gun. Shots have been fired. Raven is in her room, alone, with her door locked. That's all I know," I said.

"You are leaving now?" Cherrie asked. "I'm coming with you."

"No, you are not!" I said. "Please, stay here. I love you, but it's a long drive and besides you have to finish your Thanksgiving Special by Sunday. I'll tell you what you can do, though." The thought had just occurred to me that it would be faster to fly. "Will you please look on-line and see if there is a flight out of Metro in the next hour? See if there is a flight into Houghton, first. "Then, I don't know. You could check Green Bay or Duluth, perhaps. Where is my phone charger?" I was looking around the bed for it. I didn't see it."

"It's in the living room. I'll get it for you," Cherrie said. She left the bedroom to retrieve my charger.

I believed I had everything I might need for a few nights away from home. I zipped my bag and slipped my feet into a pair of tennis shoes that were still tied.

"Are you sure you don't want me to go with you?" Cherrie asked, as I entered the living room with my tote bag in hand.

"I'm sure. Just book me a flight as soon as you can. I'll head to the airport now. I'll rent a car when I land."

I bent down and gave my fiancée a kiss. Thanksgiving was less than a week away.

"I love you," I said and headed out the back door to my 1999 Green Jeep Wrangler. I opened the passenger door and tossed my bag on the front seat. I needed a cup of coffee for the road. I went back to into the house to pour a cup and was greeted at the back door by Cherrie. She was holding my phone in her hand.

"You might need this," she said.

"Damn!" I said. I grabbed the phone with a sigh of relief. "Thank you!" I said, as I scooted by her. "Coffee, too."

"Right," she said sarcastically. "Heaven forbid you should forget your coffee."

I poured coffee into my Detroit Lions travel mug. I spilled a bit on the counter in the process. My nerves were getting the best of me. I gave Cherrie one more kiss and headed to the Jeep. "Call me as soon as you have a flight booked. I love you!"

I started the Jeep and heard Cherrie shout over the rumble of the engine, "Be careful. I love you too." She closed the back door to the house.

I took my cell out of my pocket and searched my contacts for my friend, Detective Macy. I selected the call icon and waited for our lines to connect. Her phone rang four times before it went to voice mail.

I left a message, "Macy, its Dalen. Call me! It is an emergency! Raven is up at school and there is a lunatic on her campus with a gun. He's shooting people!" I ended the call.

I touched my 'Favorites' icon and tapped Raven's ID. She answered as quickly as it connected.

"Hello Raven. What's happening now?" I asked. My stomach churned with nerves as I spoke.

"Daddy," she whispered, "I think they know I'm in here."

I backed out of my garage, down my driveway, and into the street without checking my mirrors for oncoming traffic. Luckily, the street was clear. I threw the stick shift into first, second, then third, working the clutch and gas petals like a pro, as I headed toward Metro Airport.

"Ok, you say 'they.' So there is more than one of them. Do you know how many of them there are?" I asked. I held the phone between my left shoulder and my ear as I steered the car.

"I think I heard three different voices. They seem to be moving students into the Rec-room, down the hall," she whispered.

"Did you lock your door?" I asked.

"The door is locked. I moved my desk to block the door. The dresser made too much noise. I also wedged a chair under the door handle."

"Good. Good," I said. "That was smart. Why do you think they know you are in your room?"

"They came by and pounded on my door and said I had two minutes to come out, or they were coming in to get me," Raven said quietly, yet calm. "They may have done the same thing to every closed door, though."

"How long ago was that?" I asked.

"Maybe three or four minutes ago," she said. As she spoke, my phone made a double beeping sound.

I had an incoming call. "Raven, I'll call you right back. I love you," I said, as I used my finger to swipe the screen to answer the incoming call. It was Detective Macy.

"Reese, what's up? Tell me again what's going on," she demanded, before I had a chance to finish saying hello.

I filled her in on everything I knew, including the location of the school and that it had just let out for Thanksgiving break. I informed her that most students would be picked up tomorrow, though some were supposed to be picked up tonight, usually be their parents. I told Macy that there had been numerous gunshots. The safety of the students, though, was unknown. I said that I planned to take a flight out this evening. She didn't seem to care about that.

"I'll call a friend of mine in Houghton," she said. "I'll call you back." She ended the call.

I tapped an icon on my phone and said, "Call Cherrie."

She answered on the second ring, "Hi Babe."

"Is there a flight, soon?" I asked.

"I checked Metro. There is not a flight that will get you into Houghton before Saturday evening that leaves from either Metro or Flint Airports. Now, if you take a flight tomorrow morning out of Metro, you can get into Green Bay at noon, but then you'll have a four hour drive. You can probably make it in 3 ½ hours. Likewise, if you fly out of Flint tomorrow morning, you can land in Duluth, Minnesota at 9:00. Those two are both taking the time change into account. Duluth to Houghton also has a four hour drive," Cherrie said. She spoke clear and had covered all of her bases. She knows her way around the internet and can find the metaphoric needle in the haystack that is the World Wide Web.

"So, I'll be better off driving?" I asked. The question was rhetorical.

"Not so fast," Cherrie said. "The last option is flying out of Metro tonight at 11:00 and flying into Rhinelander Oneida County Airport and after the layover, they have a flight that will get you into

Houghton at 9:30, or you could drive from Rhinelander and get into Houghton at 8:30 Saturday morning. That's a 2 ½ hour drive," Cherrie said.

I thought about that as an option. "Or I can drive and get there in seven hours."

"Dalen," Cherrie said with concern, "according to the DistanceBetweenCities website, the drive is eight hours and fifty minutes."

"I can make it in seven," I said with confidence. "That'll get me there at 2:00 AM." My mind was made up; I was driving. "Thank you for your help. I love you. I'll keep you posted." I hung up before she could respond.

I was sitting at a traffic light when I redialed Raven. She answered on the first ring. I was about to say, "Hello Raven," when she interrupted me and said, "Daddy, they cut the power off. All I have is the light from my phone and my window. But, it's dark outside, it's cloudy, and it's going to rain."

"Raven, how much battery life do you have?" I asked.

 More sweat was beading on top of my head. I took my Detroit Tigers ball cap off and tossed it into the back seat. The light turned green. I shifted faster than I should have. I was pissed. I accidently grinded the gears so I let up off of the clutch. My tires had squealed. I slowed down a bit and got the car under control. I wanted to be with her. I hadn't felt this much adrenaline run through my veins since I had chased The Trench Coat Rapist through the streets of Detroit a few years back.

I knew Raven was scared. The only time she ever called me "Daddy" was when she batted her eye lashes at me because she was trying to get some cash from me or when she was frightened. Right now, she wasn't asking for money.

"My phone is at 30% though it never seems to last long after it hits 25%. So I really don't know how long it will last," she said. Now her voice sounded more concerned than afraid.

"Ok. Can you tell me what is going on outside your door?" I asked.

"Right now, it is very quiet. But I think I can hear some muffled voices. Oh, and now someone is crying. I think it's Linda, next door. I don't hear the men, though," she replied.

"Ummm," I tried to think of something else to ask. I was drawing a blank. "Ok. Honey, I am in the car now. I am driving up tonight. I should be there by 2:00 AM. Do you remember Detective Macy? I spoke to her. She is calling someone in Houghton. I didn't ask her who, but I assume she is calling the police. What else? What else?" I was racking my brain. "Oh, I know. Roll a towel up and lay it at the bottom of the door to block any light in your room from shining into the hall. Turn your phone off completely and wait a half hour turn it back on and call me."

"How will I know when a half hour is up?" she asked. "I'll just guess. But, if I need to call you before I believe a half hour is up, Daddy, you better bet your sweet life I'll be calling you."

"I love you, Raven. Stay strong and keep silent. I'll talk to you in a half hour," I said through a lump in my throat. Tears were forming in the corners of my eyes. Raven ended the call. I punched the steering wheel repeatedly as I let out a string of expletives loud as I

could. I had another daughter in danger; only this time there wasn't much I could do to save her.

Thanks to Macy's help and the cooperation of other law enforcement agencies, I had been given six police escorts through seven different counties on my way to Houghton. Through the others though, I had to follow the speed limit. I had stopped four times to fill up my gas tank. Raven's phone had died hours ago, but Macy had put me in touch with a police officer who had kept me up to date, every hour, on the horrific events unfolding in Raven's dormitory.

By the time I had arrived at Finlandia University, four students were dead, seven more were injured and the two gunmen had been arrested. Raven and I packed her belongings, crammed them into the Jeep, and drove all the way back home. She was able to finish her classes on-line, but dropped out of Finlandia University at the end of the semester. She is currently enrolled at Wayne State University, just a few minutes away via the John Lodge Expressway. She is in therapy, now. It is helping her cope. I feel better having her home.

Chapter Seven

First I lost Tara, then Olivia was raped, Raven was held hostage, and now my friend Mark Smith has gone missing. I'm not sure how much more I can handle. Thank God I have Cherrie in my life. I would be lost without her.

As I sat in my Jeep, trying to keep my mind on my missing friend and what else we could do to find him, my phone rang. It was a number I did not recognize. I swiped the green icon. "Dalen Reese speaking," is all I managed to get out before a woman's voice interrupted me.

"Mr. Reese, this is Salma Jackson from Ohio. Brenda said you might like to have a word with me."

"Mrs. Jackson, thank you for calling me so soon. I really wasn't expecting a call until Friday, if at all. So, thanks again," I said. "Did Brenda mention why I want to speak to you?"

Salma Jackson said, "It's all anyone around these parts is talking about. First that man gets kidnapped from the diner, and then they found his car around the bend. I'm sorry, had you been told about the car, yet?"

"Yes Mrs. Jackson," I said. "Is there anything you can remember about the men that sticks out in your mind? Did you happen to get a license plate number? Did you know if Mark drove his car or if he shared a ride with one of the other men? Mrs. Jackson, anything you can remember might be helpful in helping us find Mr. Smith." I had dug a note pad out of the small glove compartment in the side of my door. I had placed the phone on speaker and was balancing it on my left thigh while I held the note pad on my right. I had a pen in my hand, ready to write.

"Mr. Reese, I already told the police officer everything I could remember. What I told him, I'll tell you. The men arrived in the same car. They were dressed alike. They both wore dark grey suits. One wore sunglasses, the other man did not. They walked into the diner and walked straight up to your friend and his mother. They drove a dark sedan; I do not know what kind of car it was. I can't tell the difference between a Ford and a Chevy. They stood at the end of your friend's booth and spoke to him and his mother, though I assume they probably spoke more to him," she said. It sounded as though she had rehearsed the information she was giving me.

I wrote as fast as I could, trying to keep up. I was managing.

She continued. "After about a minute, your friend's mother went to the powder room. Your friend walked out of the diner with the other two men. He walked out between them, single file like. Your friend stood in front of the sedan and exchanged words. I could tell he was not happy. Now I can't say for sure, but I think one of the men might have showed your friend a hand gun of some sort. But I can't even be sure of that. I didn't actually see it. Whatever it was, it was inside his suit coat. The other man, not your friend, opened his coat up. Your friend removed his car keys from his pocket and let the other man, not the one with the gun, but the other one, have the keys. That man got into your friend's Jeep and backed out of the parking spot."

I listened and wrote frantically.

Mrs. Jackson continued, "Then without another word, that I could tell, your friend got into the passenger seat while the man that I think had a gun, got into the driver's seat. He started the sedan, backed it up and drove away. The Jeep followed."

"Wow," I said, impressed. "That is very good Mrs. Jackson. You obviously have an eye for detail. Thank you. I have to ask, is there anything else you can remember? Maybe one of the men said something you managed to hear, like a name of something. Perhaps you can remember if one of the men had a visible scar of a tattoo or the color of their shoes or anything like that." I felt as if I was grabbing at straws, but you never know.

Ian had climbed into the Jeep and sat next to me. This time he sat in the front seat. He was careful to be quiet as he shut the door.

"Well, Judas Priest!" Mrs. Salma Jackson shouted. "I didn't remember it until now but when you mentioned tattoos, you triggered a memory."

I looked at Ian. "Judas Priest?" he mouthed to me. He was laughing but he was doing so silently. His face was turning a dark shade of red. I slugged him in his arm, hoping to get him to stop. He didn't.

Mrs. Jackson continued, excitedly, "Both men did have rather large tattoos on the back of their hands. They were black tattoos. I can't say exactly what they were of, but I believe they were of letters. And each of those men had one tattoo on one hand only. And I also can't remember for certain, but I believe one had the tattoo on the back of his right hand while the other man had the tattoo on the back of his left hand."

I could tell Salma was proud of herself.

"Mrs. Jackson, you have been very, very helpful. Thank you so, so much. May I call you if I have any other questions?" I asked.

"Yes Mr. Reese, you may. And, if I remember anything else, anything at all, I will be sure to call you back."

I could almost feel the smile on her face through the phone. "Thanks again, Mrs. Jackson. Enjoy the rest of your day."

She ended the call.

"Judas Priest?" Ian repeated. "Judas Priest? Who the hell says Judas Priest instead of Jesus Christ?"

"I don't know," I said. "Apparently Mrs. Jackson does. But she can say whatever she wants if she is going to give us all the information she knows." I handed Ian the note pad.

He read my scribble and said, "Judas Priest! She saw everything." He looked at me while he handed the pad back to me. "Do you know anyone with tattoos on the back of their hands? That's gotta ring a bell to someone. There can't be too many people with back hand tats that wear suits, can there be?"

"I doubt it," I said. "I'm calling Macy." I did.

She answered on the third ring. "What do you want now, Reese?"

"Quick question; do you know anyone that has large letters tattooed on the back of their hands? There would be two men. They may wear suits," I added.

"It sounds like it could be the Royboys," she said. "I'm assuming these men are Caucasian?"

"Yes," I said. "Who are the Roy boys?"

Lieutenant Macy corrected me, "Not the Roy boys. Their last name is Royboy. Mickey Royboy is the father of the Royboy brothers, Donnie and Terry. Mickey runs the numbers and the powder on 8 Mile. His sons are the heavies. The tattoos on their hands are their initials. I don't know a lot about them, other than that. I'll make a call. I know someone that knows enough to help you out. I'm not sure what you are involved in, but if the Royboy brothers are involved, it can't be good."

The phone went silent. I looked at my screen. She had hung up. I placed the phone back into my pocket.

Ian asked, "Hey, I was thinking, why do you suppose Mark actually took this iPad into the diner, if he wasn't using it, like Mrs. Smith said? He took it in and didn't use it. Why wouldn't he have just left it in his car? I mean, it's almost as if he knew he'd be leaving his mom there and, as she said, he left the tablet there, under the placemat, for us. How does that make sense?"

"That's a valid question and one I do not have an answer for." I told Ian what Macy had told me about the Royboy's. "Have you ever heard of them?"

Ian shook his head. "Nope."

"Macy's going to have someone else call me that knows more about them than she does," I said. "I'm going to go to the cemetery now. Do you want to ride with me or stay here?"

"I'll tag along. I haven't seen my sister in a few months," Ian said. His sister, Victoria overdosed on heroine two years ago. She had been in and out of rehab for years. Her husband had committed suicide when their son, Ian's nephew Tommy, was only 5. She never got over it.

Our investigation of Mark's disappearance had stalled. I was waiting to hear back from the reporter and the person Macy was calling on my behalf. We didn't know what any of the photos on my phone had to do with our missing friend; not the pictures of gay men or the ones of Mark's car. The other stuff on his tablet weren't helping us either, yet. So, I shifted the car into drive and we went to visit Tara and Victoria.

We pulled through the wrought iron gate of the cemetery. I followed the dirt road as it wound through trees and tombstones, past a small pond and white brick chapel. Victoria's gravesite was about 50 yards to the left of Tara's. I dropped Ian off near his sister's tombstone and then drove around a very slight curve to park closer to my wife's headstone.

I have come here to visit Tara's gravesite every other Thursday for the past 10 years. I quietly closed the Jeep's door and walked slowly past a half dozen other sites before I reached Tara's. Her headstone is a white marble with a large pink ribbon engraved under her name and her birth and death years. Under the ribbon are the words "Tara didn't count the days, she made the days count."

I looked over at Ian. He was on his knees saying a prayer. I sat down on the cold dead grass. I watched my breath float from my mouth. I stuffed my hands deep into my hoodie's pockets. I wished I had put on my leather Lion's jacket. It's much warmer. I looked at the stone and, as I always did, I read the words that were in front of me. As they always did, my eyes filled with tears. I never tried to hold them back. I blinked. They slowly ran down my cheeks. I used my shoulders to wipe them away.

I bowed my head and whispered to my love. I quietly talked to her and filled her on what had transpired since my last visit. When I was finished, I stood and placed my hand on the top of the headstone. "I love you," I said. "I will always love you." When I turned to walk back to my car, I noticed that Ian was standing a few feet behind me. He placed his hand on my shoulder and we walked to the car in silence.

Once inside, I started the car and turned the heat up high. I looked at my phone. I had a missed call from Macy. I called her back. I put it on speaker.

"He'll meet you in an hour at the Wicker Bar on 8 Mile. You'll know him by the fedora hat on his head," Lieutenant Macy said. "His name is Robert Stonewall. Oh, and you are buying him lunch. Have fun!"

I waited for her to say something else. She didn't. I looked at my phone. It said the call had ended.

"Let's go eat!" I said to Ian.

"At the Wicker, really?" Ian asked. "Have you ever been there? That place is nasty."

"Nope, but we are out of clues. We gotta follow this lead." I shifted the Jeep into gear and we headed to the Wicker Bar to meet Robert Stonewall; whoever he is.

Chapter Eight

We parked the Jeep next to an old Olds Delta 88. It was white and rusted. A bungee cord held the trunk closed, from the busted out key hole to the bottom of the rear chrome bumper. It was a real gem. We walked into the musty, dark, and smoke filled room.

"Shit, you can cut the smoke with a knife," Ian said. He was right.

We looked around. Through the dimly lit barroom, we could see a man sitting at the bar. He was wearing a fedora. He was the only person in the room. We walked up to him.

"You Stonewall?" I asked. I felt like we were in a bad 70's movie.

"Reese?" he asked in return. He knew I was.

"Yeah and this is Parker," I said, pointing my thumb at Ian.

Stonewall downed the last swallow of his drink, stood up, grabbed his cane from the back of the stool next to him, and said, "Let's go eat. Macy said you're buying!"

I looked at Ian, he looked at me. We both shrugged our shoulders and followed the limping man with the cane out the door, into the cold brisk air. It felt good to breathe fresher air.

"You want me to drive?" I asked.

Stonewall didn't answer. Instead, he walked across the crumbling parking lot to a Coney Island next door. We followed.

Once inside the packed diner, we stood near the door and waited for a table. We didn't have to wait long before one opened up. Stonewall pointed to it with his cane, as if he was calling dibs on it. We sat and ordered. Within a few minutes, the three of us each had a plate with two Coney dogs, each topped with chili, onions, and mustard.

I sat across from this man with the fedora still on his head. He wore a green and white flannel shirt, underneath a grey corduroy sport coat. He had on a black tie. Years of hard work and stress were deeply imbedded in the deep wrinkles on his face. He used a fork and knife to cut his Coney dogs into small bites. He chewed with his mouth closed and never spoke with it full.

"Macy said you have questions about the Royboys," he said after he rinsed his mouth with a drink of water.

"What can you tell us about them?" I said.

Ian flagged the waitress down and ordered two more Coney's with everything on them.

Stonewall finished off his second dog, drank the rest of his glass of water, wiped his mouth with a paper napkin, then answered. "Macy said you might suspect them in the kidnapping of your friend. Is that correct?"

I spent the next few minutes telling him everything I could remember since I had received the phone call from Mrs. Smith yesterday morning. I asked Ian if I had left anything out. With his mouth full of the last of his fourth Coney dog, Ian shook his head.

"These are some bad people," Stonewall said. "I know. I work for them. Well, I work for their father, Mickey. I'm kind of a consultant or an advisor for the family. Between you two and me, because Macy says I can trust you both, this bum knee I've got, I owe that to them."

Ian and I sat and listened to Robert Stonewall talk. He spoke clearly, but in a deep whisper. I sipped my second glass of water. Ian fidgeted with his napkin and the burgundy paper wrapper that held the silverware inside the napkin at our place setting.

Stonewall continued, "Terry Royboy took a pipe wrench to it," he said, referring to his knee. "I have a gambling issue. I often lose my bets with Mickey and can't pay them off. Two years ago, I was too far in debt with my third double or nothing. When I couldn't pay, Terry followed his father's orders. The next day, I pointed my loaded piece at my knee and pulled the trigger. I said it happened in the line of duty. It was never proved that it didn't. I received my papers early; full pension. Now, I do what I can to make ends meet.

Sometimes I have to work for the wrong side of the law, but I do so without breaking it."

We stood and walked to the register to pay the bill. Stonewall didn't wait for me. He walked straight outside and stood. Ian left the tip on the table. I grabbed a toothpick and placed it in the corner of my mouth. We joined Stonewall outside. It had started to snow. It wasn't sticking to the roads yet, but the grassy areas were covered with the white flakes. The three of us walked to our vehicles and stood between my Jeep and his Oldsmobile.

As I stood and watched this retired officer lean on his cane, I couldn't help wonder how miserable his life must be.

"Do you want me to set up a meeting with you and Mickey? I can't guarantee he'll accept, but I'll try to be persuasive," Robert said. "He usually doesn't leave his house."

"Do what you can do," I said. "The longer Mark is missing, the more dire his situation becomes. That is only an assumption at this point, but history has proven this to be true."

I watched Robert shift from one leg to his other and back again, all the while, leaning heavily on his cane. Ian reached his hand into my coat pocket and grabbed the keys to the Jeep. He went around to the driver's side, leaned in and started it up. He turned up the heat and started the wipers. Stonewall followed suit with his car.

"Linda says I need to rid myself of the poison that is the Royboys. I have less than a hundred grand to work off of my debit. When it is clean, I'll take her advice. But, until then, I have no shot of reconciliation with her," Stonewall said as his breath visibly floated away from his mouth, in the cold air. "Linda is my ex-wife. I don't remember if I had mentioned her today or not. She says I have to clean up my life and become a better person before she'll even consider taking me back. I'm trying to. She said the number one thing I need to work on is being less honest."

"What the hell does that mean?" Ian asked.

"I know, right?" Robert Stonewall asked. "But I understand her point of view. As long as I can remember, I have always spoken my mind. Linda says I speak before I think. That's gotten me in trouble more times than I can count. So I have been working really hard to think about what I am going to say before I say it. I think I'm making progress." He removed his black clip-on tie folded it in thirds and tucked it into his sport coat pocket. He unbuttoned the top button of his shirt.

"Ok," I said. "Well good luck with that." I offered him a fist bump. We tapped knuckles. "It is nice to meet you. Give me a call or ask Mickey to call me or have Macy get in touch with me or whatever when you set up a meeting. I know you don't use a cell phone, so...yeah. Thanks."

"Ian," Stonewall said. They shook hands. "It's nice to meet you too." Robert climbed into his car. Before he closed his door he said, "Macy is one of about five people on this planet I can trust."

Ian interrupted him, "But there are people on other planets that you can trust?"

I elbowed Ian in his ribs. He let out a grunt.

Stonewall continued, "Look, Macy says you two are good people and she trusts you. She has trust issues, too. Hell, all cops do. This is a shitty business to be in. But, if Macy says she has trust in your corner, I believe her. So until you prove otherwise, I'll be by your sides. I only have a handful of people on my side, so I hope I can count on you as well." He closed his car door, put his vehicle in reverse and backed out. He stopped his car before he put it in drive. He rolled the window down on the passenger side. He leaned across the passenger seat and said, "This situation may not have a happy ending. Just prepare for the worst and hope for the best." He rolled the window up as he drove away.

After we got into my Jeep, Ian said, "Man Dalen, this shit just got real! Are we actually prepared to deal with the local Mafia or the Kingpin or whatever the hell Mickey Royboy and his family are? I mean, we are just two small time private investigators from the suburbs."

I said, "I thought you liked to refer to us as private detectives."

"You dick!" he said. "But no, seriously, can we do this. I know we can find Mark, that will be the easy part, but they took him for a reason. They aren't just going to hand him over when we do find him. This isn't Hide and Seek. The Royboy's want him for something, probably the pictures, but we don't know that yet. And by the way Stonewall talks, I assume they'd kill him to get it, too."

"You know what assuming does," I said. "It makes an ass out of you…"

Ian said, "…and me!" He paused for a second. "Man, I fell for that again."

I laughed. Ian laughed. I pulled the car onto 8 Mile, made a Michigan left, and headed for McCatty Drive.

"I don't know, Ian. I don't know if this is way over our head or not. If it is, we'll bring Macy and Larkin in on it. They are much more equipped to handle it. From the sounds of it though, Stonewall will help us out, as long as we do not break the law. But, we'll keep digging until we can't dig anymore. If we begin to bury ourselves, we'll turn it over to the cops. Now, I'm heading home. Do you want to be dropped off at The Coffee Cabin or at your house?" I said.

"You can take me home. I'm going to go for a run. I need to clear my head some more. I'm tempted to call Nixie, so I'll run the feeling away," Ian said. He was already staring ahead. She was on his mind now. I quit talking to him so he could think.

I took my phone from my back pocket and carefully called Miss Colavino while I kept the Jeep in one lane. Her phone rang once before going straight to voice mail. I said, "Miss Colavino, this is Dalen Reese again. Call me as soon as you have a moment. It is important. I have some news I'd like to share with you about a mutual friend. Thank you." I ended the call.

I noticed I had received a text from Cherrie. I waited until I stopped at a traffic light before reading it.

It read: My boys won't be able to make it up for the wedding. It's a long story. I'll explain it to you over dinner. Though, long story short, can we go see them over Easter break for our honeymoon?

I texted back: Yes. I'll be home in a few.

The light turned green. I proceeded. A text came back. It read: I am at the studio filming two episodes. Crash says hello. I'll see you for dinner. How about Andiamo's? We haven't been there in a few months.

At the next red light, I responded: Sounds good. 6:30?

Her next text said: Yes. I luv U.

Just before I pulled onto McCatty, I saw a late model black BMW with the driver side window rolled down. As I drove past it, I got a good look at the man behind the wheel. It was Robert Samuel Johnson. He was wearing a Detroit Tigers baseball hat. I was pretty sure it used to be mine. He had taken it from me the night we had fought in the alley, when I stopped him from raping and killing Olivia. He looked directly at me and tipped the cap in my direction, as if to say, "Good day to you, Sir." When I was past his car, the window went up. Sweat bubbled on my head as adrenaline shot from my heart and ran through every inch of my body.

I pulled the car into our garage and closed the door. I turned off the engine and called Macy.

"What's up Reese?" she asked after the third ring.

"Johnson is parked on the curb at the end of McCatty Drive," I said.

"What is he driving?" she asked.

"A black BMW. I don't know the year. It looks new. He had his window rolled down so I could see him as I drove by," I said. My heart was still racing. My voice sounded shaky when I spoke.

"I'll send a car. We have one on your daughter now. Don't worry. Call me if he makes contact with you," she said. "I'm in a meeting. I have to go." She ended the call.

I felt somewhat better. I went into the house and locked the door behind me. I called the restaurant to make reservations for this evening. I spent the next hour tracing my steps, jotting down a timeline of the past two days. I filed the paperwork away in a file box I keep in our home office. I took a shower, dressed, and checked my phone repeatedly for a missed call or text. I was at a stall in our investigation for finding our friend Mark Smith, aka Frownie Mae.

Frownie Mae is a unique performer. Mark has devised an alter ego for himself. He raps politically themed songs over Industrial music, music such as that of Nine Inch Nails. His first hit was a cover of Elvis Presley's *In The Ghetto*. As if that weren't enough, he named himself, mockingly after Fannie Mae, one of our country's largest banking institutions: one that had to look to the government for bailout money. Frownie Mae is also portrayed as a hobo clown complete with a ratty trench coat and a bolo hat. Mark who is a dark skinned black man also uses black make up to cover his face. He paints on rather large blue eyes surrounded by large white circles and a big white frown over his lips. He somewhat resembles Al Jolson's *Mammy*. Al Jolson was a white jazz singer in the 10920's that painted his face black saying that, "Working behind a blackface mask gave him a sense of freedom and spontaneity he had never known." Very few people actually know the real identity of Frownie Mae, much the same way almost no one knew what the actual members of the 1970's rock group KISS looked like.

I went to my vast CD collection, found Frownie's first album *In the Ghetto,* and slid it in the player before hitting play. I lay down on the floor and listened to the first track with my eyes closed.

As *In the Ghetto* played, I remembered:

"Pass the puck, man! I'm open!" Ian kept shouting from the in front of the net. "I'm open!"

We were probably eight to ten years in age. I, being one of the older kids on the ice, was the team captain for the players on our street. There was a pond behind the houses in the cul-de-sac at the end of McCatty that separated our street and the street Mark Smith lived on. He was on the opposing team, though we were all friends. Ian and I played on The McCatty Drive, that's what we called our 6 man hockey team; The Drive. We were playing the Panthers, Mark's team. It was Christmas break. There was at least a foot of snow on the ground. We had shoveled the pond down to the clear ice. Two hockey nets set on opposite ends of our rink.

"Come on Dalen, hit me!" Ian shouted as, I skated circles around our opponents. I was trying to show off.

I raised my stick back as far as I could and swung down with force. I shot the puck toward Ian, who stepped to the side and knocked the puck past their goalie, Mark Smith, and into the net. We had just tied the game. We didn't have a timer, so we were playing until any of our parents called one of us in for dinner. It was already getting dark outside.

The puck bounced out of the net just as fast as it had gone in. Ian started to celebrate. "Goal! Goal! Goal!" he shouted as he jumped up and down on the ice.

"It didn't go in! It didn't go in!" Mark yelled in protest. "It's not a goal!"

"The hell it ain't," Ian shouted, inches from Mark's face. "You're blind!"

I skated over to them. The other players followed. "It was a goal," I said. ""Everyone saw it go in. Right guys?" I looked around for support. The other players on our team agreed with me and Ian.

 The six players on the Panthers team all disagreed. An argument broke out between the 12 players on the ice. No one was going to win this flair up. Before I knew what was happening, I saw Ian and Mark shoving each other. Mark grabbed Ian's jacket. A few punches were thrown. I tried to step in between them and break it up. They each managed to land a punch on me, as well.

With a little luck and a little strength, I extended my arms and actually separate Ian and Mark, though they weren't finished trying to get around me to get at each other. Ian somehow connected one final blow to Mark's chest, sending Mark tumbling backward. Mark extended his arms behind himself to help break his fall. The force of his landing on the ice caused the ice to crack. Through all the yelling and commotion, we all heard the thunderous cracking of the ice, under Mark Smith.

Mark tried to stand up. As he leaned forward and climbed to his knees, the ice gave way under him. Down he went, into the frigid pond. Water splashed up, soaking those of us that were close enough to the hole. For a moment, Mark was out of sight. I went to the edge of the hole, careful not to fall in myself.

Mark's arms appeared from the water as he began trying to pull himself up. "I can't swim! Help me! Help! I can't swim!" he yelled, frantically swinging his arms.

"Stand up," Ian yelled.

Every time Mark slapped the ice with his arms, the ice would again, break from the force. The hole kept getting bigger. Mark panicked more. "Help! Help me! I can't swim!" he continued to plea.

"Stand up!" Ian yelled again, in response.

Mark yelled some more. He continued to slap the breaking ice.

"Do something," one of his teammates yelled to me.

As I skated a few feet over to the edge of the hole, I knelt down on the ice to grab his flailing arms. I tried, but kept missing them as Mark was now in complete panic mode.

Suddenly, Ian skated past me and jumped into the hole, next to Mark. The water only came up to his chest. He waded behind Mark, placed one arm under each of Mark's armpits and lifted Mark to his feet. Ian stood behind Mark and said, "I told you to just stand up!"

All the other kids, kids from both teams, began laughing.

I stood up, leaned forward and grabbed Mark's hand. I pulled him out of the water as Ian lifted him from behind. Mark's clothes, including his ski mask were soaked. His face was dripping with water, though I knew a lot of the wetness was tears. The game was over. Everyone else went home. Ian and I walked Mark back to his house, where we helped him get out of his wet clothes and into some dry ones, while Mrs. Smith made hot chocolate for the three of us, on her stove.

That evening Cherrie and I had an incredibly romantic dinner at Detroit's finest Italian restaurant. When we got home, we spent some time in front of the fireplace and watched some television.

Cherrie fell asleep in my arms. When the fire was down to a smolder, I closed the glass doors, leaving them open just a crack, in front of the glowing embers. I carried my bride to be into the bedroom and tucked her in. I washed up before climbing into bed. I noticed Cherrie was awake, lying next to me, on her side. Her arm was extended under her head, in the shape of an 'L'. The only thing she had on was the smile on her face. I slithered under the covers and for the next hour, we created enough body heat to keep us warm, long after we had fallen asleep.

Chapter Nine

8 Days Before My Wedding

Day 3 of Frownie Mae's Disappearance

When we awoke in the morning, I still had a smile on my face. Cherrie was not in bed. I went to the kitchen where she handed me a fresh cup of black coffee. Steam was still rising from the brim. I thanked her. I took a sip; it was very hot. I looked outside and noticed that it was snowing. It wasn't snowing hard, but it was snowing, none the less. I was ready for this winter to be over. Spring Training was underway in Florida and the Detroit Tigers were once again predicted to have a strong season.

"Go sit down. I'll bring your oatmeal in to you in a moment," Cherrie said.

"Thanks," I said. I gave her a kiss and headed for the couch. I turned on the television; Sports Center. I waited for the commercials to finish. My breakfast was brought to me just as the last "word from their sponsor" wrapped up. Cherrie sat next to me and cut the pancakes she had made for herself. I was jealous. But, I was battling high cholesterol and following the doctor's orders, at least when Cherrie was around.

"Do you know what you are going to do today?" Cherrie asked.

"As far as the case is concerned; no I don't. I'll make another attempt to contact the reporter. I'll give that Dick Clark sounding fella another call, though I don't anticipate he'll have much more information to give me. I'll wait around to hear from either Stonewall with word about Mickey Royboy or I wait to hear from Macy telling me where to get in touch with Stonewall. Did I tell you that Stonewall doesn't use a cell phone? He doesn't even have one. He doesn't want anyone to be able to track him. He drives a beat up Oldsmobile too. He can, but won't upgrade to a car with a GPS. They might be able to find him," I said. I laughed at the idea. But it was almost a nervous laugh. Stonewall might not be crazy. Technology has a way of holding all of us hostage, nowadays.

"Well, it sounds like you have your plate full," Cherrie said.

"Actually, I don't," I said. "Not unless more leads come forth. But, just like the Karen Carpenter said, 'We've only just begun.'"

I waited for Cherrie to laugh but she didn't. Oh well.

"What?" she asked, while looking confused.

"What?" I said.

"What?" she asked again.

I thought about explaining my comment. Instead I said, "What?"

She shook her head, returned her attention to the sports highlights from the night before, and put more pancakes in her mouth. I sat quietly by her side and ate my plain oatmeal. Cherrie had put four dashes of Frank's Hot Sauce on it. That's how I like it. When we were finished eating, I took our dishes to the sink and washed them. I refilled my coffee cup and then went to take a shower. When I was finished and I had dressed, I checked my cell phone. I had a missed call from Victoria Colavino. I sat on the edge of the bed and played the voice mail.

It said, "Dalen, this is Vicky Colavino. We need to talk. Please meet me in front of The Spirit of Detroit at 1:00 today. Do not call me back." The voice message ended. I deleted it from my phone.

The Spirit of Detroit is a large bronze statue of a man, sitting with his arms outstretched from his sides. In one hand he holds a ball that symbolizes the rays from God. In his other hand he holds another that symbolizes family. The figure sits in front of the Coleman A. Young Municipal Building, off of Woodward, in downtown Detroit.

Maybe I would have something to do today, after all. It was still early in the morning. I called Senior Patrol Officer Dale Fontana. He had nothing more to contribute to the case of my missing friend, Mark Smith. I called my Ohio waitress friend, Brenda. I spoke to her for only a minute yet she could have spoke to me for an hour and not have had anything more to say about the case. I thanked her for her time. I wanted to call Lieutenant Macy and talk to her about Robert Stonewall. I opted not to bother her. I call on her enough, as it is.

Cherrie came into the bedroom to get dressed. I sat on the bed and watched her do so. I liked what I saw. Yet, at the same time, I was playing a music trivia game on my phone. I had downloaded it from the app store. Because my music knowledge is so vast, I was very good at it. When Cherrie was dressed, she took the phone from my hands, tossed it on the bed, and climbed on top of me. We started making out like a couple of kids from junior high school. She keeps me young.

My phone rang. It was Ian. I told him we had a date with our reporter friend this afternoon and I would meet him at The Coffee Cabin in an hour.

Cherrie and I repeated our actions from last night. We finished, cleaned up and re-dressed. I kissed her good bye and headed for The Coffee Cabin.

As I made a right off of McCatty Drive, a black BMW pulled up behind me. I looked in my rear view mirror. The man driving the vehicle behind me was Robert Samuel Johnson. He smiled and waved at me. I slammed on my brakes. He swerved his car onto the right shoulder and drove past me. A patrol car followed him. My heart was pounding but I was glad to see the police car. Macy was true to her word, as I was sure she would be. I had thought that someone would be watching Olivia, but I'm glad that an officer was sticking with Johnson instead.

I parked my Jeep in front of The Coffee Cabin, next to the 7-eleven. I went into the convenience store to say hello to my friend Anush. I bought a pack of Black Jack chewing gum and a pineapple flavored Towne Club pop. I was about to head into The Coffee Cabin when I received a text from a private number. The text read: Beware of The Older One.

"Alright," I said to myself. "I have no idea who The Older One is or why I received that text, but there is no doubt in my mind, I will eventually find out. And, I'm pretty sure I won't have to try too hard to do so. I put the phone back in my pocket. Ian drove into the parking lot, parked under a street lamp near the road, and joined me on the sidewalk near The Coffee Cabin. We sat on a bench under the window.

"Do you know who 'The Older One' is?" I asked Ian.

"The older one?" he said.

"I just got a text that told me to 'Beware of The Older One.'"

Ian said, "I'm assuming you don't recognize the phone number it came from."

"It came from a private number," I said.

"Can I see the text?" Ian asked.

Now, I could have just handed him my phone so he could see it, but instead I said, "That's all the text said."

"You won't show it to me?" he said.

"I'm telling you, the text came from a private number and all it said was 'Beware of The Older One.'"

"Why won't you show me the text?" he asked, sounding a little perturbed.

I could have let this play out a little longer, but I didn't want to fight. I retrieved my phone from my pocket and handed it to him. He looked at the text, with a smirk on his face. He read the text aloud, "Beware of The Older One."

"That's exactly what I said it said," I said.

Ian said, "I have no idea who The Older One is, but I bet we find out."

Ian stood and opened the front door to The Coffee Cabin, looked inside, and shouted, "Does anyone in here know who The Older One is?"

I didn't hear anyone answer. Ian must not have either. He let the door close and he rejoined me on the bench. "No one in there knows either."

"Why do you suppose each word in The Older One was capitalized? It's as if it is a title or something." I grabbed my phone and searched the web for answers. There were three books, two song titles, one album title, four movies, and a poem each titled The Older One. The web wasn't much help. I put my phone back in my pocket.

"Did you eat breakfast?" Ian asked me.

"I had a bowl of oatmeal," I said.

"So, that's a no," Ian said.

I shrugged my shoulders.

"Let's go eat," Ian said. "I'll drive."

We climbed into his car. He turned the ignition over. The Backstreet Boys were playing pretty loud through the speakers... "Backstreets back, alright."

Ian reached for the volume knob and turned it down, but just a little.

"Why is it that every time I get into your car, you have the Backstreet Boys Greatest Hits blaring from the speakers?" I asked, as he pulled onto the main road.

"No. It's not every time," Ian said.

"Yeah, every time," I said. "For the past ten years, every time I have gotten into your car, this CD has been playing."

"Well, it's a great CD," Ian said as a matter of fact.

"Fair enough," I said. I reached for the volume knob and turned it up even more.

For the next seven minutes, Ian and I sang as perfectly out of tune as two forty something men could possibly sing, at the top of our lungs. We even managed to get most of the words wrong. We didn't care. When we arrived at Rosie's Diner, we went in and ate a large breakfast. We spent the rest of the morning at Gordon's Food Center, Costco, and Sam's Club, picking up stock for The Coffee Cabin. Ian's trunk and back seat were pretty much full.

At 12:30 we parked curbside, fed the meter, and walked to the Spirit of Detroit. We hung around the statue like two men with nothing better to do. We each held our phones in front of our faces while we surfed our apps, played games, and checked our emails and texted people from our contact list. When I glanced at the time on my phone, I noticed it was 1:15. We were both freezing cold. It was still lightly snowing and was beginning to accumulate on the ground.

I was about to mention the time to Ian, when a blonde woman approached me from my left. She was wearing a pink knitted scarf with a matching ski cap. She wore a wool coat over her hoodie. The hoodie was covering her hat. Her long dark hair hung in front of her chest. She wore pink mittens as well.

"Dalen," she said.

Ian looked up from his phone.

"Were you followed?" she asked.

I looked around. "I don't know," I said. I wasn't expecting that question. "Ian, were we followed?"

He shrugged. "Beats me! I wasn't paying attention."

"Me either," I said to the brunette.

She looked around. I assume she didn't see anyone that posed a danger. She put her hand out for us to shake. We obliged.

"My name is Vicky Colavino. Walk with me," she said.

We started walking down the street, staying on the sidewalk. Ian was on her left, I was on her right.

"This is Ian Parker, my partner in crime," I said to Vicky.

"How do you know Mark Smith?" she asked.

"We grew up in the same neighborhood," Ian said. "We've known him since we were in grade school."

"Mark and I met at Oakland University a few years ago. We had many of the same classes together," she said. "We became friends. It's just a coincidence that I covered the Finlandia University shootings last year. How is Raven?"

"She's good," I said. "She's at Wayne State now. It's much better. She's living at home. She's still in therapy, but that's to be expected. It was a tragic event."

"Good. I'm glad for her," Vicky said. Then, with the formalities out of the way, she got to the point. "Last year, I was covering the Governor's annual New Year's Eve party at the Michigan Governor's Mansion, in Lansing. I was there as 'Press'. I was not an invited guest. There were about 20 'Press Reporters' there doing fluff pieces for their local papers. There were Congressmen, Senators, and people from the House of Representatives in attendance. Everyone who was anyone in politics in the state was there; spouses and significant others we all there as well. There were about two hundred people there. It was rockin'. The ladies wore their finest garbs and most of the men either wore suits or tuxes. There was a classic Jazz band providing the entertainment."

Ian and I let her speak without saying a word. Our hands were tucked deep into our pockets. We all seemed to have our heads bowed as we walked. We were trying to keep the wind from smacking us in the face. I watched my feet hit the pavement, step after step.

Vicky continued, "About an hour into the evening, I needed to use the restroom. I went to the one near the entrance, but all of the stalls were full. I didn't want to wait. Near the front door, there is a staircase. I decided to see if there was a restroom on the second floor, right above the one that was full on the first floor. No one stopped me from going up the stairs. There was a restroom at the top of the stairs, but the door was locked. I decided to venture down the hall to see if there might be another restroom I could use. There was. I went in and used it. Seeing as it was closer to the other end of the hall, I walked down the stairwell opposite the one I had walked up."

We had stopped at an intersection. We waited for the crossing light to give us the go ahead.

"I walked down the steps, but the door to the first floor was locked. I walked back up the steps to the second floor, but the door I had used was also locked from the stairwell. So, I walked up one more flight to the third floor. That door was propped open with a wooden triangle door jam. I headed to the exit staircase at the other end of the hall. However, and this is where it gets interesting, one of the offices on the floor was open. On the desk, facing the hall was a computer screen and a keyboard. I assume it had recently been used because the screensaver was rolling. I stopped in the doorway and watched the pretty pictures roll by on the screen. Most of them were of a family on vacation in warm climate; there were many palm trees in the back ground of most of the pictures. Anyhow, as I stood there, suddenly, the theme of the pictures changed," Vicky said with excitement.

"Were they the pictures of our Lieutenant Governor; the pictures Mark sent me?" I asked. The question was rhetorical.

Vicky moved on with her story. "So I went into the office, closed the door, grabbed a thumb drive from my purse, and I copied the pictures to it. I got the hell out of there as fast as I could. Needless to say, I didn't stay to watch the clock strike midnight. I sent the photos to Mark that evening. I wasn't sure exactly what I was going to do with them. I wanted Mark's input. He has really struck a nerve in the political community with his blog. Everyone involved in politics, locally, statewide, and nationally, knows of Mark Smith. What they don't know is that he has a secret identity as well."

"Frownie Mae," Ian and I said in unison, just to have something to include in the conversation.

"So, I waited to hear from Mark. When he called me a few months ago, he said he had a hot lead on who the other people in the photos were."

"Are you talking about the woman that took the photos as well as the obvious other two?" Ian said. He reached behind Vicky and punched me in the arm. "See Dalen, I told you there was a third person in the room."

"I never disagreed with you," I said.

"So, I let Mark do his thing while I waited to hear what our next move would be. He called me last week and said, 'Shit might get pretty hairy, real soon. I contacted Ralph Dixon. I have a meeting set up with him tomorrow.' That's what Mark told me. I asked him to let me know how it went and what was going to happen. He assured me he would. He also made it very clear that he would not reveal how he obtained the pictures. I trust him. I waited. Two days ago he sent me your number in an email and said to call you, 'Just in case'".

"But I called you first," I said. "Do you know that Mark has gone missing?" I asked her. I looked at her when I asked the question. I wanted to see her reaction.

Her cold red face lost most of the color. She nearly went pale. She stopped walking. We stopped with her. The three of us formed a small huddle, each facing the other two. Ian and I spent the next minute giving her a brief rundown of the past three days.

"So we know that the Royboys took Mark," she said, trying to piece our information together.

"We assume that much, based on the description we got from the woman at the diner," Ian said. We can't say anything for certain.

"But, we don't know why," I said. "At this point, we can only assume that Mark's kidnapping is related to the pictures you had downloaded from the computer at the Governor's party. What do the Lieutenant Governor and Mickey Royboy have to do with each other?"

"That's a good question," Vicky said. "I had never heard of the Royboy family before today. I'll do some digging and see what I can come up with."

We continued to walk the streets of Detroit and made our way back to our cars. She had parked just around the corner from Ian.

"I'll call you when I have something," Vicky said. "But, you should know, I will not have a discussion about this, or anything else I am working on, over the phone. There are a lot of powerful people in politics and the can pretty much do anything they want. At least they think they can, until they get caught." With that, she got into her car, started it up, and drove away.

When we were back on the road, Ian said, "I was going through Mark's tablet last night. I came across some new music from Frownie Mae's next album. He has set a release date for June 15th. I played the songs. They are damn good. They are a little less Industrial sounding and more danceable. He actually covers, or samples anyway, Marvin Gaye's 'What's Going On'. He wrote some killer lyrics that apply to the cop killings of innocent victims going on in the country over the past few years. It's pretty powerful."

I said, "Is it as powerful as 'We Didn't Start The Fire'?" Frownie Mae, covered Billy Joel's classic for his last album. He had updated the lyrics to continue from 1989 through the 2014. He was grateful to Billy for letting him keep the original chorus, sung by Billy himself.

Ian broke out into his best Frownie Mae impersonation rapping, "Jay Z...Beyonce'...50 Cent...and Kanye,...iPods...Apple Stores...Microsoft and Tech Wars,...Obamacare...It's not fair...Something...something...something..." He had forgotten the words but moved right into the chorus anyway,... "We Didn't Start The Fire..."

When he was finished singing, I said, "He struck gold with that one, literally. He sold a million copies of it."

"Well, based on what I heard last night, 'What's Going On' should sell at least that many. I'll play it for you when we get back to The Coffee Cabin," Ian said.

Chapter Ten

When we arrived back at our coffee shop, I helped Ian unload his car. Tondalaya and Aunt Lonnie were both working. They helped us put the stock away. When we were finished, I drove to Wayne State University to meet Raven for an hour or so between her afternoon and evening classes. We walked to the D.I.A. and had coffee in the cafeteria. Raven had a salad, too. We checked out the new Pop Art exhibit. We saw art from Edward Hopper, Andy Warhol, and the like. Then I walked Raven back to her class and went on to meet Cherrie at the studio.

I picked her up at the front entrance of her building. When she closed the car door, she leaned over the gear shift and gave me a kiss. She looked beautiful. Her hair and makeup were perfect. They were perfect whenever she taped an episode for her show. But to me, she looked perfect with or without makeup on. I could tell she had on a low cut V-neck sweater, under her coat. It showed off her ample cleavage. I liked the look. After all, am I not a red blooded male?

"Not only do you look amazing, you smell fantastic," I said to Cherrie.

"It's vanilla; French vanilla, to be precise. I made a triple layered French Vanilla beer cake with an almond glazed icing," she said. "It took everything I had not to devour the whole thing. Tommy loved it more than most of my baked goods. You should have seen it, it was absolutely stunning. I'd say it is probably in my top 10 favorite creations."

"Don't you say that about all of your creations?" I asked.

She gave me a punch on my right arm. She huffed. She said, "Maybe."

"Are you hungry?" I asked.

"I could eat you up," she said squeezing my thigh. "But seriously, do you feel like Chinese food tonight? I can write a review for a new place on Griswold Street. It's called Jon Lee's. It's supposed to be fabulous. I just have to give him a call."

"I'm game, but can you see if we can get in a little later? I'm not really hungry right now," I said.

"Shit! Somebody call The Guinness Book of World Records. Take note of the time. Dalen Reese is NOT hungry for the first time in, what, ever?" Cherrie said, smiling big and laughing to herself.

I laughed at her attempt to be funny; not so much at what she said, but that she tried. She took out her phone and called Jon Lee's. When she ended the call, she said, "Will you be hungry at 9:00 tonight?"

I said, "By 9:00 tonight, I'll be starving."

"We have a few hours to waste, do you want to catch a movie," I asked.

"Yes. Hang on." Cherrie scanned the movies app for show times at the local AMC Theatre. "There isn't anything new I want to see, but we can catch 'The Bride of Frankenstein' at the Corktown Cinema."

I loved the classics; especially ones staring Boris Karloff. "Will we be done in time to make our reservations for dinner?" I asked.

"Absolutely," Cherrie said, as a matter of fact.

"I'm good for both," I said. I put the car in drive and we were off for another romantic evening.

Chapter Eleven

7 Days Before My Wedding

Day 4 of Frownie Mae's Disappearance

The next morning, after breakfast, I was on my way to The Coffee Cabin when I was flagged down by Mrs. O'Flannigin, at the end of

McCatty Drive. She was standing curbside in a pink terrycloth robe and matching Deerfoam slippers. She had a rolled up newspaper under her arm. I slowed the Jeep to a stop and rolled my window down.

"Good morning Mrs. O'Flannigin. How are you doing?"

"Dalen, I just want to remind you that you and that little red headed boy are going to come over and move my couch. You haven't forgotten have you?" she said. She had her teeth in her mouth this time.

"No, we haven't forgotten. I'll try to get over tomorrow evening. Will that work for you?" I asked.

"Bring that little red headed boy with you. Don't forget," she said.

"We'll see you tomorrow," I said as I rolled up my window and drove away. In my rearview mirror, I watched her say something to someone that wasn't me. Soon enough, she was out of sight and out of mind.

Aunt Lonnie was already hard at work when I arrived. She handed me a cup of coffee seconds after I walked in the door. I gave her a kiss. Raven was taking an order from a couple of college students, both men. They were doing their best to flirt with her. For a decent tip, she played along. I took my coffee to the office and said good morning to Paul Newman as I woke up my laptop.

My screensaver was currently a picture of Jimi Hendrix from the Monterey Jazz Festival. It was taken in 1967. I opened the Google Chrome search engine and began doing research with the information I had been given over the past two days. So much of the P.I. work that Ian, Tommy, and I do is research conducted on the computer. We take photos of cheating spouses and people on workman's comp trying to screw the system. Rarely do we have a run-in with the subject under surveillance, though it has happened. We once followed an asshole that had jumped bail as he rode ride after ride at Cedar Point while we waited for the Bail Bondsman to make the drive to Ohio. It rarely gets very exciting.

 I jotted down as much information as I could find on the people that attended the Governor's New Years Eve party. I could only find six articles that had actually been written on the subject. Most of them were about the Governor himself and his wife. Two articles were just about what the women in attendance were wearing. I made a list of every name mentioned in each piece. I did a search of each individual. I went through article after article of their elections, the bills they proposed, passed or didn't pass. There were few photos of any of them, other than the studio photos that were used for their campaign posters and the like.

I looked at the few people in all of the photos I could find. None of them matched the man that posed naked with our Lieutenant Governor Ralph Dixon. For now, the African American man would continue to go unnamed, though I thought of giving him nickname for the time being; I kinda liked John Dick. As I was tossing names around in my head, Raven knocked on the office's opened door. She had a full pot of coffee in her hand.

"Morning Daddy!" she said with a smile. "Refill?"

"Please," I said. There was a small amount of cold coffee in the bottom of my mug. I poured it down my throat and placed the mug on the desk for her to refill, which she did.

"Any luck finding where Mark might be?" she asked.

"Not yet," I said. "Hey listen, do you know how, when you can call someone and have it show up as a private number on the recipient's phone, can you do that with a text too?"

Raven looked somewhat confused. She repeated the question back to me for clarification. "Ok. I understand the question now. Um, I have never sent or received a text to anyone using the private number block. I have never texted anyone I didn't know. And I can't recall ever getting a text from anyone I didn't know, unless it was from a business, and those texts usually show up with, like, a five or six digit number. I assume you received a text from a private number and you obviously don't know who it is from. What does it say?"

"Beware of The Older One," I said.

"Can I see it?" she asked.

Really? Why don't people believe me when I tell them this? So instead of telling her that it says exactly what I have already said it says; I handed her my phone.

She swiped the screen with her finger a few times. She read the text out loud and read it exactly as I had already told her. Then she said, "How can it come from a private number? I have never heard of that happening. I didn't know someone could do that. When you figure it out, tell me how it's done. I'm dying to know." She handed me my phone back then said, "I'll let you get back to investigating." She left and took the coffee pot with her.

"Hey Raven," I shouted before she had gotten too far. She reappeared in the office doorway. "What does it mean; Beware of The Older One?"

"I have no idea Daddy. I have no idea," she said.

I had already been sitting at my desk for nearly two hours, investigating the politicians from the New Year's Eve party. I needed to stretch. I walked out the back door to the parking lot behind the strip mall. Feena, Anush's wife, was taking out a bag of trash and tossing it into a dumpster.

"Good morning, Dalen," she said with a pleasant smile. A puff of cold air was blowing from her mouth as she spoke. She cupped her hands over her mouth and blew into them to warm her up a bit.

"Good morning to you, Feena," I said. "It's a bit chilly out this morning. Hey, will Cherrie and I be seeing you and Anush at our wedding next weekend?"

"Oh, absolutely. We have our nephew Matthew covering the store for us. We wouldn't miss it for the world. I have to get back inside," she said. "It is very good to see you. Have a nice day, Dalen."

"You too, Feena. You too," I said, as I watched the beautiful lady disappear behind her closing door. I was getting cold. I went back inside.

I sat back down at the desk and Goggled Mickey Royboy. I read article after article on the Kingpin but I never found any that mentioned him as one. Every article I found and read talked about his many charitable contributions. He comes from a long line of wealthy French Canadian families. His family made their money in fur a century ago. From what I could tell, Mr. Royboy owns a handful of drycleaners in the Detroit area.

I came across pictures of Mickey with auto executives, sports figures, and a few local but nationally know celebrities such as Kid

Rock and Berry Gordy. For the most part, Mickey Royboy flies under the radar. There were no articles of arrests or run-ins with the law. I found it very odd. But what I did find interesting is that one article listed the phonetic pronunciation of his last name. They listed it as Wah-boi; Mickey Roy (Wah)-boy (boi). I didn't care. If he has anything to do with the abduction of Mark, I am going to call him Roy-boy with a strong 'R', just for spite. Then I might kill him.

Next, I looked into his sons; Donnie and Terry Royboy. There was even less in the press about these two. There were photos of them, in suits. They were good looking men. In one picture with the boys, they were standing on either side of rapper Eminem. They were each throwing up a sideways peace sign with their outside hands. Eminem did not make a sign with his hands, nor did he have any kind of expression on his face. The brothers, on the other hand, were each sticking out their tongues, ala Miley Cyrus. I saved the picture to my laptop. On the back of the peace hand of each of the Royboy brothers was a tattoo of large black letters.

In all of the research I had done this morning on the Royboy family, I was surprised to find very little illegal activity from them. When I say little, I mean, all there was, was one mention of Terry Royboy being in a car that was in an accident a few St. Patrick Day's ago. Alcohol was involved, but Terry was not driving. That's it. I wonder how in the world can a family that allegedly runs a major gambling ring for the North side of Detroit, as well as the cocaine and other major drugs, not have any arrest records. How have they managed to evade the law?

Robert Stonewall made it very clear that these are very bad people. He said he knows. They are the main reason he walks with a limp and uses a cane. He is currently working off a major debit for them. I'm baffled.

I located the picture I had just saved to my computer, emailed it to myself, saved the picture to my phone and then texted it to Senior Patrol Officer Dale Fontana. I attached a memo that said: I believe these two men, in suits, are the two men that abducted Mark Smith. Please show the photo to Brenda and Mrs. Salma Jackson to verify. Their names are Terry and Donnie Royboy, Terry is on Eminem's right. I hit send.

Seconds later I received a text from Fontana. It simply said: Ok. I will do so ASAP.

I sent Fontana one more text: Do you know what 'Beware of The Older One' might mean? It was a shot in the dark, but I was getting desperate.

His response was quickly returned: NO!

I shut down the laptop and went into the lobby to converse with my Aunt Lonnie and Raven. I grabbed a homemade muffin from the few that were left. I refilled my coffee mug and had a seat at the end of the bar. Just before I was about to unwrap the muffin, Aunt Lonnie came over and took it away from me.

"Shame on you Baby Boy," she said. She had called Ian and I that since birth. "Cherrie would tan your hide if she knew you were eating this. I, for one, will not be held responsible for your high cholesterol. How dare you." She had a lovely smile on her face the whole time she spoke. She put the muffin on the cutting board, sliced it into quarters, put one piece on a paper towel and put it on the bar in front me. "We can't let it go to waste, though." She slid a quarter of a slice into her mouth and said, "But, I am not watching my cholesterol."

"I love you Aunt Lonnie," I said.

"I love you too, Baby Boy."

Raven came around the bar, picked up one of the two remaining quarter slices and put it in her mouth. One quarter of the muffin, which happened to be chocolate chip, sat on the cutting board. The three of us stood there looking at it. Then we each looked at each other, as if we were in a gunfight, in the old west. We looked back at the muffin piece. I moved my hand, ever so slightly in the direction of the prize. More eye contact. Then out of nowhere, Ian's hand swoops in and grabs it out from under all of our noses. He shoves it into his mouth and smiles.

"Too slow!" he said with a laugh, as he sat down on the stool next to me. "Did you find anything out this morning?" He was referring to the research I had told him I was going to do.

"Not too much," I said. "I found a picture of the Royboy Brothers with Eminem and I texted it to Officer Fontana."

"With Eminem?" Ian said. "How does that happen?"

"Money! Oh, and I found out that the correct way to pronounce their last name is Wah-Boi," I said.

"Wah-Boi? What the hell kind of stupid name is that?" Ian asked with a wrinkled up face. "Ohhhh, I get it. Wah, like Patrick Roy (Wah) of the Colorado Avalanche. Man, that fight between Roy and Chris Osgood is still the best fight between two goalies ever. Damn, I hated Patrick Roy; but what a rivalry the Wings had with the Avs.

That was the last hurrah for the NHL. When they took the fights out of the game, it just jumped the shark. I still love it, though it's just not the same."

"I agree. On the plus side, now that the Wings are in the Eastern Conference, the road to the Stanley Cup got easier. I was thinking of getting Cherrie a Dylan Larkin jersey for a wedding present. She loves her Red Wings. He just may end up being the next Yzerman," I said. "Whatda'ya think, about the jersey I mean? Is that something that is appropriate for a wedding gift?"

"I don't know. But I do know she'd like it," Ian said. "Yeah, that's a good idea. Let's go get one."

"Now?" I asked.

"Let's make a run to Hockeytown. I'll bet they are open for lunch," Ian suggested.

"I'll drive," I said. "I don't feel like listening to the Backstreet Boys." I laughed.

We were almost to Hockeytown when I got a text from Renee Macy. It read: Can you meet Stonewall and Mickey Royboy at Old St. Mary's Catholic Church in 30 minutes?

I handed the phone to Ian. "Ask her if that's the one on Monroe in Greektown," I said.

He did. She responded with a: Yes.

"Do you think we have time to get the jersey before we go to the church?" I asked.

"Not if you want to eat, too," Ian said.

"Damn." I rerouted the car and headed towards Greektown. We arrived a few minutes later. I parked on Saint Antoine Street. We walked to the front steps of the beautiful historic landmark and sat down. The cement steps were freezing on my backside. I leaned back, resting my elbows on the step behind me. We waited. Exactly thirty minutes from the time I received Macy's text, Robert Stonewall walked around the corner, leaning heavily on his cane.

"Let's go inside," Robert said. No "hello." No greeting at all. Just, "Let's go inside."

He walked past Ian and me and entered the church. A few patrons were occupying the pews, though there weren't two people sitting next to each other. Near the back row was the man I recognized from the pictures I had looked at this morning. He was sitting alone, looking straight ahead. Robert Stonewall entered the row behind Mickey and sat directly behind him. Robert nodded his head, instructing Ian and me to sit next to Mr. Royboy. I entered the pew first.

"Mr. Royboy," I said, "My name is Dalen Reese. Thank you for meeting with us today. This is my associate Ian Parker. I'm sorry; it is pronounced Wah-boi, correct?"

"Very good, Mr. Reese," he said. "You have done your homework." He paused for a few moments, and then said, "How can I be of assistance to you this afternoon?"

I don't like to waste time bullshitting around so I said, "A friend of ours has gone missing. He was abducted from a diner in Ohio, this past Wednesday."

"I'm sorry to hear that. I hope he is okay," Mickey said. The inflection in his voice showed no concern.

"I hope he is too," I said. "Witnesses at the diner say two young men, fitting the description of your sons, may have been his abductors."

As I sat next to this man, I looked him in his eyes as I spoke. He breathed heavily for a man that was not overweight, mostly through his nose. His salt and pepper hair was just beginning to thin on the top of his head. It was cut into a crew cut: a flat top. His eyebrows were grey and long enough to curl at the ends. His turtle neck shirt was black. He wore a long brown leather coat that tied at the waist with a leather belt. His brown leather gloves were placed neatly on his lap. His eyes were as blue as Paul Newman's. He needed to trim the hair in his ears.

"My boys are good boys. They would never do such a thing," he said. His breath smelled of garlic. "But, if it will help you feel relieved, I will ask them for you. I'm certain my sons had nothing to do with the disappearance of your friend. After I ask them, whatever their answer is, I will inform Mr. Stonewall. He can share the information with you. Is there anything else I can do for you?"

I was actually getting nervous. I tried like hell to keep my composure. I literally felt like I was in the movie The Godfather or Goodfellas or something like that. I took a deep breath. I needed to find Mark and I knew that the Royboy's had him. I know they had taken him because he had something they wanted. I know Mark. There is no way he would give it up, without a fight. He takes his careers very seriously; both of them. He makes good money as a political blogger. He is well respected in his field. He has ruffled more than a few political feathers. He is also very serious about his music career, though I doubt he was kidnapped because he is a rapper. I knew what I had to do. I had one hand left to play and I had to go all in.

"Mr. Royboy," I said, as I stood. My heart was racing. "I hope for everyone's sake that my friend Mark Smith is not in any danger. I will find him, with or without your cooperation, regardless of what your sons tell you."

Mickey Royboy used the back of the pew in front of us to pull himself up. As he stood, so did Ian. Mickey said, "Mr. Reese, I do not like your implications. If my sons have anything to do with your friend's absence, I will inform Mr. Stonewall. However, if they say they had nothing to do with it and you continue to be a nuisance, I will see that this matter is completely laid to rest. I hope I make myself very clear."

"Listen here, Mickey," I said.

I heard Ian say, "Damn!" under his breath.

My voice was shaky, as were my hands. Under my Detroit Tigers baseball cap, sweat was dripping down my bald head. I was already disrespecting this man by not referring to him as Mr. Royboy. But, with butterflies in my stomach, I continued, "I haven't even begun to be a nuisance."

Mickey interrupted me, "Tread lightly, Mr. Reese!" That was definitely a warning.

I leaned into Mickey Royboy's personal space and whispered to him, "Mark Smith is not the only one with copies of the pictures." I straightened up and met his eyes with mine. I wanted to say, "Don't fuck with me!" but I knew I had already crossed the line; so I didn't.

Mickey's face turned a dark shade of pink. His breathing was visibly heavier and much louder. He didn't expect me to say what I had just said. He didn't respond. I could tell the wheels in his head were spinning. His eyes darted away from mine and back again; several times.

I was running on adrenaline and appearing calm at the same time. "I'll expect to hear from Mr. Stonewall in the very near future. Enjoy the rest of your weekend, Mr. Royboy." I emphasized a hard 'R' when I said his last name. Then I turned and pushed Ian out of the row and into the center aisle. We didn't look back as we exited the church.

"Holy shit," Ian said. "I can't believe you fucking played it like that! That was awesome!"

We walked as fast as we could, toward my Jeep, while trying not to run. When we got into the car and the doors were shut, I started the vehicle and we pulled away from the curb. I drove two blocks and pulled over. I took off my ball cap. I whipped the sweat off of my head with my bare hand. Some of it ran down the back of my neck and into my shirt.

"Oh my God!" I said, with my heart still pounding. "I can't believe I did that either. Shit, I'm probably going to wake up with a horse's head in my bed," I said referring to a scene in The Godfather. "I had to say what I said. We have to find Mark. That's our main priority."

"I know," Ian said. "I agree. Are we even sure that they took Mark because of the pictures?"

"I don't know. But, we will find out. Won't we?" I said.

"Man that was a ballsy move, Dalen. You played that like a pro." Ian started laughing. "Dude, that was so badass!"

Chapter Twelve

When we arrived back at The Coffee Cabin, I texted Cherrie and let her know I would be working until the rush slowed down. With it being Saturday, that would probably be well into the evening. Before Ian and I returned, we stopped at Hockeytown, had lunch, and I bought Cherrie the Larkin authentic Red Wing jersey.

I went to the jukebox, located near the front door. I slid $3.00 into money slot and chose a dozen songs to play. The televisions were on in each corner of the lobby, mounted near the ceiling. 21 Jump Street was playing; the movie with Channing Tatum, not the television series starring Johnny Depp. I left it playing, but I muted the volume on the screens.

Tondalaya was working the afternoon shift. She was currently being helped by two of our newer waitresses, Hazel Hathaway and Chante' Ramsey. Though they did have things under control for the time being, it would get busier. Ian had a few things to take care of but he said he would come back in a few hours. I sat on the last barstool at the end of the bar and nursed my coffee.

As the calm before the storm began to wind down, John Cougar's 'Jack & Diane' played through the speakers.

I remember:

I'm not exactly sure how old I was, but I was in junior high school. It was a warm Saturday in the springtime. I had spent the night at my friend Jason's house. He lived about a mile and a half from my house on McCatty Drive. The sun was already shining bright. I had to be home early that morning. I had to attend a Reese family reunion. All the cousins, aunts, uncles, and grandparents would be present. My dad said my attendance was mandatory.

I awoke early, showered, and ate a bowl of Kellogg's Rice Krispies. Jason's mother had finished the half gallon carton of milk, so I poured orange Tang over my cereal. I had seen my dad do so on several occasions. I liked it. The rice still spoke to me; 'snap, crackle, and pop!'

Jason couldn't pull himself out of bed, so I ate alone. His mother didn't drink coffee but she did drink a warm caffeine free coffee substitute called Postum. I mixed a spoonful into a mug of hot water. It made me feel like a grown up. When I was finished with my breakfast, I slipped my feet into my Velcro strapped grey tennis shoes, grabbed my Puma tote bag, told Jason I would be back after the "stupid family reunion", then I headed for home.

I stopped on his front porch, dug into my bag and pulled out my Walk-man. I placed the little foam padded headphones on my head and pressed play on the cassette player. John Cougar, who later became John Cougar-Mellencamp and then simply John Mellencamp, began to play to my delight. As his 'American Fool' kept me company, I quietly sang to myself as I soaked up the sun.

I wasn't quite halfway home when the Postum and Tang hit me. I had to pee and I had to pee right then. I quickly considered my options as I started to walk faster. I could stop at Tony's house, which I had just passed. I really didn't want to see Tony so I quickly ruled that option out. I could turn back and return to Jason's house but that would make me late getting home, and I knew my dad would not be happy with that. So, I decided to continue my trek, hoping to make it without incident.

As I got closer to home, I passed a vacant lot that I had considered using to relieve myself. The grass and weeds were tall enough, but I didn't feel comfortable as houses on either side of the lot had upstairs with windows overlooking the lot. So I walked faster.

As I was three blocks from McCatty Drive, I noticed Ginny Lee and Shannon Springer walking toward me. Ginny and Shannon were two of the most beautiful girls in our junior high school. They were extremely popular and well liked by people of every group in our class; the beauty queens and jocks, the brains and the geeks, as well as the burnouts and losers.

Ginny was a redheaded beauty queen that developed early. Shannon was a blonde that looked a lot like Farah Fawcett. They were absolutely sweet and kind to every person they knew. As I walked faster, they inevitably got closer to me. They smiled and waved when they saw me. John Cougar started singing Jack & Diane. That was the only bright spot I could conjure up at that moment.

The closer I got to them, the faster I walked. My walk became a jog, then my jog became a run, and my run turned into a sprint. Ginny and Shannon were only a few houses away from me when they stopped walking. I can only imagine what they must have been thinking as I hurried toward them. At the pace I was moving, they must have thought I was going to run them over.

I didn't say a word as I passed them because I was too embarrassed. As I was fifty feet in front of them and closing the gap quickly, I lost all control of my bladder. I was wearing a pair of light grey jeans. In the matter of moment, my left pant leg became soaked with urine. I left a trail of warm yellow liquid behind me. My tennis shoe was soaked and squished every time my foot pounded the pavement.

Ginny and Shannon stood still with a dumbfounded look on their faces, as I approached. I didn't look back to see their reaction after I passed them. I continued to pee my pants while running as fast as I could. I don't think I had ever run that fast in my life. My baseball coach would have been proud.

I ran into house and darted for the bathroom. I tried to get by my dad without his noticing. I didn't make it. It must have been the river I had flowing behind me. He grabbed my arm as I attempted to pass him.

"What the hell happened?" he said referring to my accident.

"I just became the laughing stock of junior high," I said, as tears filled my eyes.

"Get cleaned up," he said. "We're going to be late. We'll talk about it in the car."

My dad wasn't mad. He was sympathetic. He was really cool about the situation. But he was not near as cool as Ginny and Shannon were. I expected to walk into school on Monday and have everyone make fun of me. But the thing is there was never a word uttered about my incident. Not one. I had Shannon in two of my classes. She honestly acted like it didn't happen. I was beginning to think that maybe they hadn't noticed. Five years later on our graduation day, Ginny and I had a nice and private laugh about the event. They knew. They were just cool enough to never have discussed it with anyone else. For that, I have always been thankful.

As the customers began to slowly fill The Coffee Cabin, I was forced to leave the stool and my memories behind. I had sandwiches, coffee, and ice creams to make. I was behind the bar working steadily, when Ian joined me about an hour later. We were all enjoying our evening as much as the atmosphere in our little coffee shop would dictate. The music was playing and setting the mood. Laughter and conversations filled the room. Every so often I will stop, look around, and soak it all in. People always seem to be happy here.

At 9:07 p.m., my phone vibrated. I pulled it out of my back pocket. I had another text from a private number. I could only assume it was the same private number that warned me about The Older One. This text read: The Closer You Get, The Greater The Danger!

I took a deep breath. I slid the phone across the counter so Ian could read it.

"Again, each word begins with a capital letter," Ian said. "I assume it is from the same person and number."

"I assume it is," I said.

Ian asked me a question I hadn't thought of. He said, "Do you consider these two texts, from this unknown person, as a threat or a warning?"

"A threat or a warning?" I asked as I tried to think about the answer.

"Yeah," Ian said. "What if they are not from the bad guys, per se? What if they are from a friend trying to warn us about the older one, instead of threatening us? What if they are from Mark?"

"Why would he send us such a vague warning? Why would he send them from a blocked or private phone number?" I asked.

"What if he was sending them from one of the Royboy's phones?" Ian asked. "I only ask because I'm pretty sure this new text is the title of one of his new songs from his new album; the one on his tablet."

"If that is the case, and they are from Mark, why would he be using such vague statements as clues?" I said. "

"Hell, I don't know," Ian said. "You're the detective. You should try to figure it out."

"Shit. I'm trying to." I said. "But what if they are from someone else and they just want us to think they are from Mark?"

Ian said, "Knowing Mark, he hasn't let anyone see or hear his new music. No one would know the song titles of his new album. The texts have to be from Mark. They just have to be. That's why he left the tablet with his mother."

"So he could send us song titles as clues as to his whereabouts?" I asked. "I'm clueless. Where is he then? What are some of the other song titles then? Maybe they will tell us."

"Is the tablet still in the office?" Ian asked as he headed for the back room.

I followed.

Ian sat at the desk and turned on the tablet. Ian had found a charger that fit it to keep it charged. It was plugged in. I stood behind Ian and looked over his left shoulder and watched as the tablet booted up. When it did, Ian swiped and tapped at the screen until the new songs from Frownie Mae's new unreleased album were visible. Ian read off the list of titles we were looking at. *Beware Of The Older One* was not one of them. *The Closer You Get, The Greater The Danger!* was indeed one of the tracks.

"It just can't be a coincidence," I said.

"We'll have to wait until we get another text from our unidentified friend before we know if it is or not," Ian said. "I still have no idea who the older one is. Should we just assume, for now, that the texts are from Mark? If we do, does that help us at all?"

I thought about that for a moment. I looked at Paul Newman, hanging on the wall. "What do you think, Luke?" I asked the blue eyed man staring back at me. He didn't answer.

I sat down on the '57 Chevy's seat couch. I thought some more. Ian played one of the tracks from Frownie Mae. It was an original. I listened as I thought about our missing friend. Mark rarely sang on his songs. He was a rapper. He rapped. However, on the song Ian was playing, Mark was singing. He really has a great voice. The song was a ballad.

"What is the name of this song?" I asked.

"Long Live the Innocence of Memories Fading," Ian answered. It's a bonus track that wasn't listed. I read some of the liner notes about it. It plays 30 seconds after *In the Wake of the Cyber Storm*, the last track on the album."

"He may not send us a text that says either but the *Cyber Storm* title is probably a reference to the shit that got him kidnapped. Did you listen to that song? Does he have the lyrics typed up somewhere on that thing?" I said.

Ian said, "Yeah, he does. Give me a second."

I waited. "I'll be back in a minute. I need to hit the can."

When I came back into the office, I handed Ian a fresh cup of coffee in his Detroit Lions mug. I had a cup for myself. Mine was poured into an orange and blue Detroit Tiger's coffee mug. It just so happened to match the hoodie I was wearing.

"Thanks," Ian said. "Here, check this out." He read some of the lyrics from the *Cyber Storm* song. He said, "A cyber storm waged over some nudie pics. That black bro be swinging his big trophy dick. It's dangling around in a white man's world. The chick in the pic with her tasseled tits, be tossing em round as their lives unfurl."

"You are a lousy rapper, Ian Parker!" I said.

"Hey, I was just reading the words. But it is obvious that he is talking about the pictures he sent to you. So it is safe to assume, then, that he sent the text messages to your phone," Ian said.

"I agree. He must be trying to help us find him. What bothers me still is that he must have known that he was going to be kidnapped. Right? I mean, if you look at how this whole thing has unfolded, it is as if he left this tablet with his mother so we could decipher his clues. But why would he do that?" I asked. It was pretty confusing to me. "Can you print out all the lyrics to the tracks on the album?"

"Give me a few minutes," Ian said. "I'll start with *The Closer You Get, The Greater The Danger!*"

I texted Cherrie. I told her I would be home in about an hour. The girls had the business covered out front. They really didn't need Ian or me there for help. Cherrie texted me back saying that she would be waiting with bated breath. She attached a picture of herself in a sexy blue nightie.

I texted back: I'm on my way!

"Ian, I gotta go!" I said. And I left!

Chapter Thirteen

6 Days Before My Wedding

Day 5 of Frownie Mae's Disappearance

The next morning I picked Ian up at his house. We were going to pay our Lieutenant Governor a surprise visit. Miss Colavino and I spoke last night. She said he typically has breakfast with his wife at a diner in Lansing before they head to Sunday morning mass. It was 5:30 in the morning when Ian climbed into my Jeep Wrangler.

"Are ready to do this?" Ian asked me.

"Yes I am. I have no idea how it will play out, but we are getting desperate. We've got to find Mark. I'd feel like shit if we didn't cover every avenue we had. Whenever we see our flame go out, we've got to stoke the fire. Maybe this will be a dead end. I don't know," I said.

"Did you get the text I sent you last night?" Ian asked.

"The one you sent at 3 A.M.? Yeah, I got it. So, you are convinced that based on the lyrics from Frownie's songs that he is convinced that the finger of the girl in the photos belong to the daughter of Mickey Royboy," I said trying to clarify Ian's text.

"Yeah," Ian said. "And that is the connection between Lieutenant Governor Ralph Dixon and Mickey Royboy. Mickey's daughter's name is Lisa Stewart. I don't know if it is a married name or her mother's maiden name. I was not able to find that out. I still do not know the name of the black fella in the photos either. Perhaps Dixon can shed some light on that for us."

"Do you want me to stop and get coffee before we get on the road?" I asked.

"Not for me," Ian said. "I'm wide awake. I just got back from running 5 miles."

"Ok, well I'm gonna get some," I said as I pulled into a Speedway gas station.

When I was back in the car, I handed Ian a cup of coffee he didn't want. He thanked me and took a sip. I sipped mine as well as I pulled the Jeep onto the road. We had been on the road for about half an hour when my cell phone started playing, "Play That Funky Music."

I handed Ian my empty coffee cup which he tossed into the back seat. "What the hell?" I said. "I could have done that." I answered the call. It was an area code number from the 313.

"Dalen Reese, Detroit's sexiest private eye. I am off the market as of this coming Saturday. How can I help you?" I asked.

The voice on the other end of the wireless line started laughing. He laughed harder than he probably should have, even if he did think I was being funny. I waited. After about fifteen seconds, the voice said, "Lou said you thought you were funny."

"Lou who?" I asked. I honestly had no idea who Lou was nor did I know who I was talking to.

"Lou. Lieutenant Macy. She said you got a kick out of yourself. I'm sorry, I should have introduced myself. This is Detective Cody Simpson from the DPD, Missing Person's Division. I have been assigned the case of Mark Smith. Do you have a few minutes to talk? I'd like to get started as soon as possible."

"Is your name really Cody Simpson?" I said, trying not to laugh.

"Yes sir, Detective Cody Simpson of the DPD," he said again.

"Yeah, I got that. I guess I never thought about it, but sooner or later you kids with all these young names were going to have to get jobs. I just never thought I'd actually hear of a detective with the first name of Cody or Colton or Colby or Zack. I think of detective's names and I think of strong names like Mike Hammer and Thomas Magnum or I don't know, just stronger sounding names than Cody," I said.

"Sir, my name aside, I can assure you, I have earned my title." The light hearted laughter had left his voice. "Now, if you have a moment, I'd like to talk to you about your missing friend, Mark Smith."

"I'm sorry," I said. "What do you need to know?"

For the next 15 minutes, Detective Cody Simpson filled me in on what he already knew. He didn't know anything that I didn't already know. I filled him in on everything else. He asked a ton of questions. I was able to answer most of them. The questions I couldn't answer were the questions I was still trying to find answers to myself, most importantly, "Where is Mark Smith?"

I did not keep the whole Frownie Mae secret from him. I couldn't do that. But he gave me his word that he would keep it out of the investigation, the reports, and from the press as long as possible. He did say he hoped he could keep it entirely a secret, but he had to do his job and he made no promises.

When he had all he needed, he thanked me for my time and ended the call. I actually felt better about our chances of finding Mark.

Just a short time later, I parked the Jeep on Riley Street. Ian and I walked around the corner and into the 24 hour Fleetwood Diner. The place was half full with patrons. The floor was covered with black and white checked tiles. The chairs were red and tables were speckled black and white. It both resembled and smelled a lot like Rosie's, my favorite diner near Detroit. Ian and I took a seat at a table near the back. We sat so we could both see the clientele; those that were present and the others as they arrived. We ordered coffee.

Our waitress's name was Serena. I said, "Honey, we may be here a little while. This is for your trouble and possible loss of a table in your section." I handed her four Jackson's.

"Stay as long as you'd like," she said with a smile. "I'll be back in a moment with your coffee."

"How much did you tip her," Ian asked curiously.

138

"I gave her $80.00," I said.

"You did not!" he said in disbelief.

"No, I just gave her twenty," I said.

"You better have only given her twenty!" he said. "Cherrie would have your nuts in a vice if she knew you tipped a waitress $80.00."

"We might be here awhile," I said. "I don't want her missing out on her tips."

"Yeah, but $80.00?" Ian asked.

I nodded at our waitress so Ian would be quiet. He got the hint.

Serena returned with our coffee. "What can I get you two this morning?"

Outside, the sun was shining brightly through the front windows of the diner. It was a cloudless morning, with a bright blue sky. The sunrise had been a beautiful pink and orange, on our way here. It is supposed to reach 45 degrees in Detroit today. Spring was just around the corner.

"I'll have the meaty Hippie Hash," I said.

"That's good for your cholesterol," Ian said, as he rolled his eyes. "I'll have the veggie covered hash browns. And can I get some Frank's Original Red Hot Hot Sauce with that?" Ian said. "And give me two side orders of bacon. I like bacon!"

"Sure Honey. I'll put your order right in," Serena said before she left our sides.

"Talk about my cholesterol, you might want to get yours checked," I said to Ian. "That reminds me, I've got to remember to pick up my new glasses. They called Friday and said they were in. I'll get them tomorrow," I said.

"You have to wear glasses full time now?" Ian asked.

"With bifocals, too," I said. "I think I'm gonna shave my beard before the wedding."

Ian started laughing. "Why bother? It's so white now, you can barely see it. And, you don't have a chin. Remember the last time you shaved it, how young you looked?"

A moment later, Ian tapped the table to get my attention. I looked up. Walking through the front door was Ralph Dixon and his wife. They were accompanied by two young children; both girls, wearing their Sunday dresses. They sat at a table near the middle of the diner.

"Let's eat, then attack," I suggested. As I did, Serena brought our breakfast, placed our plates in front of us, and then refilled our coffee cups.

"Did you see that family that just walked in? That's the Lieutenant Governor and his family. He's so dreamy," she said with much sarcasm. "Actually, he gives me the creeps! I won't wait on him. Tami gets that privilege." Serena placed our bill on the table between our plates. "I can take that up when you are ready." She looked at Mr. Dixon and gave an exaggerated shutter with her whole body. She smiled politely at Ian and I, then went to fill more coffee cups for the other non creepy customers.

Our food was delicious. We both cleared our plates. When we were finished, I placed a twenty dollar bill on the table and asked Ian if he was ready to make Dixon's day.

"Let me hit the can first," Ian said.

"Good idea." I followed him into restroom.

When our hands were washed, we let the restroom door close behind us. I grabbed my cell and opened the file with the naked pictures of our Lieutenant Governor, Ralph Dixon. I took a deep breath. "Let's do this."

Ian asked, "Do you know what you are going to say to him?"

"Not really. Let's play it by ear."

Ian followed me as I walked up to the Dixon's table. I stopped just to his right. Ian stood at the table next to Ralph's left. Dixon looked up at me. Then he looked to Ian.

"Good morning," Ralph Dixon said with a large smile on his face. He had been eating a spinach and feta cheese omelet. He had a small green spec of spinach stuck between his front teeth. He looked somewhat confused by our presence. "What can I do for you two gentleman?"

His wife, a very attractive young lady in her early thirties, spoke up. She said, "Ralph, would you like to introduce me to your friends?"

I was pretty sure she knew her husband didn't know who we were. She was trying to lure our names out of us.

"I'm sorry," I said. "We haven't been introduced. My name is Dalen Reese. This is my associate, Ian Parker." I extended my hand to the missus. She gingerly shook my hand. I moved my hand to Mr. Dixon. We shook. Ian did not offer his hand. It's an intimidation factor.

"Can I help you?" Ralph asked.

"May we have a word with you? In private, please," I said.

"I'm having breakfast with my family right now." He reached into his suit coat jacket pocket and removed a business card. He tried to hand it to me. I didn't take it. "You can reach me at my office tomorrow." He waived the card in front of me, hoping I would reconsider.

"Mr. Dixon, please, this will only take a moment," I said.

"What is this about?" Dixon asked.

I had my phone in my hand. I tapped the screen to wake it up. One of the nude pics of Dixon and his male cohort appeared. I placed the phone in front of his face, so his wife couldn't see it. He had to pull his head back to focus on the picture. When he realized what he was looking at, his eyes grew wide open. He wiped his mouth with his napkin and slid his chair back, so he could stand.

 As he did, Mrs. Dixon asked, "Dear, what is it? What's going on? Where are you going?"

Mr. Dixon grabbed my arm and pushed me away from the table, away from his family.

"Remove your arm!" Ian said in a threatening voice. Dixon complied.

I lead us outside onto the sidewalk. Through the window, I could see Mrs. Dixon trying to explain to her daughters where their daddy was going with the two strange men.

"What do you want? Where did you get that picture from?" Lieutenant Governor Ralph Dixon had an incredible amount of fear in his voice.

"Mr. Dixon," Ian said. "I believe you have some information as to the whereabouts of our friend Mark Smith!"

"Who is Mark Smith?" Dixon asked.

A cool breeze kicked up and sent a chill through my body. I slid my hands deep into my jean's front pockets. I stepped close to Dixon and said, "Maybe you should ask Mickey Royboy." I asked, pronouncing it phonetically.

Dixon shook his head. "I don't know a Mark Smith and I have never heard of Mickey Royboy." When he said Royboy, he goofed and pronounced it as Royboy, with a hard R. I guess he hadn't read the article online that I did; the one that spelled it phonetically. He, like me and most other people, had seen the spelling and assumed it was pronounced with the hard R. He caught himself and said, "I mean Wah-boi. That is how you pronounced it, isn't it? Either way, I do not know either of the men you are asking about."

"Mr. Dixon," I said, "I don't have time for your bullshit. You know as well as I do that Mickey has my friend Mark."

Ian stepped in saying, "Our friend. Mark is our friend."

"Ian is right. Mark is our friend. Now let me tell you what is about to happen. You, Mr. Dixon, are going to contact Mr. Royboy and encourage him to locate and release our friend, Mark Smith. And, as a thank you for your cooperation, I will not email these pictures to your wife or the press."

"Don't you threaten me," Dixon said. "I have no idea who your friend is or who the person is that has him. Do you know who I am?"

He had something else to say but I interrupted him. I removed my right hand from my pocket and shoved Ralph Dixon into the window of the front of the diner. I stepped closer him. Our eyes were just inches from each other.

"Don't fuck with me!" I said. "Make the call, pay a visit, or do whatever you have to do to get Mark released. I have many pictures of you and your fuck buddy. I know Mickey's daughter Lisa is in the pictures too. I will fucking destroy your career if Mark is not released by this time tomorrow. He better not be harmed, either." I was spitting on his face as I talked. I really didn't mean to do so, but I couldn't help it. He tried not to blink or show fear, but his bottom lip was beginning to tremble. I continued, "I will see that Victoria Colavino prints the pictures tomorrow if I don't get Mark Smith back, unharmed. You do know who Miss Colavino is, don't you. You'll be seeing your ass all over the news tomorrow. Literally!"

I tapped my phone again and showed him the picture again. "There are more, too." I slid my finger to the left on my screen. "See this one? Maybe your wife wants to see this." I took a step back and acted as if I was heading back into the diner. I looked in. His wife was standing at the table trying to watch her husband and his two friends.

"Wait!" Ralph Dixon shouted. "I'll call Mickey. Give me until tonight. Mark will be released; just don't do anything with the pictures. You have my word. You'll get your friend back. I give you my word."

I looked at Ian, wondering if I should take Dixon at his word. Ian shrugged then nodded.

"Ok," I said in agreement. "You have 24 hours." I stepped back a few steps, satisfied with the progress Ian and I had made.

"You'll get your friend, but I want the pictures," Dixon said without any fear in his voice. In fact, his cocky political confidence had returned.

"What?" I said. "Fine, once I know Mark Smith is safe, I'll delete the pictures. Agreed?"

"With his release, I want your SD card, with the pictures on it," Ralph Dixon said. He had obviously given the matter some thought.

Then, like a jackass I said, "Fine. I'll get you the SD card. The pictures are in the cloud anyway." As soon as I said it, I realized I had just opened a larger can of worms. "24 hours!" I shouted.

Ian said, in a polite voice, "Hey Ralph, you have something between your teeth." Ian clinched his teeth and opened his lips and pointed to his own mouth to show Dixon an example of where the spec was located in Dixon's mouth.

Ralph Dixon imitated Ian's mouth's movements. Ralph used his tongue to try to remove the spinach.

"No," Ian said. "You didn't get it. It's right here." And with a quick snap, Ian raised his fist and popped Dixon in the mouth. Dixon's head snapped back as blood sprayed from his lip. Then Ian said,

"Sorry, it's my mistake. I thought it was spinach, but it was just my ring."

I walked back into the diner and up to Mrs. Dixon. I smiled at her and said, "I'm sure we'll be seeing each other again. Have a nice day."

On my way out, I passed Dixon, who had just stepped back into the diner. I shoved him again. He fell back into Selena. She had a carafe of hot coffee in her hand. It spilled. "Watch it asshole," she shouted at Ralph Dixon, our Lieutenant Governor.

Mrs. Dixon shrieked. Ian and I left.

Chapter Fourteen

Adrenaline was still pumping through my veins when we climbed into my Jeep.

"I can't believe you popped him in the mouth. That was funny," I said to Ian. I did my best impression of Ian, "I thought it was spinach, but it was just my ring!" I started laughing. Ian joined me.

"What about you? Dude, you killed it back there. I didn't know you had it in you. You were awesome. We are going to get Mark back. You did good, Dalen. You did good."

"Yeah, but I might have messed up when I mentioned that the pictures are in cloud. It won't matter if I give them the SD card from my phone or not. If they hadn't realized the photos will always be in the cloud, they know now," I said with concern. "I don't know what the hell is going to happen. I mean, think about it. The only way to guarantee that the pictures never see the light of day is to make sure that the people with access to the password for the cloud's account can never open the account."

Ian said, "And knowing what's at stake for the Lieutenant Governor and Mickey Royboy, they would have to know exactly who has access to that account. They know Mark does. They know you do. And didn't you tell Mickey, at the church, that Mark wasn't the only one with the pictures?"

"I did," I said. "But I was implying that I had copies of them too. The only way he would know that Victoria Colavino had the copies is if Mark tells him."

"Or Stonewall tells him," Ian said as a matter of fact.

"Right," I said in agreement. "Mark isn't going to tell him. They'd have to kill him to get him to talk."

"That makes a lot of sense," Ian said with a chuckle.

"You know what I mean. And Macy said we can trust Stonewall," I said. "We should be ok."

We were already on the expressway, on our way back to Detroit, when my phone rang. I answered it before my ringtone finished playing.

It was Macy. "Where the hell are you?" she demanded.

"I'm on my way back from Lansing. Why?" I asked.

Someone posted a Vine of you and Ian having a talk with Ralph Dixon. It ends with Ian socking Dixon in the mouth. What the hell were you thinking?"

"What's a Vine," I asked. I truly had no idea.

Ian and Macy gave their explanations at the same time. Though it was difficult to hear both, I managed to get the gist. A Vine is a short video that plays repeatedly, on a loop. I asked Macy to hold on for a second. I told Ian what Renee Macy had just told me. Before I finished, Ian had brought the Vine up on his phone and was watching it.

"We're going to be famous," Ian said.

Macy said, "This is not good news Dalen. I don't know how, but this is going to raise a lot of questions. It isn't going to help us find Mark. It is a setback. Someone is going to want answers. You guys just can't punch the Lieutenant Governor in the face and not expect there to be consequences. I'll do what I can do on my end. But, neither of you can talk to the press or anyone else about the incident. If the authorities contact either of you, tell them to call me."

I felt like I was being scolded by my mother. "I understand."

"Wait," Macy said. "I'm not finished. Until fifteen minutes ago, when I saw the Vine, I thought you were keeping your eye on Olivia."

"Why would you think that?" I asked. I had a bad feeling about the impending answer as I asked the question.

"Ryan Larkin has been watching Olivia this morning. He actually thought you were in the gym with her. She is at Planet Fitness. Ryan said you went in a few minutes after Olivia went in. Then I see the Vine and I called him to get his feedback. He said you were in the gym. It didn't add up. Wait a second. Hang on, Larkin is calling."

My cell went silent. I waited. One minute later she was back. She said, "Shit! Larkin went into the gym. The man he thought was you, is actually Robert Samuel Johnson. He has his head shaved, just like you. He is wearing a Tiger's hoodie and a Tiger's ball cap. Larkin actually thought Johnson was you."

"What the fuck?" I said. My heart was racing. "Did Livy know he was in there?"

"Ryan didn't say. So, I doubt it," she said. "But Ryan escorted Johnson out of the gym, without incident."

"Did he talk to her?" I asked. "Did Larkin say if Johnson spoke to Olivia?"

"I don't know," Macy said. "What were you doing talking to Dixon, anyhow?"

I took a minute and filled her in on the conversation we had with Ralph Dixon.

"Did Detective Simpson contact you yet? Lieutenant Macy asked.

"Yes. He called me this morning."

"Dalen, do me a favor. Let us take care of this. We'll find Mark. You have got to leave this alone. Mickey Royboy is not someone you want to be fucking around with. Detective Simpson is good at what he does. He has my support. Detective Larkin is working the case as well. Just step back and let us take care of it. We will find Mark." Macy spoke sternly.

"Do you know what the cloud is?" I asked her.

"What, like the internet cloud?"

"Yeah. Well, I might have complicated the situation a little more. I let it slip to Dixon that it didn't matter if I turned my SD card over to him or not. I said the pictures were already in the cloud." I let her think about what that might mean.

"Mickey isn't going to settle for the SD card. He's going to want you. If you have access to the cloud account, he's going to come after you; once he figures out what the cloud is." Macy was only half joking. Mickey probably knows what the cloud is. "Watch your back, Dalen. Don't do anything stupid. In fact, don't do anything at all."

"Macy," I said. "Victoria Colavino also has access to the pictures."

"Shit. That's right," Macy said. "Have you spoken to her?"

"We talked last night. That's how I knew where to find Dixon this morning," I said.

"Do you have her number?" Macy asked. "I need to talk to her."

"I'll text it to you," I said. "Anything else?"

"Just send me her number and stay out of trouble." Macy ended the call.

I handed Ian my phone. "Send Macy Victoria Colavino's contact information, please."

He did.

When Ian was finished, he handed my cell phone back to me. I called Olivia. It went to voicemail. I hung up. I knew that if she saw she had a missed call from me, she would call me back. I didn't see a reason to leave a message.

"Do you remember playing Superhero Wars when we were kids?" Ian asked, out of the blue.

"Against the Panther's, yeah I remember. We were always the heroes; the Panthers were always the villains. I like the way that worked out," I said. "I was just remembering our hockey matches and the time Mark fell through the ice." I started to laugh.

"All he had to do was stand up. The water was only waist deep." Ian was laughing as well. "Mark kept slapping the ice trying to grab hold of it. It kept breaking. I remember yelling, 'Just stand up!' He just kept slapping and breaking the ice. Man that was funny. Yeah, we had some great times growing up."

"I was always Batman. You were always Robin. Ricky was Shazam. Joey was Superman. Scott was Spiderman. Mark always had to be Rocket Racer. He always got to use his skateboard." I said, "He almost had to be Rocket Racer; that was the only black villain around at the time."

"Mark hung onto that one Spiderman comic like it was gold; the one that had Rocket Racer in it. If he hadn't showed it to us, we probably wouldn't have believed that there was a black villain," Ian said.

"I know," I said. "And he showed it to us, like, a hundred times. Every time we played Superhero Wars, Mark said, 'And I get to be Rocket Racer!' He said it with pride."

Ian said, "Can you blame him?"

"No. I can't." I said. "We chose Superheroes every time we played, like it was a draft. We all always chose the same characters; our team and the Panthers, too. Yet, whenever we chose, you always picked Robin. Why is that? You could have been Batman. I would have let you. You could have been Superman, Aquaman, The Hulk, The Thing. You could have chosen any one of them but you always picked Robin. Why?"

"You don't know?" Ian asked me. "You really don't know, do you?"

"No, I don't. I always wondered, though."

Ian said, "Batman and Robin always stuck together. When we played, the Superheroes always split up, except for Batman and Robin. I got to stay with you by default. Batman always looked out for Robin. You always looked out for me. Whenever a member of the Panthers jumped out to shoot one of us, you were always there to protect me. You were always bigger and faster and stronger than me. Batman would never have let anything bad happen to Robin. You never let anything bad happen to me. I always felt safe following you around."

Ian was just staring out the front window. I let him continue. "Do you remember the one time we actually used BB guns to play? I remember we all had one. I had my rifle and you had yours. Everyone had a BB gun except for Mark. He had a slingshot. Still, he was shooting BB's with it. We all agreed not to aim for anything above the armpits. Shit, we actually agreed to be shot at with real BB guns. There were two dozen kids, playing Superheroes, running around two streets, shooting guns at each other. That shit was crazy, man."

I knew the day Ian was talking about. "It was," I said in agreement. "Do you remember when Paul, who was playing Lex Luther, was sitting in the tree in Mr. Sanchez's front yard and he called your name when we snuck under the tree to use it as cover? We both looked up and he said, 'You're dead Robin!' and he fired at you from, like, maybe, ten feet high in the tree."

"Yeah, that's right. He did, didn't he? But you know what, you threw me down to the ground and jumped on top of me. The BB hit you in the back of the thigh. Shit Dalen, that's what I'm talking about," Ian said as he looked at me. "Batman literally took a bullet for Robin. You took that bullet for me and you did it without even thinking about it."

I said, "They were BB's, not bullets."

"No," Ian said. "When we were kids, those BB's were fucking bullets, man. You know that as well as I do. That's why I was always Robin."

"Then, I climbed up that tree as fast as I could, to kick his ass."

Ian was laughing. "You literally dragged him down that tree, by his shirt collar, one branch at a time. Then, you threw him to the ground and stood over him, pointing your gun at his leg. You kept saying, 'I should do it! I should shoot your ass! I should!'

Now I was laughing, "He was crying, begging me not to pull the trigger. He had tears, a runny nose, and spit all over his whinny face."

"But you didn't do it. You let him up. You let him go. Remember? And as he was running away from you, he shouted, 'Next time I see you, I'm going to kick your ass!'"

"Yeah," I said. "Then, when he was in the next yard, I fired my gun into the air and he dove for cover and covered his head. He scurried to his feet and ran all crouched down until he was out of sight. Those were good times."

A few minutes later I pulled the Jeep into the parking lot of The Coffee Cabin.

Chapter Fifteen

We were sitting in our office, drinking coffee, and still reminiscing about our youth. I was drinking my coffee black. Ian had put a scoop of vanilla ice cream in his coffee. We were laughing and enjoying our morning when Hazel popped her head into the office, through the doorway.

"Dalen, there is a gentleman here to see you," she said.

"Who is it?" I asked without moving from the couch.

"He didn't say. Although, I didn't ask him either," Hazel said. "He's a really nice looking African American. I mean, he is really a fine looking man."

"Finally," Ian said, "because Dalen has been looking for one. And not just a really nice looking one either. He's been holding out for a real fine looking man."

"Dick!" I said to Ian. I didn't feel like getting up. "Go find out what his name is, please," I said to Hazel.

She left.

"Are you expecting a fine looking African American male to visit you this morning?" Ian asked.

"Nope."

Ian was resting his elbows on the desktop. He had his fingers pointing up. He tapped the fingertips of his left hand against the tips of the fingers on his right. "The suspense is killing me! Who could it be? Who could it be?"

Just as Ian started with his diabolical laugh, Hazel reappeared in the doorway. "He said his name is Jerome McMillan. He is here with his associate, Tyreke. No last name given. Shall I send them back?"

"This ought to be good," I said to Ian. "Yes Hazel, please send them back. Thank you."

Moments later a real fine looking African American male stepped into the doorway of our office. His shaved head reflected the ceiling lights.

"Which one of you is Dalen Reese?" he asked. His voice was a few octaves higher than I expected it to be, but it wasn't as high as Mike Tyson's.

"I am," I said while looking up at him. I did not stand to shake his hand.

A second man entered the doorway but did not enter the office. He stood with his arms folded and his legs spread. He took up most of the doorway.

"Which one of you is Jerome McMillan?" I said. Judging by the look of the bigger man, I pretty much already knew the answer. He was not a good looking man. Though Hazel was right, Jerome was good looking.

Jerome said, "I am." He sat down on the couch next to me, making me feel uncomfortable. I stood up. Jerome did not. Instead, he slouched down on the red leather, making himself more comfortable. I sat on the edge of the desk and swung my legs back and forth, much like a child might do.

"To what do we owe this visit?" I asked. Ian stood up from the desk chair, walked around the desk, and stood to my left.

"I am here on behalf of Lisa Stewart," Jerome said. "It has been brought to her attention that you have something she wants. She is willing to pay you handsomely to get it." Jerome removed a small switch blade knife from the front pocket in his slacks and using it he began to clean under his fingernails.

"Who is Lisa Stewart?" I asked.

"Don't be coy," Jerome said without looking up from his fingers.

"I am not coy. I am Dalen. This red headed fella here is my associate Ian. Say hello, Ian."

And as expected, Ian said, "Hello Ian!"

Ian and I both began to laugh. That did not make Jerome very happy. Jerome instantly took his knife and stabbed my classic, one of a kind, 1957 Chevy, red leather rear seat couch. I felt blood rush to my head. I felt as if it were about to boil. Sweat began to bubble on the top of my shaved scalp. It took everything in my body not to react to what Jerome just did. I kept my composure. Ian did not move. Tyreke, the beast in the doorway, did not move either. I continued to swing my legs.

"That was uncalled for," I said.

Jerome began to slowly raise and lower his switch blade knife into the cushion of the couch, moving it forward with every motion. The cut was getting longer. Jerome McMillan stopped for a moment as he spoke, "As I was saying, Miss Stewart would like you to turn over what you have and in return, she will pay you handsomely." He held onto the handle of the knife but didn't continue with his slicing.

I knew he was sent to get the pictures I had. I was assuming Lisa hadn't spoken to her father or to Lieutenant Governor Ralph Dixon. If she had, by now, she would have been told that the pictures are in the cloud. Again, I could only assume, but Lisa must think that I have actual paper prints of her and her sexual exploits.

I removed my phone from my pocket. Jerome and Tyreke watched as I tapped the screen. They were both watching with curious eyes as I texted Ian. Our guests could only have assumed that I was attempting to retrieve the pictures. I hit send on my phone. Then I deleted the message.

Ian's phone vibrated. He looked at his screen. He read my text. It said, COULD THIS BE THE BLACK MAN IN THE PHOTOS WITH DIXON?

Ian sent me a response. YES!

"What the hell are you two doing?" Jerome asked. He stood up, bringing his knife with him. He was pretty confused. Tyreke took one giant step forward. He was now just a foot to my right.

I stood up as well. I slid my phone into my back pocket.

Ian didn't move. He was very calm.

"I am not screwing around. I want those pictures, Reese, and I am not leaving here until I have them!" Jerome said in a loud and somewhat nervous voice.

Tyreke unfolded his arms and dropped them to his sides.

You could cut the tension in the room with Jerome's switch blade.

"How much?" Ian asked, with a steady tone. "How much is handsomely?"

"Twenty G's!" Jerome said.

My stomach sank. I could sure use twenty grand, I thought.

But before I could say anything, Ian said, "If she is willing to pay twenty large, she'll pay a hundred."

Holy shit! I wanted to elbow Ian in his gut and say, "Shut up!" But I didn't. Instead, I kept my cool and let Ian deal with our negotiations.

"I'm sure you know who Mark Smith is," Ian said. "We want Mark and one hundred grand, in cash. We want Mark to bring the money to the Belle Isle Bridge tonight at 9:00. When we have the money and know that Mark is safe and unharmed, you'll get the pictures. If you fail to deliver on this arrangement, the pictures will go viral before morning."

"I did not come here to negotiate with you," Jerome McMillan said. "Miss Stewart will pay you twenty grand for the pictures. Take it or leave it!"

"That's a no go!" Ian said firmly. "Take our terms back to Miss Stewart and tell her she needs to deliver."

Mr. McMillan raised his knife, stepped toward me and placed the tip of the blade under my chin. He raised it. It was sharp, but he didn't put enough force into it to puncture my skin. I let out a little whimper. It wasn't very manly of me, but I couldn't help it. Ian reached behind his back and pulled a pistol out from his waistband. Ian raised his gun and placed it at the temple of Jerome's head. Tyreke had pulled two guns out of thin air and had one pointing at my head and the other at Ian's. All of this happened in a matter of a second.

"Now you get no money," Jerome said. "Now it's the pictures for your life!" Jerome was taller than me but shorter than Ian. Tyreke was nearly a whole head above Ian.

"Our terms have not changed with this little threat," Ian said. "You'll get the pictures when we get Mark and one hundred grand. Not a moment sooner. Now go tell your friends to get their shit together before I pull this fucking trigger."

Jerome pushed the knife higher. I did not raise my head. I felt the tip of the knife pierce a hole into skin. I looked to my left as Ian pulled the hammer back on his gun. The click was loud. I could feel blood run down my neck and over my Adam's apple. I swallowed. I tried not to shake, but I was scared shitless. Ian actually pressed the muzzle of his weapon into Jerome's temple.

"Get the fuck out of here. Bring the money to the bridge, tonight!" Ian said. He pressed the muzzle harder into Jerome's temple, causing Jerome's head to tilt to his left.

I moved my eyes to Tyreke without moving my head. He was fast on the draw, but he didn't look to be very smart.

"Boss?" Tyreke said, looking confused.

"Ok!" Jerome said. He pressed the switch on his knife and the blade retracted with a click.

My chin dropped. I wiped my beard with the back of my fingers. Blood smeared on them like they had been painted with a brush.

"Move!" Jerome said to Tyreke, as he pushed him out of his way. Jerome left the office.

Tyreke put both of his guns back into his waistband, under his very large Barry Sanders Jersey. He turned and followed his boss out of the office and into the lobby of the coffee shop.

"Damn!" I said with a huge sigh of relief.

Ian and I moved quickly into the lobby to make sure our friends left without any more issues. There weren't any. They walked right through the coffee shop, past a handful of customers and out the front door. They climbed into a black Ford F150. The windows were tinted so we couldn't see into the vehicle. As they pulled away, I noticed that the license plate on the truck read BLKIRSH. Black Irish. It made sense for a guy named Jerome McMillan.

Ian handed me a warm, damp, white towel. He pointed to my neck. I wiped the blood from my neck and chin. I held the towel under my chin for a moment. I glanced at it every few seconds. I hadn't stopped bleeding.

"What happened?" Hazel asked.

"I cut myself shaving," I said. I took my bloodied white towel with me as I returned to the office I shared with Ian. He followed with two more cups of hot coffee. He handed me one.

"Man, I can't believe he backed off so easily," Ian said.

"You did have your pistol held up to his head," I said. "Maybe that had something to do with it."

"No. I doubt it. That big dude was fast. He would have taken us both out. No," Ian said shaking head, "Jerome must have realized he wasn't going to get the pictures today; at least not here. I don't believe for one second that they will bring us a hundred grand either. Mark isn't going to be there tonight. I have no clue what is going to happen. We have opened a huge can of worms."

"I know," I said. "Did you see his license plate?" I asked.

"No. No, I didn't. What'd it say?"

"Black Irish."

Ian chuckled. "Creative."

I went around the desk and had a seat. I opened my laptop and woke it up. I typed in the words *Black Irish*. It was suggested that I click on sites about dark haired phenotype appearing in people of Irish origin. That was no help. I then typed in Jerome McMillan. There were a few suggestions under his name. I followed the list. Jumping out at me was a link titled Diamonds and Pearls. I clicked on it.

Diamonds and Pearls is an elite escort service out of Windsor Ontario that is owned operated by one Jerome McMillan. They offer high end escorts for everyone, regardless of gender. They claim to be safe and extremely discreet. The site had a link to the women and the men that were available for service. I clicked the ladies link. I started to scroll through them. One immediately caught my eye.

I clicked on Miss Eliza. There is no denying that she is a Royboy. She looks just like her brothers, only feminine and very beautiful. "Eliza. Liza. Lisa," I said out loud.

Ian walked behind me and looked over my shoulder at what I had found. "That's got to be our Lisa Stewart! Is there a picture of her finger? We could compare it to the one in our picture." Of course Ian was joking.

"I'm going to call Macy," I said.

Chapter Sixteen

"Lieutenant Macy," she said when she answered. She must not have looked at the gorgeous picture of me she has on her phone before she answered.

"Renee, it's Dalen," I said. "Do you have a second?"

"It always takes more than a second when you call. What do you need now?"

I told her what had transpired in the last two hours.

"What have you gotten us into, Reese?" she asked, only half kidding. "Alright, let me talk to Ryan. We'll go with you in case this thing actually plays out. Damn it! I was going to get my nails done tonight. Dalen, do not go out there without us. Do I make myself clear? Shit, now I've got to find Stonewall. Thanks for messing up my day. I'll call you later to go over our plan." With that, Lieutenant Renee Macy hung up.

I told Ian what Macy had just said. Then I had an idea. "Do you know where Mickey Royboy lives?" It actually gave me joy to say his name with the hard 'Roy' as opposed to the soft' Wah'.

"No." He removed his phone and searched the World Wide Web to see if he could locate an address. He did not have any luck. "We can go to his offices off of Livernois. They are located on the west side of Detroit. I'll drive."

"No!" I said. "I'll drive. I'm not in the mood for The Backstreet Boys. I have no idea what we'll do once we get there, but we can play it by ear."

"That's how we roll, isn't it?" Ian said. "They say it's never good idea to wake a sleeping dog. We are about to poke a damn bear. This should be fun."

I checked the towel one more time. It looked as though the bleeding had stopped. I tossed it into the trash can under the desk. I put the computer back to sleep. I drank the rest of the coffee in my cup and used the restroom one last time before we climbed into my Jeep.

"Let's go poke the bear," I said. I shifted the car into gear and we headed for the west side of the greatest city in America, Detroit. "Hey, why do you think Jerome has his business in Windsor?"

Ian said, "I don't know. Prostitution is not legal in Detroit. Is it legal in Canada? Hang on." He checked his phone. Thirty seconds later her said, "According to Yahoo, it is still legal but there are many concerns about the wording of the new laws, which as I can surmise, mean it is legal but you cannot talk about it and I guess women can't charge for sex but they can accept donations. Well, that's what this one article says anyway. There are a ton of articles on the new laws, so yes it is still legal in Canada."

"Ok. That makes sense as to why McMillan runs his business out of Windsor," I said.

"Don't you mean Black Irish?" Ian said in a mocking tone.

"Oh, yeah, you're one to talk," I said. "That statement is coming from a guy that has THEIAN on his license plate!"

"Hey, ladies love The Ian," he said.

"That may be, but you do know that when people read your plate they don't see The Ian. They see theian. Theian is not even a word." I started to laugh.

"Screw you!" Ian said.

"Where is this place?" I asked as we were entering the industrial district off of Livernois.

"According to Google Maps, it should be just ahead on the right," Ian said. "Make a right at the next entrance."

I slowly pulled the Jeep into the drive. We were facing a row of cement and steel buildings with many smoke stacks that were polluting the sky with thick pillows of black smoke.

"It's this one on our left," Ian said. "This is an odd place for an office building, especially for a dry cleaner. Don't ya think?"

I pulled the Jeep along the grass partition near the road and put the car in neutral. I pulled the parking brake and removed the key. I placed it into my pocket. Ian and I climbed out and shut the doors behind us.

"Lock it?" Ian asked.

"No," I said. "I have the key." I removed my phone from my pocket and took a few pictures of the building. I wasn't exactly sure why I did this; but in this line of work, I've learned, you can never have too much information. I slid the phone back into my pocket.

We stood at the side of the Jeep and stared at the building.

"What now?" I asked Ian.

"Well, let's go poke the bear!" he said.

We walked up to the one single door, located in the front of the building; it had a window in it so I glanced in. All I could see was a wall that leads to two other doors; one to the right and one to the left. Ian pulled on the handle to the outside door. It was locked but there was bell button to the left of the door. Ian pressed it. I didn't hear it ring, so I pressed it; still nothing. I started to walk around the building. Ian followed.

"I've never actually had a gun pointed at me before today," Ian said in a whisper. "That shit was scary. I had sweat drip from my arm pit down my side when I cocked the hammer back on my gun."

"You have been shot twice. So, I'm pretty sure you have had a gun pointed at you," I said in a whisper, although I wasn't sure exactly why we were whispering.

"Well yeah, but that was different. That was from a sniper. I never actually saw him point the rifle at me. I'm saying, like, up close, like Tyreke did today. That shit was wild. I didn't know if he was going to pull the trigger or not. Though, I did a pretty good job of not showing how scared I actually was."

"Man, you were tough as hell. You woulda frightened me. You looked like you had been in that situation many times. I didn't know you were so fast on the draw. I was impressed. I felt safe having you by my side," I said. "But in all honesty, I almost shit my drawers."

We moved from the front of the building to the left side of it. We made our way around to the back. I followed Ian staying just a few steps behind him. He reached behind his back and put his hand up the bottom of his shirt and placed his hand on the grip of his pistol. He stopped and raised his arm, in the shape of an L, showing me the back of his fist signaling me to stop. I did. He pointed to two men loading white cardboard boxes into the back of a blue Chevy pickup truck. We backed up; back around the corner to the left side of the building.

"Why are we afraid of being seen?" I said. "This is hardly poking the bear."

I stepped past Ian and walked around to the back of the building. "Hey," I said without whispering.

The two men looked at me. They looked at each other and back to me. Ian stepped to my left.

"This is private property," one of them said. "You two need to leave."

"I'm looking for Mickey Royboy. Is he here?" I asked.

I took a few steps closer to them. Ian moved with me. His hand was still on his pistol grip.

"Don't know who that is," the same man replied.

"You's two need to leave here," the second fella said. He raised the bottom of his shirt, exposing the pistol he had tucked into his waistband.

"So, Mickey isn't here?" I asked, taking a few more steps closer to the men. "How about we go inside and ask the people in there if they know who Mickey is?" I said motioning to a back door that had been propped open with a similar white cardboard box. I assumed the contents of the box had to be heavy enough to hold open a steel door, since one box was doing the trick.

"I'm not telling you's again," the second man said. "Get the hell out of here." He put his hand on the grip of his pistol.

I heard Ian click the hammer of his.

I put my hands up. "Hey, we come in peace. I'm just looking for the owner of this establishment. I have some clothes I need pressed."

"Get!" the first man said, as he pulled his gun out of a holster on his left side. He pointed the gun at us.

"Ian, they want us to leave," I said.

Ian un-cocked the hammer of his pistol; he showed both hands to the men.

"Tell Mickey we'll see him tonight," Ian said. He turned around and walked back to the Jeep. He never looked back in the direction of the two gunmen. I followed him.

We climbed into the Jeep and drove away without saying another word, at least until we were off the property and a few blocks away. I stopped the car on the shoulder of the vacant road. There were a lot of buildings around but nary a car in sight.

"That's the second time today we've have had a gun pointed at us. I don't like this at all," I said. I was still shaking a bit. My adrenaline was still rapidly flowing through my veins.

"Remember why we are doing this. We need to find Mark. Don't lose sight of that. Things are getting more intense because we are getting close. Mickey, Dixon, Lisa, and Jerome are all getting nervous. They apparently think we have more pictures than we actually do have. They are all afraid the pictures are going to be released to the press or on line or whatever else they think we can do with them. They do not want them getting out. They will do whatever they have to do to see that we can't release them, including kidnap Mark. We don't know what they have done to him. Hopefully they will exchange him tonight for the pictures. I don't care about getting the money. I just want Mark back." Ian's voice was starting to crack when he talked, so he quit. He had a tear hanging on his lower eyelashes on his left eye. He did not try to wipe it away.

"We'll get him back. We will!" I said.

My phone vibrated. I had a text from Raven. It read: Can I bring a date to the wedding?

I texted back: Sure. Who?

Her response: Gaston

My response: The guy from Beauty and the Beast?

She typed: Same name, different guy. So it's ok?

I typed: Yes. I love you.

Raven responded: Thanks Daddy. I love you too.

I returned the phone to my back pocket. As I did, the blue Chevy truck with the two gunmen in it drove past us. They paid no attention to us. Ian watched them pass us as well.

"You want to go back?" Ian asked me.

I didn't answer. Instead I put the car in first gear and pulled a Michigan left. Moments later, I parked the Jeep in the lot next door to Mickey Royboy's office building. We snuck around the back of his office. The door was still propped open with the same white box, though now it was only opened the width of the box. Ian retrieved the pistol from under his shirt and held it to the side of his thigh and pointed it down at the ground. He motioned with his head for us to enter the building.

Now, I am just a simple man that owns a coffee shop and also happens to run a PI firm. Basically I spend my time pouring coffee or taking pictures, from a distance, of people trying to scam insurance companies. But somehow, today, I have had several guns pointed at me, which is scary enough in it's own right. Now I am entering a building, on a Sunday afternoon, with my partner who has his gun drawn. My heart began racing and sweat started to bubble on my head, under my Detroit Lion's ball cap. Ian spent two tours in the United States Army and has done and seen things in his deployment that he still doesn't want to talk about. I trust Ian with my life. I followed him into the building and stayed a few feet behind him. He moved like a cop in a movie looking for men that might spring up out of the blue and shoot at us. I expected him to yell "Clear!" as he looked in every room and down every hall. He kept two hands on his pistol as he moved.

Ian stopped abruptly. I wasn't expecting him to do so, so I walked right into his back. I let out a loud, "Umph!" I laughed as I did this.

"Ssshhh!" he whispered. He was holding his left arm up, in the shape of an L. He was making a fist with his hand. "Didn't you see my hand? This means stop," he explained.

"Sorry. I was looking at the floor," I said.

"Ssshhh," he said again. Ian nodded his head in the direction of the room to our left, near the end of the hall. "Voices."

I listened. I heard the voices. It sounded like two men arguing, though there might have been three. They sounded Hispanic.

Ian turned his fist into a wave and motioned for me to follow him. He moved slowly but he moved with purpose. He had raised his gun and held it at arm's length in front of him. He had both hands back on the grip. My heart pounded faster.

Ian arrived at the room with the voices inside. He stopped and rested his back against the wall. He held this pistol against his chest. I stood beside Ian with my back also against the wall. I began to wish I had brought my gun as well. Ian stepped to his left, peeked into the room and quickly resumed his resting position against the wall.

Ian held up two fingers and then pointed at the room. Two men were inside. I nodded. I didn't have a clue what was about to happen. So I followed Ian's lead. He extended his arms again, gun in hand, and stepped quickly into the doorway. I inched closer to the door, still unsure what I was supposed to do.

"Hey asshats," Ian shouted. "Drop the boxes and step away from the table!"

"Asshats?" I said to myself. I started laughing again. I probably shouldn't have, but I couldn't help myself.

"Now!" Ian yelled.

I poked my head around the corner of the door jam, to look inside.

The two Hispanic men did as Ian had ordered. The room was filled with tables and white boxes that were stacked three or four high on each table. There were probably twenty tables. They were covered with the boxes.

"You are the asshat," the taller, skinnier man said. He was wearing a black beanie and a black North Face jacket. He had a thin face that had twenty years of beard growth on it. His beard might have consisted of thirty-seven hairs, each about five inches long. His mustache was just as weak.

The second man easily had a hundred pounds on his taller friend. He stood a head shorter than the skinny man. "Who the hell are you?" he asked Ian and me.

I expected Ian to come back with a smart mouthed comment, but instead he said, "Demitri? Is that you? What are you doing here?" Ian lowered his gun.

I was confused. I thought we were headed for a gunfight but instead I watched as Ian gave Demitri a one armed hug.

"How have you been? It's been too long. How's your sister?" Ian started to laugh at the situation.

"Demitri, who are these clowns?" the bowling ball on legs asked his associate. He was squeezed into a flannel shirt that unlike Ian's was stretched taught at the buttons; they were buttoned up to his neck. His pants were a foot too long and had been rolled up at the ankles.

"This is Ian. He dated Marlina, when, about 15 years ago?" Demitri told Shorty. "You remember? I told you about him. He's the guy that did, you know, that thing."

Shorty said, "That thing?"

"Yeah," Demitri said, "that thing." He bent down and whispered into Shorty's ear.

Shorty smiled. "Oh yeah. This is the guy, huh? The man, in the flesh." He stepped toward Ian and extended his hand. Ian shook it. Shorty stepped back.

Ian looked back at me and smiled.

"Demitri, can I have a word?" Ian asked. Ian put one arm around Demitri's neck and led him to a corner of the room. The two men whispered. Ian still had his gun in hand.

Shorty looked at me and smiled. It seemed uncomfortable for him. He didn't know me. I didn't know him.

I stood tall and folded my arms in front of my chest. I felt like I needed to look as tough as I could.

"So, are you getting time and a half for working on a Sunday?" I asked Shorty.

He squinted his eyes and looked confused while doing so? "What?" he asked.

"Well, you're working on a Sunday. Most companies pay time and a half on Sundays. Doesn't Mr. Royboy pay you extra on the weekends?" I asked.

"No. It doesn't really work like that. We get a flat rate." Shorty didn't like the conversation we were having.

"But, you do work for Mickey Royboy, right?" I said. "I mean, this is his office, is it not?"

Shorty looked around. He shrugged his round shoulders. I can assume he knows Mickey by his reaction, though he didn't seem to know much more than that.

"What's in the boxes?" I asked.

Shorty looked over his shoulder at Demitri who was speaking softly to Ian. Shorty looked back at me and shook his head.

"Mind if I take a look?" I asked. I stepped toward the table closest to me.

From behind me I heard Demitri yell, "Don't do it amigo!"

I put my hands up and turned around. This is me not doing it. Shorty had pulled his weapon and was pointing it at me. For a split second, I thought Demitri might have been talking to Shorty. He wasn't. Ian had raised his gun and was pointing it at Shorty.

"Don't do it amigo," Ian said to Shorty.

"Come on now; everyone lower their weapons and calm down. We don't want any bloodshed today," Demitri said. He took his hand and helped Ian lower Ian's arm.

"It's all good," Ian said. He walked back to my side. "We're good here." Ian motioned with his head toward the door. He walked out. I followed him. We left the building through the front door and walked next door to my Jeep.

When we were on the road, heading back home, I said, "What were those guys talking about?" Curiosity was getting the best of me.

"Oh, that was nothing," Ian said.

"Don't give me that. Who is Marlina? I don't remember you dating anyone named Marlina. And just what was that thing that you did that they know about that I don't know about? What the hell? I'm dying over here. You gotta tell me."

"What? Can't a guy have a secret?" Ian asked.

"Yes, but, I didn't think we had any secrets. Just tell me," I said.

I'm sure Ian would have told me if I hadn't been making a big fuss over not knowing. He knew it was killing me too.

"Don't worry about it, Dalen," Ian said. "So, do you want to know what was in the boxes?"

"Yeah," I said sounding somewhat defeated.

"The boxes with the green labels have bags of powered laundry detergent in them. If the boxes have a red label on them, they consist of laundry soap plus bags of cocaine in them. The blue labeled boxes have soap plus bags of weed. All of the boxes get delivered to Mickey's many dry cleaners and Laundromats." Ian said, "I also asked Demitri about Mark, to see if he knew where Mark is being held. He assured me he knows nothing about Mark or about anyone that has been kidnapped. Demitri is an honest man and I believe him. I've known him for a long time. I trust that his is not lying to me. He is just a runner. The short fella's name is Pacco. All they do is deliver the boxes. They are not really involved with the day to day operations of Mickey Royboy or his crew. They are contracted out a few days a month."

"How come I've never heard of Demitri before? You two seem like you were pretty chummy at one time," I asked.

"I dated his sister; that's all!" Ian said. "Now can you let it go?"

"I can, but..."

Ian shouted, "Drop it!"

"Ok," I said. "Damn, I was just..."

"Dalen, stop it! I'm asking you nicely. Just shut up about it, alright?" Ian's face was turning a dark shade of red.

"Fiiiiiine!" I said. We sat in silence the rest of the way home. I dropped Ian off at the end of his driveway and drove away without even a "Good-bye."

Chapter Seventeen

I parked in the garage and went into my house through the back door. I was still pretty perturbed by the situation and exchange I just had with Ian. Why wouldn't he have told me? What was the big deal about it anyway? It has been a while since I have had a stressful day like this. The night wasn't shaping up to be much better.

Months have gone by since I last thought about having a drink. But today, right now, I really wanted to pour a pint of Jack Daniels down my throat. I took a deep breath, removed the phone from my pocket and called my AA sponsor. She answered on the third ring. I paced around the kitchen as I spoke to her. Before I knew it, a half an hour had passed and I was feeling better about myself. My urge to drink had passed. I had opened a new family size bag of Better Made BBQ potato chips, which I managed to completely consume during my phone call. I licked my finger tips clean and tossed the bag into the trash. I thanked her and ended the call.

Cherrie, Naomi, and Raven came in through the back door as I was making a fresh pot of coffee.

Cherrie gave me a kiss and said, "I have a surprise for you."

Normally when she says that, we end up in the bedroom, but Raven and her friend Naomi were home so I didn't anticipate getting any nookie from my fiancé. Though to be honest, I could have used some right about now.

"What is it?" I asked.

"Wait right here," Cherrie said. She went into the garage for a quick minute and then said, from the doorway, "Close your eyes and put your hands out."

I did as instructed. I was shocked when Cherrie placed a puppy in my hands.

"Open," Cherrie said.

I did. In my hands was the cutest little puppy I had ever seen. He was a black and white spotted cocker spaniel. He trembled in my hands. He wasn't much bigger than a throw pillow. His ears were long and floppy. His eyes were a dark brown. He was frightened to death. I pulled him close to my chest and began to stroke his back. He stopped trembling. He rose up and tried to lick my chin. I let him.

"Do you like him?" Cherrie asked with hope in her eyes.

"I love him," I said. "Where did you get him? Why…"

Cherrie interrupted me saying, "He's your wedding present. I thought we could name him Elvis"

Raven and Naomi came to my side and started petting him as well.

Naomi said, "I think you should name him Grandpa. 'Come here Grandpa.' 'Grandpa, do you have to go potty?' I think that would be hilarious."

I laughed but said, "Elvis. I like Elvis. Let's go with Elvis."

I gave him a kiss on his little face and put him down on the floor. Elvis started to sniff the floor and followed his nose as he began to wander the kitchen and then the living room. Raven and Naomi followed close behind him.

"I love him and I love you," I told Cherrie. I bent down and gave her a long kiss. "Thank you," I said to her. That's a much better gift than a stupid jersey, I thought. I wished I had thought of it. The girls had taken Elvis into the back yard to begin his potty training.

My cell phone began playing 'Play That Funky Music.' I looked at the screen. It was Lieutenant Renee Macy. I swiped right. "Don't mess up my good afternoon Renee. I just received my wedding gift."

"I don't care about your sex life Reese," she said, with a slight chuckle. "Listen up. Ryan and I will be present at the bridge tonight. You won't see us but just know that we will be there. Stonewall has other plans and can't make it. I think he's up to something but I couldn't get what it was out of him. Are you home?"

"Yes."

"Stay there. I have a friend dropping off a hoodie and a flannel jacket. They have tracking devices sewn into them. Wear them tonight."

"What color is the hoodie?" I asked. I don't know why I asked the question. It really didn't matter to me.

"Just wear it," she said.

We spoke for a few more minutes and discussed our plan for the meeting with Demitri, Mickey, and hopefully Mark Smith that was to take place on the Belle Isle Bridge, tonight.

"Is everything alright?" Cherrie asked with a strong look of concern on her beautiful face.

"No. It really isn't," I said.

I opened the refrigerator and removed a can of Faygo orange pop. I pulled the tab and poured half of the can down my throat. I asked Cherrie to join me on the couch.

I updated her on the events that had unfolded today. I even told her about the uncomfortable conversation I had with Ian on our way home.

"This is a lot to take in. Are you doing alright? Should I be more worried about the exchange tonight than I already am? This really sounds like a dangerous situation."

"Look, I've got to be honest with you," I said. "I am scared to death. I know Ian has got my back and it is incredibly reassuring knowing that Macy and Larkin will be there too, somewhere. I just want to get Mark back safely. That's our endgame here, to bring him home, dare I say it, alive. We just want to bring him home alive." My stomach churned as I said that. I felt empty inside.

"We have done everything in our lawless power to find him. The DPD are working his case. I trust Macy. She isn't going to give up. Detective Simpson is working his ass off. We are so close to getting Mark," I said. A lump appeared in my throat as I spoke. "There is a strong case against Mickey Royboy and his sons for kidnapping. But we have to get Mark first. I still hold hope that he is alright."

Raven and Naomi brought Elvis back into the house. Naomi was carrying him.

"He has legs," Cherrie said to her.

Naomi put the puppy down. He wandered the house with his nose to the ground. His small tail moved from side to side at an alarming pace. Raven and Naomi sat down on the love seat opposite Cherrie and me. They each had their phones in their hands.

"So, how is work?" I asked Naomi. I was still trying to wrap my head around the fact that the young woman sitting across from me was working at one of the many local strip clubs in the area. I remember when she and Raven were in kindergarten.

"It's going well. Thanks for asking." Naomi could tell I was uncomfortable but liked the fact that I cared enough to ask. "Oh, my gosh, Father Reese. You'll never guess who started working with me at the club."

Naomi started calling me father Reese about ten years ago. She grew up referring to me as Dad. At some point it was switched to Daddy 2.0. Shortly after that Raven thought it would be funny to call me Father instead of Dad and Naomi started calling her dad Father as well. So I became Father Reese. It stuck.

I shrugged in response.

"Ophy Vanderhagen! You know, the girl down the street?" she said pointing over her shoulder. Apparently she was referring to a girl that lived on McCatty Drive.

I couldn't place the name.

Naomi continued, "She has a brother. You know them; Ophelia and Oedipus. Ophy and Eddie. The Vanderhagens!"

I didn't know who she was talking about. But since we moved back to McCatty, I haven't become acquainted with every resident of the street, yet. I was making my way through the families on the street. It takes a long time, though. It is important to know your neighbors.

I shrugged again. I held my palms up at the same time.

"Anyhow, she knows who you are. She makes a ton of cash; much more than I do. I do pretty well though. I have my classes paid for and I have enough saved for the next two semesters. You two must come down for lunch sometime," she said to Cherrie and me. "They have a buffet during the week. The food is fantastic. I wait tables

180

during the afternoon. I only strip on the weekends. I'll take good care of you, I promise."

"We'll see, dear," Cherrie said as she patted my thigh, trying to make me feel more comfortable. It worked, kind of.

Raven, being so much like her dad, turned on music through her cell phone. The sound was refreshing. The mood in the room became lighthearted as the Spice Girls started to tell us what they "Really, really wanted!" Naomi and Raven jumped up from the couch, they each grabbed a remote control from the coffee table, used them to mimic microphones, and started singing and dancing to the song, as they had undoubtedly done a few hundred time before.

As I sat there and watched these best friends entertain us, I started to remember taking Raven to her last Daddy Daughter Dance in elementary school.

"Daddy, how do I look?" Raven asked. She was standing in front of Tara in a new white dress with blue trim. I looked down at her standing in the doorway of my bedroom. Tara had her hands on Raven's shoulders. They both had beautiful smiles on their faces. I had been tying my tie, looking at the mirror on Tara's dresser. I turned around. Raven had her hair done to resemble that of Shirley Temple's hair with spiral curls. She took my breath away.

"You look beautiful, Honey; absolutely beautiful!" I said.

"Mommy did my hair like this. Isn't it lovely?" Raven asked as she bounced the curls with the palms of her hands.

"It sure is," I said. I looked at Tara when I said it.

Tara had her head wrapped in a pink bandana. She was waiting for her hair to grow back from the rounds of cancer treatment she had recently received. She looked more beautiful to me than I could ever remember, even though she looked tired. The bags under her eyes were darker that day than normal. But, her positive attitude and beautiful smile shined through. She had a sparkle in her eyes. I never wanted to forget this moment. Our little girl was growing up so fast. She looked so much like Tara. My heart was filled with love for these two ladies.

"How do I look?" I asked as I slipped into my sport coat.

"Very handsome Daddy; we are going to be the best dressed daddy and daughter at the dance," Raven said. "Are you ready?" Raven held her hand out for me to take.

I took her little hand in mine and followed as she led me into the living room. "Sit down Daddy. I have a surprise for you."

I sat on the sofa. Tara stood near me as Raven hurried into the kitchen and opened the fridge. Moments later, she returned with a corsage and a boutonniere. "Mommy got these for us. See, they match the blue in my dress and in your tie. Mine goes on my wrist. I have to pin yours on your coat." She struggled to open the plastic containers the flowers were in."

"Let me help you with that," Tara said to Raven.

She opened the plastic boxes and handed me the corsage. I slipped it onto Raven's tiny wrist. It nearly came up to her elbow. Raven sniffed the flowers on her arm. Tara bent down and pinned the single flower onto my lapel before she gave me a kiss on my cheek.

"Stand up. Let me take some pictures of the happy couple," Tara said.

I stood next to Raven. Tara knelt down onto one knee and snapped a dozen or so pictures with our Cannon auto focus camera.

"Dalen, bend down so Raven can give you a kiss."

I knelt. Raven kissed me on my cheek. She held the pose while Tara snapped a few more shots. Raven knew how to work the scene. She loved to get her picture taken. She wanted to be the next Tara Banks when she grew up; a true Super Model. I cherished the moment.

When we were at the elementary school dance, I was sitting at a table with other fathers that I barely knew, as we watched our daughters dance to songs by Shania Twain, NSYNC, Britney Spears, and The Backstreet Boys. The dads tried to converse about our local pro sports teams and how fast our daughters were growing up. Most of it was uncomfortable small talk as we wished our daughters would come back to our tables so we could have someone else to talk to.

The night wasn't actually as bad as it could have been. I really was having a good time watching Raven have a blast. That made the night worthwhile. This dance wasn't for the dads, it was for the daughters. I was trying to convince myself of that anyway, until, the DJ announced that he wanted every father to find their daughter, so everyone could participate in the last few dances.

 Raven ran up to me, grabbed my hand, and pulled me to the dance floor. Every daughter did the same thing to their fathers. We all partook in the Hokey Pokey, the Bunny Hop, Y.M.C.A. and a quick comical version of Simon Says, though that wasn't actually a dance. When someone did something that Simon didn't say, they had to sit *on the floor. The winner, a daddy and daughter I didn't know, won a big basket of summer goodies; candies and toys.*

Then our DJ announced that the last song of the evening was going to start in just a moment. He suggested that we take a mental snapshot of the scene as it unfolds. He said, in his experience, we would really want to remember this dance. He was right. He then proceeded to play the song 'Butterfly Kisses' by Bob Carlisle.

The dance floor was crowded; no father and daughter absent. When the music started, I grabbed Raven and placed my hands on her back. She raised her arms and placed her hands on my hips. I looked down. Raven looked up. We kept our eyes locked on each other's as we took small steps and tried to sway, moving in a small circle.

Most fathers were doing the same thing, trying not to step on the little feet in front of them. I wanted more. I wanted to be closer to Raven. I bent down and picked her up. She wrapped her arms around my neck and her legs around my waist. I held her bottom with two hands. We listened to the words of the song as I swayed and danced in a circle. Raven placed her head on my shoulder. I took the moment in. A lump gathered in my throat, again. Tears filled my eyes. I danced with my daughter.

In doing so, I looked around the dance floor and noticed that almost all the fathers had done as I had done. They were holding their daughters close to their hearts as they danced and made a memory. My eyes locked with a few other men's. We smiled. There were tears in their eyes as well. None of us, not a single man, had a dry eye and none of us, not a single man, cared or attempted to wipe the tears away. These were tears of joy. This was a moment none of us, not a single man, was going to forget. Nothing mattered at that moment, except the daddy's and the daughters they held, tight, as they danced into the night.

"I love you Daddy!" Raven whispered into my ear as the song finished playing.

"I love you too, Raven," I said. "I love you too." I gave her a butterfly kiss.

My cell vibrated, returning me to the present. I checked it. I had a text from Ian. It read: I spoke to Macy. She said someone dropped a flannel off at your house for me to wear tonight. I'll be over after I grab a bite. Should we leave about 7:00?

I sent back: Yes. I'll pick you up.

The doorbell chimed. I answered the door. A uniformed officer stood in front of me holding a brown paper bag. The top of it was folded down. She handed me the bag. "Lou said to say, to make sure you and your friend wear these tonight, as discussed." She almost felt proud for delivering the message verbatim. "She said to say, 'Try not to get them wet. If it rains, wear a jacket over it.'"

"Thank you," I said. I closed the door after she stepped off the porch.

I looked into the bag. The hoodie was orange and brown with a camouflage design. I would never wear it, normally, but I would make an exception for tonight. Ian's flannel was black and gray. He probably already had one that matched it, but this one had a tracking device in it. I tossed the bag and the hoodie onto the sofa.

I went into the kitchen to make a plate of dinner. Elvis was already eating out of a small bowl. Cherrie was sitting on the floor next to him. I smiled.

"There is some leftover Irish stew in the red Tupperware container on the second shelf in the fridge. I'm not hungry. I'll eat something later. The girls are going out to eat with a few friends," Cherrie said. "I'll just stay home with Elvis and try not to worry about you."

"Thank you," I said. I placed the stew in the microwave and heated it up. "What am I doing?" I asked. I'm just an ordinary guy. I'm not cut out for this." I sat at the kitchen table. I placed my head in the palms of my hands. My elbows rested on the table. "What if we can't bring him home? I promised Mrs. Smith we would find him. Now, I'm involved in a mess with a drug lord, prostitutes, a pimp, and the Lieutenant Governor of Michigan. It's been, what, like, four or five days since Mark was kidnapped? I'm set to marry you in less than a week. Oh, and let's not forget the fact that the man that raped and nearly killed my daughter is out on parole and is stalking Olivia when he isn't following me around. And...and...Mrs. O'Flannigin wants me and the little red headed boy down the street to move a couch for her. Yeah, let's not forget about Mrs. O'Flannigin. We can't forget about Mrs. O'Flannigin."

Cherrie had stood and moved behind me. She was rubbing my shoulders. The microwave began beeping, telling me that my stew was finished warming. I tried to stand to get it. Cherrie pushed me back into the chair. "I'll get it," she said and she did.

Chapter Eighteen

I picked up Ian a few minutes after 7:00. We made our way to Jefferson Avenue.

"I want to get there early so we can figure out what our best options are," I said.

"I know," Ian said. "Are you packing?"

"Yeah, I've got it in my shoulder holster. It's under this ridiculous hoodie. I feel like I'm supposed to be deer hunting."

"The orange color is so Macy and Larkin can find you easily."

I said, "I know. This is the only thing I have ever put on that was camo. I feel like Mickey and Jerome are going to know it isn't mine."

"They don't know what you normally wear. They just met you this week," Ian said.

"I get that," I said. "It's just that…"

"Dalen," Ian said interrupting me, "I'm sorry about this afternoon."

I knew he was.

"Let me explain. During my second deployment, when I was in Egypt; Demitri was stationed over there as well. We were in different platoons. But a few times, when we had time for leave, we went to Cairo for the weekend. Many soldiers went. Anyhow, this one weekend, I met this girl, an American, Marlina. Well, we partied. Demitri joined us along with other soldiers and their dates. Things got out of hand one night. Someone had brought an eight ball."

I didn't exactly know what an eight ball was. I figured it was some sort of a drug or a way to take drugs, but I didn't question him about it. I just let him talk.

Ian stared straight ahead as he spoke. He had lowered his voice to a level above a whisper. "Things got out of hand. Clothes came off. Partners were shared. Things were attempted and other things were done that should not have been done. I drank too much and got way too high. I passed out. Anyhow, when I woke up, it was the next morning. I was alone in the hotel room. I was naked. I had a, um…" Ian paused as he searched for what words he wanted to use. "…a uh, a ladies toy, um, stuck in my, uh…" He couldn't say the words.

I didn't blame him.

Ian continued, "But lying on the bed next to me were 10 Polaroid pictures of me in uncompromising situations."

"Ian," I said, "You don't have to continue. I get the point."

"I played it off as a joke when it was mentioned around the guys at base. They all found out. But we were brothers. None of them would ever have said anything to anyone else. But Marlina told Demitri and obviously he told that fat fuck at Mickey's. I burned the photos. Marlina swears she didn't take them of me. I can only assume there weren't any more. A film cartridge contains 10 pictures. I was given 10. I hope that was all there was. I was raped that night. I was raped. I never found out who did it. Hell, I might have done it to myself. I don't know Dalen. But that's what he was talking about this afternoon. Of all the people I could have run into today, in this world that is so large, yet at the same time it is so small. Why did I have to run into Demitri?"

I promised Ian that would never bring this conversation up to anyone, ever. "On the plus side," I said, "he did tell us what was in the boxes."

"Right."

"Your flannel is in the bag on the back seat. Put it on before we get out of the car. We need to call Renee to make sure the tracking device is working," I said.

Ian reached behind me and removed the flannel shirt from the bag. He was careful not to hit me in my face with his arm when he put it on. I decided to park the Jeep at a Big Boy Restaurant on Jefferson, not far from the bridge. We crossed the street at a light.

 When we were on the bridge, Ian asked, "Do you have any idea how this might go down? Will it be like it is in the movies; like, we come from one side and they come from the other, then we'll meet in the middle? They will send Mark with the money and you'll give them your phone."

"I'm not going to give them my phone."

"You promised them the photos," Ian said.

"I didn't promise them shit. This was you're idea. You told Black Irish we'd make the exchange here. Not me. This was your doing. Or did you forget that?" I asked. "Though I did tell Ralph I would get him the SD card that had the photos on them."

My phone vibrated. I looked at the screen. It was Macy. I answered. "Well, I say there Lieutenant Macy. How does this evening find you?" I was doing my best John Wayne impression. Macy didn't care. Ian just shook his head at me and walked away.

"The tracker is working. We have both of you. You're on the bridge. Parker is walking away from you. Good. It's working. Now leave the area and don't show up until 9:00 as we discussed earlier. I hope you didn't park on the island."

"No. I parked at the Big Boy," I said.

"Good. Go there and get something to eat. Stay there until 8:50. Like I told you before, I'll be around, Larkin will be there, and I have Simpson there already. You are covered."

I looked around. I didn't see Detective Cody Simpson anywhere. "I don't see Simpson."

"You are not supposed to. He's there. Go eat. We've got your back. Text me when you leave Big Boy," Macy said. The line went silent.

"Ian," I shouted. He was near the middle of the bridge already. He turned around to look at me. "Let's go eat," I yelled.

Ian smiled and started running back to me. Food!

We crossed Jefferson and went to the Big Boy as instructed. I had already eaten so I just ordered French fries and a side salad. Ian ordered 2 Slim Jims with one order of fries. We both had coffee. At 8:40 we used the restroom and then Ian paid the bill.

I had nerves sprinting through my body. My palms were beginning to sweat. It was cold outside. The temperature on my phone's weather app read 38 degrees. It was cloudy. Rain was expected later in the night. The street lamps had hazy halos around the lights. We crossed the street and walked on the sidewalk to the center of the Belle Isle Bridge.

Ian said, "Did you know that the actual name of this bridge is the Douglas MacArthur Bridge?" I assumed he was attempting to lighten the mood.

It didn't work. I was a nervous wreck.

We stopped and listened to the water flow below us. I kept looking around wondering where Mickey or his sons were. Maybe Jerome McMillan and Tyreke would walk Mark over to us. I didn't know. Perhaps no one would show up. I checked my phone. It was 9:05. I didn't see Macy, Larkin, or Simpson. I stayed close to Ian. He gave me comfort.

Minutes ticked by. I was about to call Macy when Ian elbowed me in my side. I looked around, looking for someone to be walking toward us. I saw no one. No cars were on the bridge. Jefferson was also quiet.

"What?" I asked.

Ian pointed his thumb in the direction of the water. Below us was a boat, floating in our direction. I could see three men standing on the deck near the bow. The closer they got, the clearer I could see, though I couldn't make out the faces yet. The street lights had shown little light on their faces.

"I'm glad my glasses are ready. I'll pick them up tomorrow. I wish I had them on now. Maybe, I'd be able to see these people more clearly," I said.

Ian said, "That's Mark in the middle. It looks like Terry and Donnie, the brothers on either side of him." Ian removed his gun from his waistband. He held it beside his thigh.

I unsnapped my holster and placed my hand on the pistol grip. I didn't remove it from under the hoodie though.

 The boat seemed to slow down. I could make out the faces now. Ian was correct. Mark was between the Royboys. He looked like he had gone 15 rounds with Tommy Hearns. One of the brothers held a gun up to Marks temple. The other brother was holding Mark up by his armpit.

"Are you seeing this?" Ian asked.

"I am. This isn't what I had anticipated," I said.

Ian said, "I wondered how they were going to deliver him. I guess we are not going to get the money."

I looked around to see if Macy, Larkin, or Simpson were in the area. I didn't see them anywhere. I wondered if Macy had thought that the boat might have been a possibility. If she did, she didn't mention it to me.

"What should we do?" I asked Ian.

"I don't know, man," he said. "I don't know." Then he shouted down at the men at the boat, "Mark. Are you OK? Raise your hand if you are Ok?"

Mark didn't move. The brothers looked at each other. The one on Mark's left yelled, "He's fine. Where's the phone with the pictures? Throw it down and you'll get this guy back. No phone, no friend."

Without looking at Ian I said to him, "Should I throw my phone down?"

Ian said, "No." Then he shouted, "Where's the money? One hundred grand; that was the deal. When we have Mark and the money, you'll get the phone with the pictures." Then Ian raised his pistol and pointed it over the wrought iron fence that was waist high to him and pointed it at the men on the boat.

The front of the boat was about to float under the 30 foot bridge.

"No phone, no friend!" the brother on the right yelled in our direction.

I had to lean over the rail to not lose sight of them. I was startled when my phone started to play my ringtone. I checked my phone. I had a text from an unlisted number. The text read: The Older One says FUCK YOU! My heart sank. I gasped. Just as I did, I heard a gunshot. I looked over the rail. The boat was halfway under the bridge now. I jumped the rail, ran across the bridge's street, and jumped the rail on the other side of the bridge. I leaned over the iron fence and saw the tip of the bow float under us. The brothers waited until I could see them before they threw Mark over the bow of the boat. His body barley made a splash before it disappeared under the moving vessel.

Ian jumped the rail and stopped beside me. "Did they just throw Mark overboard?" He was removing his flannel jacket. He jumped over the rail and landed with a loud thud on the deck of the boat. Ian landed on all fours but the momentum sent him tumbling into a roll. Shocked, the brothers turned around. One of them kicked Ian in the face. His body flopped backwards like a rag doll. The other brother, the one with the gun, bent down and grabbed Ian by his shirt collar.

I had removed my hoodie and moved ten feet to my right. I heard another gunshot. I jumped over the rail and into the water. It was a long drop. I thought I had moved far enough over to avoid hitting the boat. I remember scanning the approaching water below me for Mark's body. I didn't see him. What I did see, a millisecond before my head hit it, was the rail on the bow.

In the distance, I heard sirens approaching. I sat on the dry shore; my back was leaning against Renee's chest. Renee was rubbing my arms as I sat there shaking. Ian was rubbing my legs and my hands, one at a time, trying to get me warm; trying to get me circulation flowing again. Blankets had been wrapped around me. I was in the freezing cold water for about fifteen minutes, before Ian had rescued me. I had cut above my left ear. The cut was about four inches long and rested in the middle of a bump that was half the size of a tennis ball. I have no recollection of being in the water.

I tried to speak but my lips were trembling too fast. "Sh-sh-sh-sh-shot h-h-him," was all I could muster. My face was dripping wet but I could tell which drops were water and which were tears. "Th-th-they sh-sh-shot h-him." I fell asleep again.

Chapter Nineteen

5 Days Before My Wedding

1 Day Since Frownie Mae's Death

I woke up. I looked around. Cherrie was gently rubbing my left arm. I was in the hospital, lying on a bed. I was tucked under a few white sheets and blankets. My head was propped up with two pillows. I had little white circles stuck to my chest with wires coming from them. They were used to monitor my heart rate.

"Good morning Sunshine," Cherrie said in a pleasant voice. "It's nice of you to join us." She sounded so sweet.

"What am I doing here?" I asked. I tried hard to remember. I couldn't.

A beautiful blonde nurse was standing beside me. She was checking my vitals.

When she was finished she said, "Try to get some rest Mr. Reese. I'll be back in two hours to check on you again."

I fell back to sleep pretty quick, I guess. It seemed like the very moment I had fallen asleep, my beautiful blonde nurse was waking me up again to recheck my vitals. This was repeated over and over. It seemed pretty cruel to me; going to sleep so they could just wake me up.

Chapter Twenty

4 Days Before My Wedding

2 Days Since Frownie Mae's Death

Ian came out of a bathroom that was across the hall from the foot of my bed.

"Hey, look who's up," he said.

I tried to sit up. It felt like blood had rushed to my head. "Whooah. Head rush!" I said. I lay back down on the pillows.

"Stay where you are Honey. You don't need to get up yet. There's no hurry," Cherrie said. She had stood and was trying to adjust the pillows and tuck me back in.

"I've got to pee," I said.

"Just go!" Ian said with a laugh. "You have a catheter." He laughed harder.

"Really?" I said. "Crap. I used to pride myself on the fact that I had never needed one before." I took advantage of my first cath. "So what happened?" I asked. "How did I end up in here? I didn't get shot, did I?" The events of Sunday night were coming back to me.

"No. No," Ian said. "I did. But it was only a flesh wound. Terry shot me while we were fighting on the boat." He slipped an arm out of his flannel and showed me a bandage on his right bicep.

"Shit! Did they find Mark? Is he ok?" I said excitedly. Then I felt the air go out of my lungs and escape through my lips. My heart had a sudden sharp pain. "Did he make it?" Then I whispered, "Is he alive?"

Cherrie's eyes filled with tears that instantly slid down her rosy cheeks. She placed her head in her hands and began to sob.

I could tell by the look on Ian's face that Mark hadn't made it.

"I tried to save him, man. I did. I tried," I said. I started to cry as well. I didn't hide my face. I kept my blurry eyesight on Ian's face.

"I know you did. Everyone knows you did. We both tried. We did our best, buddy. We did our best." Ian started to cry too.

The lump in my throat prevented me from saying anything for a moment. When I could, I asked, "Did they get Mickey?"

Cherrie grabbed a tissue and blew her nose. She took another to wipe her eyes. She gave a tissue to Ian and one me. Ian wiped his eyes. I did not.

"They couldn't locate Mickey. Larkin killed Terry Royboy on the boat; one shot, right between his eyes. When the shot hit Terry, he discharged his gun; that's what hit me. Donnie wasn't on the boat when it docked. I fought Donnie for a minute. When I thought I had knocked him out, I dove into the water to save you. I pulled you to shore as fast as I could. You hit that rail pretty hard. It knocked you out, man. You were unconscious, floating like a corpse. I thought we lost you too."

For the first time, I remembered the jump. I remember falling and looking for Mark on my way down. I recalled seeing the rail on the bow of the boat approach my head.

I reached up and touched the bandage tapped above my ear. I felt the bump. It was enormous. It hurt like hell, for the first time. Now that I was aware of it, my head began pounding.

"Can I get something for this headache?" I asked a male nurse as he walked by.

"I'll check with the doctor," he said, before continuing on his way.

"What is it with your family? Every couple years, one of you needs to end up in the hospital for a few days. I don't know if I want to marry you now. I could be next," Cherrie said jokingly.

"Wait. Did you say, 'for a few days'? How long have I been in here? What day is it?" I didn't remember yesterday too well.

It's Tuesday afternoon," Ian said. "Oh, here; I picked these up for you." Ian had a few bruises on his face and a slight shiner around his left eye. He handed me my new pair of glasses.

I said thank you and put them on. I was surprised how much more clearly I could see now. I liked it. Until, Mark's bruised and swollen face popped into my memory. My heart sank again.

"I let him down," I said. "I couldn't save him."

"Dalen, the M.E. said he was dead before he was shot. He's pretty sure he had been beaten to death before he was shot on the boat. I'm pretty sure they beat him to death because he wouldn't give you and Victoria up and he wouldn't give them the pictures. Sadly, he died because he had principles and they weren't going to beat that out of him," Ian said somberly.

"If I've been in here since Sunday night, what happened yesterday?

Cherrie stood and gave me a kiss on my forehead. "I'll give you two gentleman a few minutes. I'm going to go get some water. I'll inform your nurse that you are awake." Then she walked way.

"They pulled Mark out of the water early Monday morning. They found his body down by the Ren Cen." Ian was referring to the General Motor's Renaissance Center; it is located about 5 miles or so west of Belle Isle on the waterfront. "The news caught wind of the story. A reporter from *Rolling Stone* somehow discovered that Mark Smith was Frownie Mae. That somehow ended up being a bigger story than Mark's death; the fact that political blogger Mark Smith was actually Frownie Mae."

Ian continued, "Mrs. Smith is devastated by his death but she assured me that she doesn't blame you or me for it. She knows we did everything we could. She was up here yesterday and spent about an hour with you."

Ian removed his phone from his pocket, opened up his Twitter app and said, "Yesterday morning, Ralph Dixon tweeted that 'The altercation I had Sunday with Mr. Parker and Mr. Reese was just a few men settling a minor disagreement.' He said it was just 'boys being boys.' He then said, 'No legal action needs to be taken.' Dixon posted that before the story of Frownie Mae broke. He hasn't made a statement since, but you've got to believe, the world is dying to know what you and I were arguing with him about."

"And I would love to tell them. But, I won't do it yet. We still hold the ace. We've got the pictures. We can release the photos whenever we want. Have you heard from Macy in a while?" I asked.

"Macy and Larkin have been incredible through all of this," Ian said. "We are cleared of any wrong doing as far as the investigation goes. That's just an FYI. There is an ongoing manhunt for Donnie and Mickey Royboy. Their faces are all over the news. This is another national news story, once again involving the countries favorite Superhero, Dalen Reese, the man that captured the Trench Coat Rapist. You are famous all over again. There is even a cop stationed outside the ICU door. He's here to protect you. Aren't you special?" Ian said.

"I don't need this. I've got to get out of here." I tried to sit up, slowly this time. I managed. I swung my legs over the edge of the bed."

"If you are going anywhere, make sure you take your piss bag with you," Ian said laughing.

As he said that, a nurse back came to check on me.

Three hours later, I was back home and eating a grilled cheese sandwich that Cherrie had made for me. I had Towne Club cola as well. I sat at the dining room table. Raven and Cherrie joined me. They were eating ice cream.

My phone vibrated. I had received a text from a phone number I didn't have saved in my phone. It read: Mr. Reese, This is Tabitha Colavino. Can I call you, please? It is important.

I didn't send a text back to her; instead, I called the number that had sent the text.

"Hello," a sweet and quiet voice said. "Mr. Reese?"

"Yes. You can call me Dalen. What can I do for you?" I put the phone on speaker and placed it on the table. I took another bite of my sandwich and stuffed it along side my cheek, so I could chew and talk at the same time. I saved the phone number in my contacts and entered her name along with it.

"I think Victoria is missing."

That is all she had to say to cause a large knot to appear in the center of my back, between my lungs. It hurt. I tried to take a deep breath. I couldn't.

"No. Don't tell me," I winced. "Why do you think that?" I asked her. I already knew the answer. Fucking Mickey Royboy!

"I haven't heard from her in two days, well not since Monday morning over breakfast. She was telling me about the whole Mark Smith, Ralph Dixon photo thing. She said some nasty people were involved. I'm assuming it was Mickey Royboy from the news, though she didn't want to use any other names because she didn't want to involve me. But, Mr. Reese, she gave me your number and said to call you if I felt I needed to. I can't reach her. We have always been close. It isn't like her not to return my calls. I went to her apartment."

I felt like I needed to say something, just to let her know I was still listening, so I said, "And she wasn't there?"

"Mr. Reese..."

"Dalen," I interrupted. "Please, call me Dalen."

"Sorry. Dalen, I went to her apartment and it is trashed. Her computer, her desk top, not her laptop, has been smashed to pieces. Her laptop isn't here, but that is not unusual. She takes it with her everywhere she goes. But her drawers have been pulled out and dumped on her floor. Everything in all of her cupboards has been thrown on the floor. Her dishes have been smashed. It's obvious they were looking for the pictures. They didn't need to trash all of her belongings," she said. "Dalen, I think someone has taken her. I think she is in real danger. And knowing what the news is saying about Mark Smith, I fear Mickey Royboy has her too."

I tried to stretch the knot out as Tabitha spoke. It wasn't working. "Did you call the police?"

"I just did. I am at Vicky's apartment now. They are sending an officer over. I felt I needed to call you and let you know. I'm not asking you to find her. I don't want to put you in anymore danger. But, Vicky trusts you and she knows you'll do whatever you can do."

"Can I call you if I have any questions, Tabitha?" I asked.

"I hope you will. I've got to go. The police are here."

"Tabitha? I have one quick question before you hang up."

"Yes Sir. What is it?" she asked.

"Where did you and your sister have breakfast yesterday morning?"

"At the Leo's Coney Island on Old Woodward, in Birmingham," she said quietly. "We met at 7:00 am. We left around 8:00. I haven't heard from her since. I'm sorry Mr. Reese but I really must answer the door. Have a nice day." She ended the call.

"It's Dalen," I said to the empty line. "Please call me Dalen."

Raven and Cherrie laughed. I finished my grilled cheese and washed my plate. Cherrie brought her and Raven's dishes over and placed them in the sink. She gave me a kiss and said thank you. I washed their dishes as well.

I called Lieutenant Macy and repeated the conversation I had had with Victoria's sister. "Are you any closer to getting Mickey or Donnie?" I asked.

"We are working on it. Dalen, this shit has got to stop. Too many innocent people are getting hurt because some assholes had to take pictures of the shvantzes they should have kept in their pants."

"They weren't even wearing pants," I said as a matter of fact. "Though Jerome McMillan did have on a pair of chaps," I said laughing.

"Reese, stay home. Get some rest." Macy hung up.

Chapter Twenty-one

2 Days Since Victoria Colavino Disappeared

 "Shoot!" Cherrie shouted as the doorbell rang. "I forgot the Pastor was coming over tonight to talk to us about the wedding. Do you want me to tell him that we need to reschedule? If you are not feeling up to it…"

"I'm fine. Invite him in."

Pastor Gronkowski entered the living room like he owned it. He walked directly up to me, shook my hand then took a seat on the couch. He placed his briefcase on the coffee table and pulled the coffee table closer to the couch, so he didn't have to lean over as far to reach his things.

"Would you like some coffee, tea, or water?" Cherrie asked the pastor.

"Hot tea, please; nothing herbal. No cream but if you have a sweetener substitute, I would prefer that over sugar," the pastor said with confidence. He was already digging through his briefcase and removing stacks of papers. He would straighten each stack by tapping them upright on the table in front of him.

"I'll be back in a moment," Cherrie said. She disappeared to the kitchen.

"I'm sorry about the loss of your friend. If you feel you need to talk to me, I am always available to you. How are you feeling anyhow, Dalen?" the pastor asked without looking up from his task at hand.

"I'm doing well," I said. And I was. I felt like I was nearly back to 100%.

"When did people stop being good? It used to be, at least when we were younger, that everyone answered that question with the word 'good'. Then sometime in the last few years, people started saying that they were 'well'. I'm still not comfortable using the word 'well' to describe my feelings. I may be old fashioned but I'm sticking with 'good'," Pastor Gronkowski said.

"I can dig that," I said, understanding his point of view. "So, how are you doing?" I asked him, almost as a test.

He started laughing. "I'm good," he said. He put a lot of emphasis on the word 'good'. He laughed harder.

Cherrie returned with a tray of drinks. She placed Pastor Gronkowski's non herbal hot tea on the table beside his stacks of papers. He thanked her. She handed me my coffee while she had poured herself a glass of red wine.

"I didn't know wine was an option," the Pastor said.

"I'm sorry," Cherrie said. "I thought you didn't drink. Would you like a glass of wine?"

"No thank you. I'm just messing with you. You are right, I don't drink." He laughed some more. "Tea is my addiction."

"Dalen, how are you handling your addiction?" he asked me.

"Most of the time, things are good," I said.

"Not well?" he said as he laughed some more.

This guy must think of himself as a real comedian.

I gave him a courtesy laugh. "Most of the time, things are good." No emphasis. "There are times though, when things are harder to deal with than normal. I still call my sponsor and attend one or two meetings a month. But for the most part, I'm good."

He laughed some more. I'm surprised how much mileage he was getting out of this good verses well bit. If he uses it at every meeting, he's spending a lot of time laughing. I really don't think it is that funny but, to each their own, as they say.

"Shall we get started?" he asked us.

"Please," I said. The sooner we start; the sooner this evening would be over.

"Can I get either of you anything else before we begin?" Cherrie asked. She was still standing.

"Nope," the pastor answered for the two of us.

"I guess not," I said to Cherrie. I wanted some chips, but the pastor must have thought I was good without any. "Have a seat Cherrie," I said as I patted the cushion on the love seat next to me.

For the next half an hour, we discussed family, family values, marriage, what we expected to get out of our marriage, our wedding ceremony, and religion. When we started talking about religion, Pastor Gronkowski said, "Dalen, I get the feeling that your belief in God is not as strong as it used to be. Would you like to talk about that?"

"Not really," I said. "But you are correct. I just haven't had the connection with God that I had before Tara passed away."

"May I be so bold as to ask if you still believe in God?" our pastor asked.

I didn't want to discuss religion. I didn't want to talk about my beliefs. I didn't want to discuss my loss of faith. I didn't feel comfortable talking about it with Cherrie, Ian, Raven, and especially not with our pastor. But, Cherrie thought it was important to get married by a member of the clergy and not by a Justice of the Peace, so I decided to suck it up and have this discussion for her.

I took a deep breath; the knot from Tabitha's news about Victoria still hadn't gone away. I said, "Look, it's not that I don't believe in God. I want to. Will it be the God from the Bible? Maybe, I don't know. I want to believe that there is a God of some sort out there; some sort of spiritual being looking down on us. But to be perfectly honest with you, I lost faith in whatever God might be out there when Tara was taken from me. I have not lost hope that someday I may find him, but right now, I need more reassurance than the words in a book can give me."

"Thank you for being open with me. Your comments just now have reminded me of a story I heard a few years ago. If you have a moment, I'd like to share it with you?"

I looked at Cherrie. She patted my knee. I had the feeling that we were going to hear the story whether we wanted to or not.

"We would love to hear it," Cherrie said with a pleasant smile on her beautiful face.

"There once was a man, let's call him Luke and his wife, we'll call her Tamara, that were devastated when they found out that Tamara had been diagnosed with cancer; much like you were when you found out about Tara. When they found out about Tamara's unfortunate situation, they put their faith in God. They prayed often and asked God that he look after Tamara. They were confident that God would listen to them and soon find Tamara in good health. They prayed a lot. When Tamara was informed that the cancer had spread and was in terminal, she and Luke continued to pray, with hope that God would intervene and perform some sort of a miracle."

I took a deep breath. I hurt to do so, but I didn't want to interrupt Pastor Gronkowski, as he shared the story that I found, hit too close to home. But that was actually the point, and I knew it. I settled back into the love seat and grabbed hold of Cherries hand. She squeezed mine.

The pastor continued, "The closer Tamara got to the end of her life, the more Luke began to doubt whether or not God actually existed. Luke wondered that if there actually was a God, why would he put Tamara through such an awful ordeal; why was God taking Tamara away from him?

"It wasn't long before Tamara had passed away. Luke had lost all faith in God. He stopped praying. Luke was so devastated and pissed off at life in general, please excuse my foul language, that he basically gave up. He stopped going to work. He started drinking. Before long, he lost his job and soon after he lost his home. Luke felt he had nothing to live for."

I had been there, for the most part. I had been in Luke's position; kind of. I knew what Luke felt like.

"Homeless and needing a place to sleep, Luke spent his last few dollars and bought a Greyhound ticket to the west coast. He got on the bus and had taken a window seat. Before the bus departed, Luke looked out the window and saw a long haired man holding a sign. The sign read; GOD IS NOWHERE! Luke said to himself, 'You've got that right, homeless man!'

"The bus departed and drove for hours. Luke fell asleep. When the bus finally stopped at a gas station, the passengers exited the bus to stretch and grab a bite to eat. When Luke passed the bus driver, he asked, 'Where are we?' The bus driver said, 'You've got to read the sign.' Confused, Luke ignored the response and followed the other passengers into the rest stop. After eating, Luke boarded the bus again and returned to his seat. When he looked out the window, he saw the same homeless man with long hair, holding the same sign that read; GOD IS NOWHERE!"

My cell phone vibrated. I picked it up off the arm of the seat. Before I could read the text, Cherrie snatched it from my hands and placed it under her thigh. "Not now," she said.

The pastor saw our exchange but paid no mind to it. He continued, "This went on for several stops. The bus would stop, Luke would ask the driver where they were and the driver would reply, 'You've got to read the sign.' Luke would eat, re-board the bus and see the same man holding the same sign; GOD IS NOWHERE! Luke wondered why the man was following him. Luke was certain that the man was not a passenger on the bus; the man must be following him, but why? At the next stop, Luke walked past the driver again, on his way to the rest area. Again he asked, 'Where are we?' Again the driver said, 'You've got to read the sign.'

"Now, Luke was getting upset. The only sign I've ever seen is the sign that the long haired man is holding up. I've read the sign. I've re-read the sign. I agree with the sign. God is nowhere! His message could not be clearer. Frustrated, the driver said, 'Maybe you are reading the sign all wrong.'

I was riveted. Cherrie was riveted.

"Luke had had enough," the pastor continued, "Luke stormed down the steps of the bus and walked over to the long haired homeless looking man that had followed him from the beginning of the trip; the man that held a sign that read; GOD IS NOWHERE!

"Why are you following me? Luke asked the man. And don't tell me to read the bleeping sign. I have read the sign. I know. I know. God is nowhere! Believe me, God is nowhere! He took my wife away from me. He took my life away from me. If there has ever been a sign that is clear to me, this is the sign."

"The man that Luke was talking to said, 'Luke, take a step back and read the sign again.' Luke huffed but wanted to put an end to the taunting. So he took a step back. He read the sign. But this time, the words were different. Luke rubbed his eyes and read the sign again. Luke was confused. Had he been reading the sign wrong from the very beginning? Could the sign be right?"

"The man with the sign asked Luke to read the sign aloud. Luke did. He read, 'GOD IS NOW HERE!' It had never read; God is nowhere! It had always read; God is now here!

"Ya see," Pastor Gronkowski said, "Even when there is doubt, when all hope is lost, when one questions their faith, God doesn't go away, he waits until you rediscover his love. The signs are always around. All you have to do look, and sometimes, you just need to re-read them."

I wasn't sure Pastor Gronkowski had convinced me to believe in God again, but I had to admit that it was a cool story with an important message, at least from his point of view. I was sure the story would stick with me forever. I did get goose bumps when he got to it's climax.

"Thank you," I said to our pastor. I stood from the love seat and extended my hand for him to shake. "It's getting late and I really need to get some rest." I was feeling tired and my head was still pounding.

We said our goodnights and said we would see each other on Saturday at my and Cherrie's wedding. I kissed Cherrie and headed for bed.

When I was washed up and about to climb under the sheets, Cherrie walked into the bedroom. "Dalen honey, here's your phone. Remember, you received a message when Pastor was telling us the story?"

She handed me my phone. I plugged it in to charge it. The screen lit up when I did so. I noticed the unread message was from a private phone number. I tapped the icon. It showed that I had a multi-message. That meant it was a photo that needed to be uploaded. I touched the screen, the picture appeared. It took my breath away. I sat down on the edge of the bed and stared at the photo. "Holy crap!" I said, almost in a whisper.

"What is it?" Cherrie asked.

I handed her the phone. "Oh, for God's sake!" she said. "That poor girl. Who is it? Is this that reporter woman?"

"Yes it is; Victoria Colavino," I said. I started to cry. Cherrie put her arms around me, hugged me, and let me cry on her shoulder. She started to cry too.

"What are you going to do?" she asked when we had composed ourselves.

"I'm going to send the picture to Renee, and then I'm going to find Mickey and Donnie Royboy and I'm going to kill them!" I said.

I called Lieutenant Macy; it went to voicemail. "Call me!" I said. Then I sent her the picture.

I called Detective Ryan Larkin; it also went to voicemail. "Call me!" I said. Then I sent him the picture of Victoria too.

I called Ian. That son-of-a-bitch didn't answer either. I didn't leave him a message but I did send him the photo.

"Doesn't anyone answer their phone?" I asked Cherrie. The question was rhetorical. Cherrie didn't answer me.

"Where's my Louis?" I asked. "I've got to listen to my Louis."

I started looking through the stack of record albums on my dresser. Louis Armstrong was my saving grace. If anyone could calm me down and help me relax, Louis could. He always did. He wasn't on my dresser. I went into the living room and started removing albums from the bookshelf. I was tossing them on the couch, looking for Louis. I was tossing them at an alarming rate. Some were bouncing off of the cushion and sliding onto the floor. The records were sliding out of the jackets. He wasn't there.

"Where is he? I need Louis!" I shouted.

Cherrie started picking the records up off of the floor. She put them back into their rightful sleeves and stacked them neatly on the coffee table. I didn't care. I kept tossing them onto the couch. She kept picking them up without saying a word.

"Maybe he's in the basement." I headed for the stairs.

"Dalen," Cherrie said in a calming voice, "maybe you could listen to Louie on your phone. I'm sure you have his music on your phone."

"I don't need the digital music!" I shouted. "I want to listen to the record. The sound of the record is what soothes me. I need the pop and the hiss of the old record. I need to hold the album cover in my hand. Do you understand that? Do you know what I mean? I need the record. I need Louis."

"Dalen. Stop!" Cherrie shouted when I was half way down the stairs.

I stopped where I was. I sat down on the step. Cherrie walked down and sat next to me. She put her arm around me. She placed her head on my shoulder. "You are scaring me."

"I'm sorry," I said. It was painful but I took a very deep breath and let it out slowly through my nose. My back hurt, my head hurt, and rage was running through my body. I wasn't thinking clearly.

Then, from the living room, I heard a beautiful sound that instantly began to relieve the knot in my back, between my shoulder blades. I began to smile. I realized Raven had found my Louis Armstrong record and had placed it on the turntable. She turned it up. I stood. I helped Cherrie to her feet. I leaned down and gave her a kiss. I took her hand and led her to the living room.

Raven was standing next to the record player. "I'm sorry Daddy. I had him in my bedroom." I gave her a hug.

We all sat down on the couch, me in the middle, and listened to my man Louis Armstrong sing about this wonderful world, complete with pops and hisses. I closed my eyes and within a few minutes, I fell asleep.

Chapter Twenty-two

3 Days Since Victoria Colavino Disappeared

3 Days Before My Wedding

I woke up at 5:00, still on the couch, with a blanket on me. The girls had covered me up with a afghan and turned out the lights. I felt a lot better. I snuck into the bedroom and removed my phone from the phone charger, careful not to wake my beautiful fiancé. While in the kitchen, I checked my messages. I had one from Ian. It read: Now what? I had one from Macy. It read: Do not do anything before we speak. I also had one from Larkin. It read: Call Renee. My phone showed a missed call from all three of my texters.

I made a pot of coffee. While it was brewing, I looked at the picture of Victoria Colavino that had been sent to me last night from a private phone number. I sat at the kitchen table, placed the phone on a place mat. I stared at the picture while fresh hot coffee drained into the pot. My stomach churned at the sight of Victoria. She was sitting on a wooden folding chair, her arms were behind her back; probably duct taped or tied together at her wrists. She had a rag tied around her head; it was pulled tight between her lips. She had two black eyes and a cut above her right eyebrow. Blood had dripped down the side of her face but was now dry. She had tears running down her cheeks. Mucus from her nose shined on her upper lip. Her shirt was ripped and barely hung on her shoulders. Fear reflected in her eyes.

When the coffee was finished brewing, Mr. Coffee beeped twice. I stood and poured myself a cup. Steam rose from the brim. I took small sips. I opened a pack of unfrosted strawberry Pop Tarts. I ate them untoasted, all the while, barely taking my eyes off of the picture of Mickey's latest victim.

As difficult as it was staring at the photo, I tried not to take my eyes off of it, while I thought about what I should do next. I had to save her, but I wasn't sure how. I failed in my attempt to save Mark. I felt that if I didn't act quickly, the Royboy's might kill Vicky before they tried to kill me too.

I called Ian. Again, it went to voice mail. "Call me!" I said.

I looked at the photo some more. But this time, I didn't actually look at Victoria; instead I looked at the background. I noticed a familiar sign. The wall of the room she was in was very much like the room I had seen the white boxes were in on Sunday afternoon. She was in a building much like the offices of Mickey Royboy, however, there was only one room in his building that had rippled metal walls, like that of metal sheds; it was the room with the tables and boxes of powdered laundry soap with bags of drugs packed into them. The other rooms in the building had been dry walled. If Victoria Colavino wasn't in the same room, she was in a building in the same vicinity; I was sure of it.

I called Macy. Her phone rang four times before it went to voice mail. I said, "I think I know where Victoria is. Call me!"

Ian was probably out running. I could only assume that Renee was either sleeping or in the shower. I showered, got dressed, grabbed my gun, and left a note for Cherrie. I told her to have a good day and said I would call her later. I signed it with love. I let Elvis out to tinkle, then I opened Raven's bedroom door and let him into her bedroom. I locked the back door to the garage behind me, started my Jeep and headed down McCatty Drive.

It was 6:00 in the morning on Wednesday. I wasn't sure what I was going to do, but I was sure I was headed to the warehouse district off of Livernois to try to find Victoria Colavino before she wound up dead like my dear friend Mark Smith. If Ian, Renee, or Ryan weren't going to call me back, I was going to go it alone; and I was.

At least until I saw Mrs. O'Flannigin standing in the middle of McCatty Drive with nothing on but her white granny panties and her very large white bra. Her hair was in curlers and she wore her pink Deerfoam slippers. I pulled the Jeep off to the shoulder of the road and got out of the car.

"Mrs. O'Flannigin?" I said with concern.

She looked at me but didn't move.

"Mrs. O'Flannigin," I said again as I removed my dark blue Detroit Piston's hoodie. I placed it over her shoulders. "Are you alright?" It was obvious to me that she wasn't.

"Wallace?" she asked. "What are you doing out here? You need to come back in the house. It's very cold out here. You'll catch a cold."

Wallace was her husband. He passed away when I was a child.

"Mrs. O'Flannigin, I'm not Wallace. It's me, Dalen Reese, your neighbor from down the street. Come on. We need to get you inside."

I grabbed her hand and we walked slowly to her front door. She didn't say anything. When we were in her house, I noticed her nightgown was lying on the floor in the living room. I picked it up, removed my hoodie from her back and helped her on with her gown.

"Have a seat Mrs. O'Flannigin. I'll make you a cup of coffee. You are freezing. It'll help warm you up," I said.

I helped her sit on the sofa and went to make a cup of instant coffee. She didn't have an automatic coffee pot. I used the microwave to heat the water. When I finished stirring the coffee crystals into the water, I took it to her, careful not to spill any as I walked.

"Thank you Dalen," she said with a smile. "Did you come over to move my couch? Is that little red headed boy with you?"

I breathed in deeply through my nose and blew out slowly through my lips. I wanted to get to Victoria as soon as possible. It would have to wait a few minutes. "No he is not here but I can move it now." Then under my breath, I added, "Since I'm already here."

"You'll have to remove the cushions and the toss pillows first. The couch is too heavy with them on it." She started to gather the half a dozen throw pillows from the couch.

I took them from her and placed them on the Lazy-Boy recliner. I helped her up off the couch and led her to the kitchen table. I held a chair for her as she sat down. I returned to the living room and slid the sofa, the love seat, the television stand, and the two end tables to the locations where I had moved them once a year, every year, for the past 30 years or so. In six months I would move them back to where they were before I moved them today. I placed the throw pillows back on the sofa, and plugged the television, cable box, and table lamps back into the wall sockets.

"There you go Mrs. O'Flannigin. All done," I said. "Can I do anything else for you before I go?"

"Wallace, will you be home at your normal time? I think I'll make meatloaf for dinner tonight. Doesn't that sound delicious? You love my meatloaf," she said.

"Mrs. O'Flannigin, I'm not Wallace. It's me, Dalen. I live down the street. I just came by to move your furniture," I said trying to jog her memory.

"Of course you are. I'm sorry. My memory sometimes gets lost. You just look so much like my Wallace used to look when he was a young man," she said, somewhat embarrassed. "But you are welcome to come by for my meatloaf this evening, if you'd like."

"I'd love to," I said, "but I have other plans; so, maybe next week, sometime." I patted her hand. "I really must be going now, Mrs. O'Flannigin." I noticed the wedding invitation I had sent to her was hanging on the refrigerator. It was hung with a ladybug magnet. I removed the invite and studied it for a moment. "Will you be attending my wedding Mrs. O'Flannigin?"

"I wouldn't miss it for the world," she said. "Thank you so much for moving my couch. Can I offer you a glass of ice water?"

"I'm good. Thank you. I really must be going." I leaned down and gave her a kiss on her cheek.

"Ya know," Mrs. O'Flannigin said, "My and Wallace's wedding Anniversary is Saturday. He usually works a twelve hour shift on Saturdays so he'll probably be home around 9:30. I think I'll cook a nice pot roast for him. He loves my pot roast. That's the same day you'll be marrying your bride, isn't it? What is her name again?"

"Cherrie."

"She is a very lucky woman, Dalen. Now go. You must have a lot of work to do before the ceremony."

"Thank you Mrs. O'Flannigin," I said. I stuck the invitation back on the icebox door with the ladybug magnet. I let myself out.

I walked to my Jeep. Ian was walking down the street toward me.

"Where is she at?" he asked as he got closer to me.

"She's back in her house. Ya know she was out here in her underwear and slippers just a bit ago. No clothes, no nightgown, no jacket; just her undies and her slippers. She thought I was her husband," I said.

"Wallace?" Ian asked.

"Yes. Apparently I look a lot like him in his younger days."

"Do we still have to move her couch?" he asked.

"No. I just did it."

"Cool," Ian said somewhat relived. He wasn't all too fond of Mrs. O'Flannigin. He was always nice to her but he kinda feared her at the same time. "I wasn't really asking about old lady O'Flannigin, though. I was asking where you thought the reporter was."

"Get in," I said. "We'll go get her. I'm pretty sure she is being held at Mickey's warehouse."

"You call Macy?" Ian asked.

"I did. No answer, but she texted me saying not to do anything without her."

"Is she meeting us there?"

I said, "No." I shifted the Jeep into gear and we headed to Detroit to save Victoria Colavino from the evil Mickey Royboy.

Ian called Lieutenant Renee Macy and filled her in on our plan.

"They'll be there before we get there," Ian said when he ended the call.

"She'll answer for you but not for me," I said.

"I'm better looking," Ian said, laughing.

Chapter Twenty-three

We headed down the Lodge freeway toward our exit. We had a short drive ahead of us. In Michigan we have two seasons; winter and construction. Orange and white barrels had popped up alongside the road about a week ago. I had to maneuver my Jeep through the maze, down the highway, while trying not to knock any of them over. The other drivers on the road were not making our trip any easier.

"So, do ya know how my pinky fingers snap like I have trigger fingers?" I asked Ian.

"Yeah."

"Well, I've been wearing those metal splints with the blue pads on the inside of them, on my pinkies whenever I go to sleep, in hopes that they don't hurt as much in the morning. So far they haven't stayed on my pinkies any night for well over two weeks now. So the other night, I had them on when I went to sleep, and guess where they were when I woke up."

Ian didn't waist any time in answering me. "In your pillow case," he said. "I know how you like to sleep with your hands inside the pillowcase, under your head when you fall asleep."

I started to laugh. "No, but that is a good guess. Nope, they were in my underpants; well, one of them was. The other was on the floor."

Ian started to laugh. "I should have known."

"I guess my hands were cold that night," I said.

"Oh yeah, that's what you're going with; cold hands?" Ian said, still laughing. "Is that what we're calling it now; cold hands?" He laughed harder. "I know what your hands were doing in your shorts."

"I was sleeping!" I shouted. "The splints just slide off too easily."

Ian laughed some more.

"Hey," I said, "at least I didn't find my cell phone in my underpants like you did."

Ian laughed harder. Recapping the story he had told me a few times already, he said, "Oh my gosh, I almost forgot about that. I still can't believe I did that. I was sitting on the toilet, taking care of business, at the Coffee Cabin. I was playing a trivia game on my phone. When I needed to grab the toilet paper, I laid the phone inside my undershorts which were stretched between my knees. When I was finished, I just pulled my pants up and buckled my belt. I washed my hands and left the restroom." Ian was still laughing as he told the story. "I went to make a pot of coffee and I felt something hanging between my upper thighs. I thought, 'What the hell is that.' It was my damn cell phone. I had pulled my pants up with my cell phone inside my underpants. I couldn't believe it. Who the hell does that?"

I was laughing right along with Ian. "Only you, my friend. Only you!" I said.

Ten minutes later I pulled the Jeep off of the expressway and onto Livernois Avenue. Within moments we were parked behind Macy's car on the side of the street about a half a block away from the factory building where Mickey Royboy ran his operations. Macy's car was parked behind Robert Stonewall's Oldsmobile Delta 88. Renee Macy and Ryan Larkin climbed out of her car when Ian and I arrived. Stonewall did not exit his vehicle but he did roll his window down. Renee motioned with her head for us to walk up to the door of the Olds. We gathered in a half circle around Robert's opened window.

Robert Stonewall rested his arm out the opened window. He was wearing a flannel shirt with his grey corduroy sports coat over it. He had the black clip-on tie on the vacant seat to his right. The tie was next to the handle of his wooden cane, which was resting across his lap. His pistol was visible under his unbuttoned coat. He wore the brown fedora hat on his balding head.

No pleasantries were exchanged. Lieutenant Renee Macy said, "If Dalen's hunch is correct, she could be in any one of these buildings," referring to Victoria Colavino. "There are 37 of them within three square miles of here that have the rippled aluminum exterior walls. Three of the buildings are owned by Mickey Royboy's company. We do not have a warrant yet but ADA Jessica Maloney is working on that for us. Judge Hawthorne is our best bet for it. He is in court until noon." We spent the next few minutes mapping out a game plan. We then stepped away from the vehicle.

I went with Ryan. He asked if I was carrying. I patted my waist, touching the handle of my pistol which was under my Detroit Lion's hoodie.

"Don't pull it unless you feel that your life is in imminent danger," Detective Ryan Larkin said to me. "Stay behind me. Leave the premises if I tell you to. Do you understand?"

I understood, however, I didn't like hearing the words 'imminent danger' when he used them. I didn't assume we were just going to enter the building, untie Victoria Colavino, and walk out with her, but I really wasn't sure how dangerous this situation could be until I heard Ryan use those terrifying words. I wanted to act like I was not nervous and that I had been in situations like this a few dozen times, but the fact of the matter was, I was scarred shitless. I wanted to vomit. My acid reflux was getting the best of me and my stomach was churning like hot lava. But, being such a cool cat, I said, "I've got you're back!"

Detective Ryan Larkin looked at me and said, "Then I'm screwed." He paused for a moment and then he laughed.

"Ha, good one!" I said. Then for some unknown reason, I slugged his bicep which was solid. I was surprised. I felt safer for having him on my side.

It looked like Renee Macy was having a similar conversation with Ian, minus the arm punch. Ian had fought in two tours overseas. He had seen and done things he won't even talk to me about; things that keep him awake some nights. Ian knew how to handle himself and was an excellent shot with a gun. Macy was in good hands.

Robert Stonewall had climbed out of his car, with the help of his cane. He checked his guns to make sure they were both loaded; he had two on his person. They appeared to be fully stocked. He put one in his holster, under his coat and held the other one close to his thigh.

I could tell that these three officers had worked closely together a few times. They knew how to communicate with each other just using their eyes. Larkin tapped me on my wrist, once, with the tip of his service piece. He motioned with his hand to tell me we were leaving and we headed in the direction to the left of the first and closest building. He started walking at a fast pace and like he had instructed, I followed closely behind him. He smelled like he had put on too much Old Spice.

I looked back to the vehicles and expected to see Stonewall limping away from them, but he was nowhere in sight. I didn't see Ian or Macy either. I took a deep breath and exhaled slowly through my nose as I followed closely behind Larkin. When we arrived at the side of the first building, Larkin stood with his back against the wall. There was a window to his right. I stood at his left side, also with my back to the rippled wall.

I looked up at the sky. It was a beautiful bright blue. A few sporadic clouds hung like cotton balls, miles above our heads. The sun shone brightly in the distance. Our shadows were lining the ground to our right, just a few feet away from the side of the buildings. The warmth of the sun felt good on my skin.

I didn't have a headache from the accident, but my head hurt where I had a large bruise above the arm of my glasses. I thought about wearing a baseball cap to the wedding, just to hide the black, purple, red, and yellow bump that still existed on my head. Cherrie wouldn't approve, though.

Ryan Larkin took a quick glance through the window. "There are two men inside. There are a lot of white boxes on tables. I didn't see much else. It's a large room. I doubt if they would keep her tied up in a room with a window. But we do have two men counted so far."

Larkin crouched down and walked under the window toward the back of the building. I did the same.

"This isn't the same building that Ian and I were at on Sunday. That one is next door," I whispered to Ryan.

"I know. Stonewall is over there now. He has been there before. It won't come as a surprise to the employees if he shows up there," Ryan Larkin said. Even with a whisper, his voice was extremely deep, yet gentle.

As we were about to move to the back of the building, we heard voices coming from behind it. Ryan peaked around the corner. He must not have liked what he saw. He stood up straight and unlocked the safety on his gun. He took a deep breath. He held up three fingers for me to see, then he pointed to the parking lot behind the building. He mouthed the words, 'Machine guns.'

I felt my head break out into a sweat, under my ball cap. My mouth suddenly felt dry. I tried to swallow, but I couldn't gather enough saliva to do so. I licked my lips. Ryan pushed me in the direction of the front of the building. I crouched under the window as I moved catlike to the front corner of the establishment. I stayed close to the wall. Ryan was on my tail pushing me to move faster. Maybe because I was moving more like an old overweight cat.

"Move it!" he said. "Hurry!" He moved by me and pulled me around the front corner of the wall. We were crouching behind a few bushes, under another window. White stones were spread in the flowerbed around the green hedges. They crunched under our feet. Ryan popped up and looked inside the window. He returned to his crouch. He lowered himself onto one knee.

My heart was racing. I removed the gun from under my hoodie. I checked the cartridge to make sure it was fully loaded. It clicked loudly when I jammed the sleeve back into the grip. I felt safer with it in my hand. My palms were sweating. I dried them on my jeans, one at a time.

Two buildings away, where Ian and Renee Macy were, gunfire exploded. Bang, bang, bang!

Bang!

Bang, bang!

The shots we coming from different directions. They were over in less than two seconds. The shots were loud. Ryan shouted, "Get down!" and pushed me to the rocks. "Stay here!" He took off like a panther chasing it's prey. He was fast. He was quickly around the far side of the building next door; the building Ian and I had visited on Sunday. Seconds later, Ryan was out of sight.

Bang!

One more single shot had been fired. I looked behind me to see if anyone was approaching. I was alone. I peeked around the corner of the wall that Ryan and I had just come from. I didn't see anyone there either.

Then, from the back of the building that I was in front of, there was a steady stream of gunfire, likely from one of the machine guns Ryan Larkin had seen a minute ago. I wanted to be brave. I kneeled on the rocks and placed my palms on the white stones. I had laid my pistol on the stones next to my hand. I threw up between my hands, like a teenage girl that could not handle her booze. I threw up again. Then a third time. I wanted to cry.

I had no idea who had fired their guns, if anyone had been hit, or if anyone of my friends were even still alive. I felt alone and afraid. I didn't know what to do. I wasn't cut out for this kind of work. All I wanted to do was run to my Jeep, climb in it and drive home to be with Cherrie and Raven.

Bang!

Bang!

I removed my cell phone from my pocket and dialed 911. I whispered into the phone and explained to the dispatcher what was unfolding around me. I left out the part where I had just thrown up. He asked me to stay right where I was and to, please, don't hang up. I ended the call and put the phone back into my pocket.

As I did that, Robert Stonewall opened the door in front of me. "Dalen! Get in here!" he said in a loud whisper. He held the door open for me with his cane. I hadn't expected to see or hear from anyone; so when Robert opened the door, he startled me. My heart was racing so fast, I could hear it in my head. I scurried to my feet and scooted to the open door as fast as I could. So much for the search warrant, I thought.

The first door on the right was opened. Stonewall practically pushed me into the room. "Stay in here and stay low. Stay away from the window," he said as he was closing the door behind me.

"Wait," I shouted. "What the hell is going on out there?"

"Stay here!" Robert said. He closed the door.

There was more gunfire behind the building I was in. "Who the hell is getting shot out there?" I said to myself. I know Stonewall instructed me to stay away from the window, but I wanted to know what was going on outside. I walked to the window, stood to the side of it and pulled the horizontal blinds a few inches away from the window. I peeked outside. I could see our vehicles parked a short way down the street. I didn't see any people.

More gunfire. Bang, bang, bang!

Bang!

The last few shots sounded muffled; almost as though they were coming from inside a building, but not the one I was in.

There was shouting. I believe it was in Spanish. The voices were also muffled.

I peeked through two of the slats in the blinds to get a look in front of room I was in. Still, I didn't see any action.

 I walked over to the door Robert Stonewall had closed. I listened closely. Silence. Sometimes it is the worst kind of sound. I slowly turned the door knob and quietly pulled the door open a few inches. I peered through the crack, into the hallway. I was shocked to see the back of Donnie Royboy. He was holding Victoria Colavino by her left bicep. Her hands were indeed duct taped behind her back. Donnie was wearing a brown leather bomber jacket. He had a large hand gun in his left hand. He was pointing it at the ceiling, inches away from his head. Donnie was walking backwards, pulling Vicky with him. They were getting close to the door I was peering out.

I wasn't sure what made me move when I did. I wasn't sure why I didn't quietly close the door and wait for the police to handle the situation. I was afraid. My heart was beating much faster than it should have been. When I saw Donnie backing toward me, with Victoria, I didn't think about anything other than getting Vicky away from Donnie.

They didn't see my coming. I had my pistol in my right hand. I didn't really want to use it, but I wasn't going to go into this gunfight without it. I threw the door open. I lowered my head and charged at him with full force. I had taken about eight or nine large strides, gaining momentum as I moved. It only took a second.

By the time Donnie Royboy and Victoria Colavino had heard me coming, I used my head and rammed it into the small of his back. He let go of Vicky's arm and arched his back. He let out a loud scream. I had knocked the wind out of him. Vicky let out a squeal, but it was muffled by the duct tape covering her mouth.

The hit made my spine feel like an accordion that was being closed. I wrapped my arms around Donnie's waist as the momentum I had gained forced the two of us to tumble to the ground. He landed on his stomach. I landed on his back. My right knee landed between his thighs. I tried to press my knees on his bottom as I used my left hand to try to slam his head onto the floor of the hallway.

Donnie was strong. He quickly climbed to his knees and tried to buck me off of him like mad bull at a rodeo. I laid my torso on his back. I reached under his stomach with my right arm and held on for dear life. I wasn't sure what was going to happen. I hadn't planned ahead. This was all unfolding fast. I didn't see where Victoria went, I just know she had disappeared. I was just trying to not let Donnie get away. I tried to throw punches to the side of Donnie's head, using my left hand. I landed a few of the dozen punches I was able to throw.

Donnie managed to pull himself to his feet, with me still on his back. I wrapped my left arm around his neck and pointed the tip of my pistol against his stomach. Donnie jumped back as fast as he could. He used his weight to slam my back against the wall. I let out a grunt. He leaned forward then straightened himself as fast as he could, again slamming my back against the wall. I grunted loudly, again. It felt like someone had cracked a 2x4 against my spine. I pressed the gun harder into his abs.

Donnie raised his arms, reached over his head, and grabbed the back of my head, just above my neck. He pulled my head forward and threw his head back. Our heads smashed together, skull to skull. My baseball cap was knocked off in the process. He repeated the process several times, all the while, he continued slamming my back against the wall.

I kept my left arm wrapped around his neck and squeezed as tightly as I could, hoping to choke him into blacking out or something. I didn't know. I was just holding on as tight as I could. I fought to prevent our heads from colliding repeatedly. I wasn't as strong as Donnie Royboy was. He was winning.

I placed my finger on the trigger of my pistol, and with the barrel of the gun pressed into his gut, I fired. I felt a quick vibration travel up my arm. Maybe it was my adrenaline. Donnie let out a puff of air; a quick exhale. He didn't let go of my head. Instead, Donnie used force to smash my head against the wall; pinning it with his. He kept pressing. My head turned sideway. He pressed harder, digging the back of his skull into my temple. I felt my vision start to blur. My glasses snapped between the wall and his head. They broke at each joint between the arms and the lenses. He pressed his back harder against my chest.

Donnie Royboy was a powerfully strong individual.

I pulled the trigger again. He let out a whimper. I raised my gun up to his head. I placed it under his chin and pressed it up with all of my strength. I didn't want to fire it, I just wanted to press it hard into his lymph nodes. I knew it could cause unbearable pain. I pushed up with the gun's handle. I swear I didn't mean to, but I pulled the trigger. I hadn't really noticed the sound that the first two shots had made. But, maybe because this one was near my head, I heard the shot. It was almost deafening.

All the force Donnie was using to press my body and head against the wall was released. His body went limp. We both fell to the floor. There was an exit wound in the top of his skull. It wasn't really big but it appeared that his brain matter was bubbling out of it.

Donnie laid motionless on the ground. Blood started to form a puddle, both under his head and from under his jacket near his stomach. I felt like throwing up again. I felt light headed; almost weak and frail. I had just taken a man's life. As I laid on top of Donnie Royboy, just for a moment, trying to make sense of what had happened, the pool of blood had run to my hand. It was warm. I let out an, "Ugh!" I literally didn't want another man's blood on my hands. I tried to scurry away from the body. But as I did, my foot stepped in and slipped in the dark red liquid. I fell to my right knee, which also got soaked in his blood. I hated what I was going through. Vomit rose from my insides and spewed out of my mouth. It splashed on the floor just inches away from Donnie's body.

I managed to make it to my feet. I still had the gun in my hand. It, too, had blood on it. Victoria was standing in the doorway of the room I had left just a minute ago.

Chapter Twenty-four

The Day Victoria Colavino Was Found

"Dalen!" she muffled under the tape.

I ran to her side. I pulled her into the room and closed the door behind us.

"This is going to hurt," I said as I pulled the duct tape away from her skin. It ripped a good portion of her hair from her head, in the process. She didn't seem to care. Her eyes were almost swollen shut. Her cheeks had cuts on them; they were bruised and swollen as well. Her upper lip was also swollen. She reminded me of what Rocky had looked like at the end of the first Rocky movie. Her face though, was not covered in make-up. She had dried blood in her hair. Her clothes were ripped and torn.

"Mickey wants those pictures," Victoria said. "He'll kill to get them."

"Are you alright?" I said. "Besides the obvious." I grabbed a chair and asked her to sit down.

"No. I've been sitting for two days."

"But are you ok?" I asked.

"I have to pee," she said.

"Soon. We'll get you to the restroom soon," I said.

"Who else is here?" Vicky asked.

"Ian, Detective Larkin, Lieutenant Macy, and retired Detective Robert Stonewall. But with all the shooting that took place in the last few minutes, I have no idea who is still with us. I hope they all are. Did they feed you?" I asked her.

"No, and if I could open my mouth wide enough, I'd eat a Whopper. I'm dying for a Whopper."

I was appalled. "What kind of kidnappers don't feed their victims? I would have fed someone I kidnapped. Shit, it's just the right thing to do. I would have given you some bacon at least. Everyone loves bacon. I can't believe they didn't feed you anything."

"They said Mark didn't make it. I swore I wasn't going to make it out of here alive either. All this shit happened because of some kinky stuff the Lieutenant Governor, a whore, and her pimp did," she said. "That's just bull shit."

I removed my hoodie and draped it over her shoulders. She thanked me.

"I could really use a drink right now," Victoria said.

"We'll get you some water once the dust settles down out there," I said.

"I'll take it, but I really want a fifth of Jack."

"You and me both," I said. My mouth was very dry and tasted like copper. I hated throwing up. "First things first. Let's get you out of here."

I walked to the forbidden window and peeked outside through the slats again. There were three police cruisers with their lights dancing back and forth in the sunlight. No sirens were sounding. I didn't see any of the officers. Two ambulances turned down the street and parked in front of the building next door.

There was a pounding on the door to the room we were in. "Drop your weapons and place your hands on you head!" someone ordered from the hallway.

I looked at Victoria. I shrugged. I assumed it wasn't a bad guy. I placed my pistol on the floor and kicked it away from me.

"My hands are on my head!" I shouted to the door. "The girl in here has her hands bound behind her back." I'm not sure why I hadn't unwrapped them yet or why she hadn't asked me to remove the tape for her. Of course, we had only been in the room for two minutes. Still, that was no excuse.

The door opened. A very large uniformed officer peeked inside quickly before he pulled his head back into the hall. He opened the door further and stepped into the room with his gun drawn. He pressed a button on the radio mouthpiece attached to his shirt, near his shoulder. "The girl is in her. She is with Mr. Reese."

"Are you both alright?" he asked us.

"She needs a drink and she has to pee," I said. "She needs a medic and could you please have someone order her a Whopper. The girl deserves a Whopper."

"Send the medic in here," he said into the mic.

"And a Whopper. The girl wants a Whopper. Don't forget about the Whopper," I said. I put my hands down and stepped behind Victoria. "I'm going to untie her. My piece is over there, on the floor. I used it to kill Donnie Royboy. That's his body out there in the hallway."

I tried to loosen the duct tape around Vicky's wrists. I couldn't. "Do you have a knife to cut this tape off?" I asked to the officer.

Just as I asked the question, Detective Larkin and Lieutenant Macy entered the room. They were followed by two paramedics pushing a roll-a-way cot. A medical bag sat on it. Macy walked right over to Victoria and cut her wrists loose.

"She has to pee," I said to Macy.

Macy said, "Are you ok to walk? I passed a bathroom down the hall. Come with me. Renee helped Victoria steadily walk out of the room.

"Can you get her a Whopper, too?" I asked. "She hasn't eaten in like three days.

"Will you shut up about the Whopper?" the uniformed officer asked me in a loud voice.

"What?" I asked him, with my palms facing upward. "Like, you've never wanted a Whopper before? Because I'm pretty sure you have." He looked like he might eat five of them a day. But who am I to judge.

"Dalen!" Larkin said. "Shut up!"

"Well, I'm not wrong," I said to myself. "Where is Ian at?" I asked. With all the gunfire, I wasn't sure I actually wanted to hear the answer.

Ryan Larkin said, "He was trying to keep pressure on a bullet wound of this guy he used to know. The guy apparently works for Mickey now and the guy tried to kill Renee; I mean, Lieutenant Macy. The guy got one in the chest. Ian was trying to stop the bleeding. The medics are working on him now. Ian is still with him."

"Stonewall?" I asked.

"He's fine."

When all the dust had settled in the building I had found Victoria in; the building I had killed Donnie Royboy in, we had moved to the building next door. I was recounting the events of the last half an hour, in as much detail as I could remember. Macy was taking notes and asking questions. Larkin was recording the conversation with a recording app on his phone. Stonewall was dealing with the other officers. The paramedics were still tending to Victoria Colavino. There were crime scene techs taking photos and measurements of both buildings, the rooms, and the parking lots attached to the premises. All in all, there were seven dead people; all of whom worked for Mickey Royboy. All seven of them were men that had fired at either Ian or at one of the members of the DPD. Three of Mickey's men had managed to stay alive; they had all been apprehended and were on their way to booking. There had been a lot of blood shed.

Three hours had passed. My heart had finally started to slow down. Ian sat next to me on one of the white tables along the wall. The urge to chug a bottle of Jack Daniels had passed. Victoria was on her way to Saint Catherine's Hospital on Midway. She was being escorted by two other detectives.

The room was empty except for Macy, Larkin, Ian, Stonewall and myself. We were talking about each of our heroics from earlier in the day. They had to take my word for my side of the story. I could have exaggerated my actions, to make myself sound tougher than I actually was, but I didn't.

We were all startled when the door of the room we were in flew open. Dressed in a black turtleneck with a brown leather jacket and khakis, Mickey Royboy burst into the room and charged at me as fast as the old man could move.

"You fucking killed my boys. You son of a bitch!" he shouted. "I'll fucking kill you. Who the fuck do you think you are?"

Like a ninja, Robert Stonewall tossed his cane at the feet of Mickey Royboy. The cane slid between his ankles and Mickey tripped and stumbled toward me. Detective Larkin reacted, jumping between us. He swiftly scooped up Mickey and brought him to his feet. Mickey tried to break free, but his frail body was too weak for the mighty Ryan Larkin.

Mickey tossed his body around. He started screaming at me in French. He leaned in toward me, as close at he could get, and he spit at my face. He didn't miss. It landed on my right cheek. I realized at that moment, that I didn't have my glasses on. They had probably already been bagged and tagged by the crime scene techies.

Larkin pulled Mickey back, removed his handcuffs and snapped them onto Mickey's wrists, behind the old man's back. Mickey squirmed and shouted. Ryan read Mickey his Miranda Rights. Mickey didn't hear Ryan or care what he was saying. Ryan started to drag Mickey toward the door.

Mickey switched back to English. "I'm going to skin you alive, fry your fucking flesh, and eat it for breakfast!" he shouted.

"That might be a little hard to do behind bars," I said.

That made him even more mad. "We are coming for you. We are coming for your family!" he continued. Larkin stopped dragging Mickey, so he could enjoy Mickey's and my exchange. Mickey continued, "The Royboy's are coming after you, you fucking douchebag."

"Who, you and your daughter? Boy, that's frightening," I said.

"You'll be looking over your shoulder for the next twenty years. We'll get you. You're fucking dead, you motherfucker!"

"Who's gonna get me?" I said, in a calm voice. "You and your sons? Yeah, well kinda not so much. You'll be in prison and your precious sons, well, they're kinda, not so much alive anymore."

That made him even more mad. He literally moved toward me fast enough that he pulled Ryan Larkin about five feet.

"Come on," Larkin said as he successfully pulled Mickey Royboy out of the room and tossed him into the back seat of Macy's ride.

"That guy has some issues," I said. Then I looked at Ian and said, "I'm sorry Demetri didn't make it."

"Renee did what she had to do. He was going to kill her. The sad thing is, he was willing to kill her for Mickey Royboy. Demitri had it coming," Ian said. " I'm sorry I had to kill your new friend Black Irish." Ian laughed when he said that. "I almost wish our friend Tyreke hadn't escaped the line of fire. But I'm guessing he'll be right at home in Jackson," referring to Michigan's state penitentiary.

Chapter Twenty-five

It was just after 6:00 in the evening. Cherrie was making a gourmet dinner for us. We were joined by Mrs. Smith. Cherrie prepared the meal in the kitchen, while I sat to the left of Mrs. Smith at our kitchen table. We were both drinking coffee. Raven and Olivia were setting the table. I was retelling my heroic altercation with Donnie Royboy. Thankfully I made it through the whole ordeal with only a few bumps and bruises. My chest was sore. My back hurt. The bruise on my head hurt, but only when I touched it.

Donnie was no longer a threat to me or my family. Terry Royboy has been killed by Ryan Larkin on the Detroit River, so he was no longer a threat. Mickey was behind bars, awaiting his arraignment on two counts of kidnapping along with a handful of other charges. Victoria was in the hospital, but doing pretty good; all things considered. Lieutenant Governor Ralph Dixon was sitting back, hoping this story was just going to blow over without the pictures ever seeing the light of day. I intended to live up to my word, and not release them. I am pretty sure Victoria was going to let the matter rest as well. Dixon's sex partner, Jerome McMillin was in the morgue. His so-called bodyguard, Tyreke, was also in the Wayne County Jail awaiting arraignment for attempted murder. The girl with the finger in the photos, Mickey's daughter Lisa Stewart, has yet to make contact with me about any of this mess. I hope I never hear from her.

As Cherrie brought our plates to the table, the smell of eggplant parmesan filled the room. She had prepared a spinach salad and some homemade garlic bread. I couldn't wait to dig in. I hoped that Vicky had gotten her Whopper. I had lost one of my very best friends, but as I looked around the room, I was so thankful for those that were still in my life.

As we sat and ate, a slight commotion began to stir in the street on McCatty Drive. I excused myself from the table and went to the front window to see what was going on. There were three local news vans parked at the curb, outside of my house.

"It looks like the media found out about my little altercation this afternoon," I said to the women sitting in the other room.

"You should go there and speak to them now, before things get out of hand," Cherrie suggested. "They aren't going to leave until you do."

I walked back into the kitchen and stood at the head of the table. "Do you want to stand beside me," I asked Cherrie. "Two celebrities is better than one. Plus, you can keep me from making an ass of myself."

"I'll pass. I trust you to say the right thing. Just speak the truth. Oh, but you might want to avoid any mention of the pictures that started this whole mess in the first place," Cherrie said.

"Mrs. Smith, would you like to join me, what with you being Frownie Mae's mother and all?"

"I'll pass Dear," she said politely.

"How do I look?" I asked as I looked down at my clothes.

"You look nice, Daddy," Raven said. "But you might want to take off your hoodie."

I took her advice.

I walked to the front door, took a deep breath and stepped out into the bright light of the sunset that blanketed the sky over McCatty Drive.

I walked to the end of the driveway. Three news reporters scurried to meet me; microphones in hand. They were each followed by their cameramen. Two more vans pulled up. Two more reporters joined the others. The newest reporters did not have cameramen or microphones; they both had micro recorders.

"What can I help you with?" I asked the pushy group.

With the mics and recorders just a few feet from my face, they each started spewing questions at me; each one trying to out shout each other.

I raised my hands, showing them my palms. "Wait. Wait. Wait. One at a time please. I pointed to an attractive brunette that worked for Channel 7 Action News.

"Shelley Childers; Channel 7. Dalen, did your altercation with Lieutenant Ralph Dixon on Sunday have anything to do with the unfortunate events that unfolded today at Royboy Incorporated?"

I felt my blood pressure rise. My heart began to race. Sweat started to bubble on my head. I suddenly felt nervous. I took a deep breath. I resisted the urge to wipe the sweat off of my scalp. I didn't want to lie. I paused for a moment and thought about how I wanted to answer the question.

"Sunday's incident was just a misunderstanding between a few men. The events that happened this afternoon at Royboy Inc. were the result of me and my associate Ian Parker following a lead that led us to find a kidnapped victim, reporter Victoria Colavino. The people that are responsible for the tragic events that led up to it have all been dealt with in the appropriate manner," I said as proud as I could. Though I tried to keep from smiling.

I pointed to a bald reporter wearing a grey suit. He said, "Mr. Reese, I'm Jerry Madono, Channel 2 News. Is there a connection between the kidnapping and death of Mark Smith and the kidnapping of reporter Victoria Colavino? If so, what is the connection?"

"Mr. Madono," I said attempting to sound both educated and polite, "Last week Mark Smith's mother hired The Parker & Reese Private Investigative Agency to find her missing son." I was happy I could squeeze in a free plug for the agency. "During our investigation and with the help of the Detroit Police Department, we were able to find Mark Smith, but we were not able to get to him in time. Mark Smith and Miss Colavino shared information that the Royboy family wanted." I pronounced Royboy correctly, with the soft 'Wah'. "As reporters, you are all aware that sometimes it is important to keep your sources confidential. That very situation is what led to the demise of Mark Smith. He and Victoria had information that they were willing to give their lives for. They were both willing to protect their source, even if it meant surrendering their lives. They must both be commended. Fortunatly, my agency, with the help of the DPD, was able to free Miss Colavino before her life followed the path of Mark Smith. She is currently resting and safe."

Sara Burgeron asked, "Did this information have anything to do with your altercation with Ralph Dixon?"

I felt a knot appear between my shoulder blades. I tried to take a deep breath. It hurt, but I managed. "Stay calm," I said to myself.

"The incident that happened Sunday, in Lansing, was just a misunderstanding. I have nothing but admiration and respect for our Lieutenant Governor," I said in a calm voice.

Burgeron again probed further, "Yes, but how are the altercation with Mr. Dixon and Mark Smith's kidnapping connecting. Didn't your investigation into Mark Smith's disappearance lead you to Lansing to have a discussion with our Lieutenant Governor?"

Did she know more than she was letting on or was she just good at fishing for answers? She sure knew how to poke the bear. When she was finished asking the question that hung in the air, the reporters all took one step closer to me, pushing their microphones closer to my mouth. I took a step back.

"Mark Smith was kidnapped in Ohio by Terry and Donnie Royboy." I paused. I didn't know what to say. Silence filled the street. The reporters waited. Think. Think. Think. "My associate and I went to Lansing on Sunday to have breakfast. The events that unfolded in Lansing between us and Mr. Dixon are not open for discussion. It was a private matter that just got a little heated and that is unfortunate. However, Mr. Dixon and I have laid the matter to rest. The investigation into Mark Smith's disappearance kept us focused on the Royboy family and their associates." I felt good about that answer.

One of the reporters with a voice recorder shouted, "Why did you drive all the way to Lansing just to have breakfast?"

"Have you ever been to the Fleetwood Diner? Their food is amazing!" I said. The other reporters laughed. I laughed right along with them. "Ladies and gentleman, I'm sorry but I really must get back inside. My wife Cherrie has a wonderful dinner sitting on the table waiting for me. Enjoy your evening." As George Costanza once said on Seinfeld, "Leave them wanting more."

As I turned to walk back inside, I noticed a man standing in the street, a few houses down. He was wearing a Detroit Tigers baseball cap, a dark blue hoodie with an old English D on the chest, and he was wearing a pair of black horn rimmed glasses; just like the ones that Donnie Royboy had broke of mine. The son-of-a-bitch standing a few houses down the street from mine was staring right at me. He had a big smile on his face. He looked exactly like me. I mean, he looked EXACTLY like me. The son-of-a-bitch was Robert Samuel Johnson; also known as the Trench Coat Rapist. I wanted to sprint directly over to him and beat the living shit out of him, but I knew I could not do that with the reporters right here. I went back inside and closed the door.

"How did it go?" Cherrie asked me.

"He's out there," I said. "That motherfucker is right outside. He's just standing in the street taunting me."

"Who?" Olivia asked.

"Robert Johnson!"

"Good Lord," Mrs. Smith said. She placed her fork gently on her plate. She took her serviette and dabbed the corners of her mouth. "Miss Cherrie, dinner is delicious, but I believe I just lost my appetite."

"Dalen," Cherrie said in a stern voice. "Calm down. He isn't doing anything. Is he? You said he is just standing out there. Right? Doesn't Lieutenant Macy have an officer assigned to watch him all the time? Let them do their job. Sit down and we'll enjoy this meal together. Please."

"You're right. You're right," I said giving up. "You're always right. That's why I'm going to marry you in a few days."

I pulled my chair out away from the table and sat down. Cherrie had a fresh pot of hot coffee in her hand. She filled my coffee up and placed the pot on a warmer that sat on the middle of the table.

"Thank you," I said to her.

Cherrie gave me a kiss on my cheek and returned to her seat. "Now, how did the interview with the news reporters go?"

"Fine," I said. I should be on channels 2, 4, 7, and 62 tonight at 11:00. At least I assume I will be.

I ate my wonderfully prepared dinner, salad, and bread. I drank a few more cups of coffee, too. We laughed and enjoyed each other's company. We tried to avoid any negative conversation.

During dinner, I received a text from Ian. It read: Have you banged your head in the past ten years, to a song?

I responded: Yes Sir, to Master of Puppets by Metallica, just last week.

Ian responded: Isn't that kind of like waving a flagless flagpole around since you don't have hair? He followed the with 4 laughing/crying emoji's to imply that he made himself laugh so hard he was crying.

I sent him the typical LOL response.

When we were finished eating and the dishes had been washed and placed into the dishwasher, we all headed to the living room to relax for a while before we retired for the evening. It had been another long day. I was tired and sore. I just wanted to fall asleep in my bed, in the arms of the woman I loved.

Chapter Twenty-six

It was dark outside now, so I got up to close the front drapes. As I pulled the first set to the middle of the window, I noticed a figure standing in the road, staring into my house. It was Robert Johnson. There was a glare from the street lamp that reflecting off of his glasses.

I pulled the other drape closed and told Cherrie that I would be back in a few minutes.

She asked me where I was going.

"Just to the corner store. I have a hankering for some Better Made BBQ potato chips. Can I get any of you anything?"

Cherrie stood and followed me to the back door. "I'm coming with you. I could use a Coke."

I knew she knew I was up to something. "I'll get it for you. I'll just be a few minutes. I promise. Go back in there and keep Mrs. Smith company." I bent down and gave her a kiss on her lips. "I'll be right back."

I opened the back door into the garage and closed it behind me. I didn't open the car garage door, instead I snuck out the back door to the garage and closed it as quietly as I could. I walked to the neighbor's back yard, hopped the fence in one motion and snuck around their yard, keeping low and out of sight. I followed the same path in the next yard as well. I moved to the fence that separated the front and back yard. It had a gate that I chose not to open. I hopped it instead. I made my way down their drive way and into the street. I crossed McCatty and went up to the back yard of the house across the street from the last yard I was in.

I could still see Mr. Johnson standing in the street, facing my house. He hadn't moved. I didn't see a police cruiser or the car of any other officer I knew. I assumed no one was watching Robert Johnson, as they were supposed to be.

 I made my way to the yard across the street from my house; that way I could approach Johnson from behind. I thought it was best if I attacked him form behind, much the way I attacked Donnie Royboy this afternoon. I started to run at him slowly because I didn't want him to hear me. The closer I got to him, the faster I ran. When my shoes hit the pavement, they had made too much noise for me to be silent anymore. Besides I was breathing pretty hard anyway.

 I had taken three steps on the street and was just about to tackle him from behind, when Robert Samuel Johnson, sensed me coming, and he stepped to the side in one swift motion. I had my arms extended so I could wrap him up, but since he had moved to the side, all I could do was brush his body with my extended arm. Momentum had taken me right past him and into my front yard. I tripped on the cement curb and stumbled into the grass.

By the time I had turned around, Johnson was coming at me with full force. He had his right arm raised above his head. He swung it in a downward motion and with his closed fist, he struck me across my left cheek. It made a loud crack. I felt my skin split open. Warm blood instantly dripped down my cheek. Holy crap, was it ever painful!

The punch I had just taken knocked me to my right. I started to fall to the ground. I extended my right arm and used my hand on the ground to break my fall. I recovered quickly. Johnson was standing next to me. I used my right leg and swept it behind his knees. Using my right arm, I shoved him backward as hard as I could. His knees buckled. He fell backward and landed on his ass.

I jumped on his chest with my knees. He tried to roll over hoping I would fall off of him. I braced myself with my arms and the ground. I propped myself up on his chest again and quickly landed three incredibly hard punches to his face; a right, a left, and another right. Every punch hurt my knuckles more than the previous one. I knew how his face felt.

"I'll fucking kill you if you come near my family again!" I shouted.

He raised his knees and powered a blow to my back with them. God, that hurt. He managed to get his arms in between us. He started to claw at my face, hoping to dig his fingers into my eyes. I tried to pull my head back. I swung a couple more times with my fists at his face. I only managed to land one of them. I didn't hit him very hard.

"Tell your lovely daughter, Olivia, I say hello," he said with winded breath.

I used my arms to separate his. I grabbed his wrists and drove them to the ground. He tried to buck me off of him. Since both of my hands were occupied, I lowered my head and with my forehead, I head butted him square across his nose. I heard a pop. I can only assume I broke it. I hope I broke it. I raised my head to lower the boom on his face again.

But, just as I did, I felt my body levitate off of his. Detective Larkin had grabbed my sweatshirt and pulled me up, flinging me into the grass a few feet away from Robert Johnson. I jumped to my feet as fast as I could. I tried to charge at Johnson again, but Larkin stepped between us, wrapping his arms around me. He lifted me off the ground, killing my momentum.

This time I was the one squirming like a fish out of water. "I'm going to kill him. He won't leave my family alone," I yelled. "Put me down. Put me the fuck down!" I yelled.

Robert Johnson climbed to his feet. Larkin put me on my feet but didn't let go of me. He held onto my arm. Detective Ryan Larkin said, "Johnson, sit down right there on the curb. Don't move." He was pointing to the curb in front of my mailbox. Johnson sat with his knees bent to his chin. He hugged his knees and began to rock back and forth, staring across the street.

"Dalen, I'm going to let go of you. Walk directly to your front door and go inside. Lock the door behind you. I don't want to see you any more tonight. Do I make myself clear?" Larkin ordered.

I said he did. When he let go of my arm, I took two fast steps in the direction of Robert Johnson's back. I swung my right leg at him, attempting to kick him in the head. Ryan Larkin was too fast for me. He grabbed my shirt and whipped me backward. I fell to my ass. "Get the fuck inside!" he shouted. Robert Johnson was so calm, he never even turned around.

 Cherrie turned the porch light on and opened the front door. She stood behind the screen door and watched me as I walked toward her. She opened the screen and held it for me as I walked past her, into the house."

"Damn you, Dalen!" she said after she closed the door. "You forgot my Coke." She walked up to me and threw her arms around me. She had tears in her eyes. "I wish you would have killed him," she said in a whisper. "But, thank God you didn't. Come on, lets get you cleaned up. You are going to look like shit in our wedding pictures."

Raven handed Cherrie a cold wet wash cloth. Olivia was filling an ice bag with ice. Mrs. Smith was digging through her purse for a Band-Aid and some Neosporin. The women had me cleaned up, bandaged, and had ice on my face in no time at all. The ice would hopefully prevent any swelling. Raven handed me four Advil and a cup of hot coffee. I popped the pills into my mouth and washed them down with one gulp.

"Did you get the potato chips?" Raven asked, laughing.

"No," Cherrie said. "He forgot my Coke too."

Olivia looked outside. "They're gone," she said. "It's a good thing Detective Larkin was out there, huh?"

"I didn't see Larkin's car out there anywhere," I said. "He's like a ghost."

"I, for one, am glad he was out there," Mrs. Smith said. "In the heat of a moment like that, humans are capable of doing much more damage than they think they are possible of. You may not have intended to harm him, but with the adrenaline that you have, in a moment like that, you boys can really harm one another, or something even worse. Heaven for bid, if you did something worse."

"Can he press charges against you for assault and battery?" Raven asked.

"I suppose he could, but I'm pretty sure Larkin will talk him out of it. I think his being outside of our house was probably a violation of his probation or something," I said. "He is already walking on very thin ice."

I'd had enough action for one day. I excused myself, gave all four women a kiss on their cheeks, told them good night, I took a shower, and then laid down on my bed. I put Law & Order on the television in the bedroom and fell asleep before the first set of commercials were finished airing.

Chapter Twenty-seven

Two Days Before My Wedding

The Day We Buried Frownie Mae

I woke up in a relatively decent mood, all things considered. My emotions were playing a game of Ping Pong with me. I had to attend the funeral of one of my best friends, so that had me pretty bummed out. I was more sore today than any day I could remember. My hands hurt, my back hurt, my chest hurt, and my forehead was bruised; it was extremely tender to the touch. I also had a ton of other bruises on my face. Yet, I was just a few days away from marrying Cherrie and that had me excited.

When I showered, I shaved my head. I even shaved my beard off. When I was finished, I stood in front of the mirror and looked at my somewhat wrinkled yet younger looking face. The gray hair on my chin had done a wonderful job of making me look older than I felt. I splashed a little after shave on my skin and let it cool my face. I stared in the mirror at my reflection and wondered if I should have shaved my moustache off as well. I covered it with my finger, removed my finger, and covered it up again. I decided to leave the moustache alone.

I dressed in my nicest black slacks, a gray pin striped black dress shirt, and tied my solid black tie under my collar. I clean up pretty nice, I thought. I shined my black dress shoes with a magic shoe shining sponge and carried the shoes and a pair of socks out to the living room.

Cherrie was already dressed and looked beautiful in her black blouse and a black skirt that flattered her bottom.

When she saw me, she started laughing. "What the hell did you do?" she said, nearly crying with laughter.

"What? Do I look alright? You said you didn't care either way if I shaved my beard off or not," I said.

"I'm sorry. I'm so sorry!" she said, trying to compose herself. "I've never seen you without your beard. I was wrong. You should have kept it. You look like you are 12." She started laughing again. "And what's with the moustache? Are you trying to pull off the Magnum P.I. look? Wait right here, I'll go get your red Hawaiian shirt." She was kidding of course. I think.

'Well, that's just rude!" I said, somewhat joking, myself. Then, I started laughing.

Raven came into the living room. She looked beautiful. Her hair was pulled back in a braided pony tail. She had on a nice pair of dress slacks and a red and black paisley patterned blouse. She looked so much like Tara.

"What time is T.C. coming? Are we riding to the funeral in his helicopter?" she said with a deadpanned straight face. T.C. was Thomas Magnum's best friend. Raven silently gave Cherrie a little hi-five for her comment and walked into the kitchen to pour herself a glass of milk.

I had to give her props for her quick wit.

Ian knocked once on the back door and let himself in. He walked into the kitchen and poured himself a cup of coffee. "The Coffee Cabin is all locked up. Everyone will be able to attend the funeral. It's the first time since the doors opened that they have been closed."

Ian was wearing his finest black jeans and a black and gray flannel shirt.

"Is that what you're wearing?" I asked him.

"I know what you are implying, but you need to rephrase your question," Ian said. "Though, to answer your silly question; yes, I am wearing what I have on. I am always wearing the clothes that I have on. If you are asking if it is my intention to wear the clothes that I have on to the funeral today, the answer is no. I am going to take the flannel shirt off. I also have on a nice black T-shirt. I even ironed it." He took a sip of his coffee. "You kinda look like Captain Kangaroo. Are you going to be sporting your red coat to the funeral?" He laughed to himself.

"Stop being a dick!" I said.

"The red coat will go nicely with the bruises on your forehead and the cut on your cheek. When did you get those? Those aren't from Donnie, are they? I don't remember you looking so bad yesterday."

"No, I got into a little scuffle with Robert Johnson last night," I said.

"Are you fucking serious?" Ian asked.

I poured myself a cup of coffee and pushed two Pop Tarts down into the toaster. When my breakfast was finished toasting, I placed them on a plate and took a seat at the table. I picked a pastry up and attempted to take my first bite of it when Cherrie snuck up behind me and snatched it out of my hand.

"What would your doctor say if he saw you eating this?" She removed the plate from the table that had the second Pop Tart on it. She placed the plate on the table in front of Ian. "Here you go Honey," she said to Ian. "Dalen made you breakfast."

"What the hell?" I said. "Those were mine."

Ian took a large bite into the first one and said, "Thank you Dalen. They are fantastic." He laughed with his mouth full of food.

"I'll pour you a bowl of Cheerio's," Cherrie said. "You need to watch your cholesterol. You have been eating healthy, haven't you?"

"Yes Dear," I said in agreement.

"Except when he doesn't," Ian added; laughing again, as he finished the first Pop Tart.

Cherrie placed a bow of cereal on the table in front of me. She handed me a half gallon of milk. I poured some into my bowl and handed the jug back to her. I grabbed the spoon and devoured the Cheerios like Mickey devoured Life, though I ate it because I had to; not because I wanted to.

Twenty minutes later we were driving to the church where Mark Smith's funeral was going to be held. We pulled around the block and were shocked to see all the news vans and thousands of fans lining the street.

"Damn!" I said. " I knew there might be a few hundred people, but I never expected this. This is insane."

Cherrie said, "Since Rolling Stone broke the news about his true identity, his fans have been swarming the neighborhood. Haven't you noticed?"

"No. I really haven't. I guess I've been a little busy with the whole Victoria Colavino and Mickey Royboy thing."

I pulled the Jeep through the crowd and parked it in the church parking lot. There were men working the lot from the funeral home as well as local police for crowd control. The crowd was pretty tame and they were mostly dressed in black. There were a few people dressed as Frownie Mae with their faces painted like a sad clown, Mark's alter ego, wearing trench coats and bolo hats. It made me smile.

Raven and Olivia climbed out of Olivia's car and met Cherrie and me at the procession line. We exchanged hugs. Ian had pulled his jalopy behind my Jeep. The girls hugged him as well.

"This is some crazy shit," Ian said. "There must be two thousand people out here. Maybe more. Mark would hate to see this many people make a fuss over him."

"I know. He hated fame but he loved that it allowed him to get his message out there," I said.

"Did you see that MTV was going to have a tribute concert for him?" Raven asked us. "They are going to hold it at Hart Plaza. D12, Eminem, Kid Rock, Andrew W.K., Bob Seger, Ted Nugent, The Detroit Cobras, Insane Clown Posse, and even Jeff Daniels and George Clooney are going to be there. I don't know what Clooney is going to do, but hey, it's pretty cool though. That's an awesome line up. They are still adding celebrities to the list. MTV is going to broadcast it live, a week from Saturday."

"That is cool!" I agreed.

We made our way into the church. Mrs. Smith was sitting in the front pew. I walked up to her and leaned in to give her a hug. There was a box of tissues sitting next to her. Several used and wadded up tissues sat on the bench next to it.

I walked up to the closed casket, alone, and placed my hand on it. "I did my best, my friend. I tried. I'm sorry I wasn't quick enough to save you." I leaned over the casket and placed a kiss on the lid. "I'll miss you my man. I'll never forget you. You helped make me who I am," I whispered. "You changed the world. You made my world great." Tears filled my eyes as I realized that I would never be able to speak to him again. I found it hard to swallow. I tried to take a deep breath. I couldn't.

I felt a hand begin to rub my back. I turned around. It was Mrs. Smith's. I placed my crying eyes on her shoulder and she hugged me tight. She patted and rubbed my back. "He loved you," she whispered into my ear.

"I know," I squealed. "I loved him too." She squeezed me tighter.

It took a minute, but I managed to compose myself. I joined Ian and the rest of my family in the second row, behind Mrs. Smith. I looked around. I recognized so many people from the old neighborhood. Some were customers at the Coffee Cabin, others I hadn't seen for years.

Mr. Sanchez walked up to the end of our pew to say hello. He paid his respects and went to sit near the back.

The service started a few minutes later. I sat and listened to a dozen people talk about the memories they had of Mark and what his life meant to them. I wasn't brave enough to stand up in front of the congregation and say anything. I knew in my heart what Mark meant to me. Mark knew what I meant to him. He knew I would miss him. He knew I loved him. I was good with that.

When the service was over, we made our way through the crowd, like rock stars parting a sea of fans, to our cars. We drove twenty miles, slowly, in a chain of cars that stretched over a mile long, out to a cemetery in Clarkston. That's where the dearly departed Smith family members have been laid to rest.

I fought to hold back my tears as we said a prayer and watched Mark's casket get lowered into the ground. Mrs. Smith held it together like a champ. When the final tears had been whipped from the cheeks of the mourners, we piled in our vehicles and headed to Pasquale's in Royal Oak for one hell of a memorial party. Their pizza was always Mark's favorite.

Somehow, his fans found out about our gathering and they had lined the streets of Woodward near the restaurant. They held up banners and posters proclaiming their love and support for Frownie Mae. It was actually pretty moving.

When I parked the green Jeep in the parking lot, Robert Stonewall was standing by a lamp post near his car. He was leaning on his cane. He had on a solid black shirt under his gray corduroy sport coat. He was wearing his black clip-on tie along with his fedora.

I gave Cherrie a kiss and told her I would meet her inside. I loved watching her walk away from me.

"What's up Stoney?" I said in a rather chipper voice.

"Don't ever call me that!" he said with a deadpan look on his face.

"Alright then, what's up former Detective Robert Stonewall?" I tried.

"We need to talk," he said.

"This sounds serious. Are you breaking up with me? I mean, I know I haven't been around much lately, but I can work on that. Do you want to go see a movie tonight? My treat."

"Cut the shit," he warned. "Mickey is a powerful man. Just because he's caged, doesn't mean he's out of commission. I spoke to his lawyer today. He actually sought me out. He told me that you still have a target on your back."

"We'll let's see now, his sons are both dead, Jerome is dead. Tyreke is locked up. To be honest, I'm not really worried about any other peon he might send my way. Mickey's not going to be out for a long time. I'm just going to live my life as I do. He doesn't scare me all that much," I said.

"He wants you dead. Generally, what Mickey wants, Mickey gets. As I said, just because he is incarcerated doesn't mean he doesn't have people on the outside. He didn't get to where he is in life just being a nice guy. This is a man, that prior to yesterday, had never even been arrested. This is one of the most powerful men I know. He has connections. You need to be worried," Stonewall said." You need to be scared!"

I heard what Robert was saying, but I didn't really feel like my life was in any real danger. "Ok. Well thanks for the warning. I need to join my family in the mourning of a friend."

I started to walk toward the restaurant. Robert Stonewall used the hook of his cane to stop me. He hooked my right bicep and pulled hard enough, it caused me to turn around.

"What is it Stonewall?" I asked. I was getting irritated.

"I told you that his lawyer sought me. He did that for a reason. It wasn't just to tell me that you still have a target on your back."

I stepped close enough to get into his personal space. I thought I really needed to hear what he was about to say.

I said, "And..."

"And," Stonewall continued, "his lawyer made me an offer, on behalf of Mickey Royboy."

I felt a knot appear in my back again; right between my shoulder blades.

"Continue," I said. I tried to take a deep breath through my nose, slowly. It was easier on my back when I did it that way.

"I told you before that I'm into Mickey for a considerable amount of money. I also told you that as an honest man, I have every intention of living up to my responsibilities. I will pay that debt off, in full."

I didn't like where this was headed. "And..." I said again.

"According to Mickey's lawyer, I can consider my debt paid in full if I..." he paused.

"If you…? What?" I asked. The knot tightened and grew. I arched my back, trying to ease the tension.

"Mickey will remove my debt if I kill you myself," Stonewall said. He had stopped making eye contact with me and as was now staring at the ground or the bottom of his cane. I wasn't sure which, but it didn't matter.

"He's behind bars," I said, trying to process the information I had just heard. "I mean, what is he going to do if you don't pay up; break your other kneecap? Seriously though, just keep paying him or whoever you'll be paying while he's in the joint. You told the lawyer, 'No!' though. Right? I mean, you're not actually thinking about doing it, I know that much. But are you saying that someone else might be trying to kill me? Is that what you are saying?"

"Reese, there's more."

"Oh! I gotta hear this," I said.

Stonewall shifted his weight from one leg to the other. He moved the cane to the other side of his body. He leaned on it. "Mickey has given me an ultimatum. I can kill you and erase my debt. By doing that, I have a good chance of getting back with Linda. She'll likely take me back if I don't have to deal with Mickey Royboy anymore. That's all I want out of life. I just want to live the rest of my life with Linda. She makes me happy. She is the only person on the shitty Earth that makes me happy. I deserve to be happy. I love Linda. I want her back." He paused again.

"Oooooorrr?" I said with my eyebrows raised.

He whispered, "He'll have Linda killed."

I heard what he said, but he didn't say it loud enough for me to understand him. "I'm sorry, what did you say? Or ... what?"

"He'll have Linda killed." He said it louder this time but he didn't say it very loud. It wasn't easy for him to say. It was figuratively harder for me to hear it.

"Holy shit!" I said. "So, if you don't kill me, he'll have Linda murdered? Is that what you are saying?"

"That is what Mickey's lawyer told me. That's the offer on the table."

"Did you tell anyone? You gotta tell Macy. If you don't, I will," I said. "She'll know what to do. We gotta tell Macy. We gotta tell her."

"Mickey is more powerful than Macy. He has more power than the DPD. It won't do any good to tell her," he said.

"Ok. But seriously. You aren't seriously thinking about killing me. I mean, you can't be. That would just be stupid. They'll find out who did it. They'll discover it was you. You'll go away forever. You won't be able to be with Linda. Think about it. I mean, really think about it." I was getting pissed.

"They would never be able to trace it back to me," he said. "Seriously!"

"Fuck!" I said. My heart had sped up. It was racing fast now. I hadn't noticed the sweat dripping down my face where my sideburns used to be. It was dripping fast enough that the collar of my shirt was getting wet. I missed my beard. "Did he give you a time table? Do I have the twenty years he'll be locked up? How much time did he give you? How long do I have? Son-of-a-bitch. I'm getting married in two days. Am I even going to be alive long enough to get married? Are you even going to warn me first?"

"This is your warning?" he said. "I didn't have to tell you anything." Then Stonewall reached into his sport coat Jacket.

I jumped. I literally thought he was going for his gun.

"What the fuck?" I yelled. I ducked behind the rear or bumper of his Delta '88.

"Relax," he said. "I'm not going to do it now. Man. Chill out." He removed his hand from inside his jacket. He held his hand out to me. "Here," he said.

He handed me my glasses.

"Are these mine?" I asked. It was a stupid question. "I thought they needed these for the crime scene shit. How'd you get them?"

"I know people. I'm pretty powerful too. Besides, I fixed them for your you. I thought you could use them."

I said, "So, you are giving me back my glasses so I can see you kill me. Is that it?"

Stonewall just stared at the ground. He didn't say anything.

Damn. I shook my head and turned to walk into the restaurant. I had a party to attend. I needed to celebrate the life of my friend. I wondered if anyone would be celebrating my life after I was dead, in a couple of days.

Chapter Twenty-eight

When I went inside, I must have looked pale. Cherrie said, "Are you alright? You look like you've seen a ghost."

"I'm fine. Where is the restroom?"

Cherrie pointed to a corner where the men's room was located. I made my way to the bathroom, through a mob of Mark's family and friends. The room happened to be empty. I felt relieved. I went to the sink and splashed cold water on my face. I placed my hands on the sink and stared into the mirror. I took several deep breaths. Cherrie was right; I did look pale, even though it looked like a had let a 3 year old Raven paint my face with Mommy's make-up.

I walked to the urinal. With my back facing the door, I didn't see Robert Samuel Johnson walk in. He patiently stood behind me and waited for me to zip up.

 When I turned around, he said, "I see you got your glasses back." He had startled me.

Blood rushed to my head. My heart started pounding at an incredibly fast pace. My breathing became shallow. All of that happened in less than a second. I stood and stared at him for a few seconds more without saying a word as I contemplated what I was going to do or say.

He stood motionless and stared directly into my eyes with a shit eating grin on his face. He was practically daring me to strike him again. I wanted to kill him. I wanted to do it that very second. Then I thought about where I was. I knew Cherrie was waiting for me. I decided to let the moment pass. I started to walk past him and out the door.

As my hand reached for the door handle, he said, "How is Olivia?"

I paused. I took a deep breath. I wasn't going to let him get to me. Not tonight. Not here. He shocked me when he said, "I can't wait to taste her again!"

"What the fuck did you say?" I said as I turned and charged at him.

I only had to move a few feet, but I had enough strength and momentum to drive him the wall. He didn't try stop me. We hit the wall with a lot of force. He held his arms up, like he was the victim of a stick up. I grabbed hold of his shoulders and slammed him into the wall again. Again, he didn't fight me. He grunted as his back slammed into the wall.

"If you ever come anywhere near her I will end your life!" I said as I looked him dead in the eyes.

"I'll never leave you of your family alone," he said with a evil smile. "Every time you leave your house, look around. I'll be there," he whispered.

"If I ever see you near my family, I swear to God...!" I didn't know what to say.

I raised to left arm and pressed my forearm as hard as I could against his neck. His head was pinned against the wall. His arms were still raised above his head. He wasn't going to fight back.

His face was turning red. With gasping breath, he said, "I'll even be attending your wedding to that hot little red headed woman."

I pressed harder against his neck with my left arm. With my right hand, I cupped his genitals and squeezed.

Though he could hardly take a breath, he managed to say, "Were you this gentle with Tara?" He tried to smile.

I squeezed his nuts harder and twisted. He shrieked what I thought was his last breath.

I hadn't heard Ian come into the restroom. Ian walked over to me and said, "Dalen, stop." He gently pulled my arm away from Johnson's neck. I didn't resist. Ian grabbed my right arm and pulled it away from Johnson's groin. I didn't resist that either. I backed away from Robert Johnson and he fell to the floor, gasping for air. He grabbed his own neck, as if it was going to help him breath.

"Come on," Ian said. "Leave this shithead alone. Let's go join the party." He placed his hand on the small of my back and steered me through the bathroom door. "He's not worth it," Ian said. "He's not worth it."

"I might have killed him. Twenty more seconds. That's all it would have taken. I wanted to do it. I did. I wanted to kill him. I tried. He would have deserved it," I said as a matter of fact.

"Sssshhhh," Ian said, trying to clam me down. "He's not worth it. Ok? You understand that, right? He's just scum. He wants to provoke you. He gets off on you attacking him. It's sick. But, you are better than this. Just let it go. Let it roll off your back. Just chill. You are about to be married to a beautiful, smart, sexy woman that loves you to death. She needs you. We all need you." Ian and I were still standing in a small hallway, outside the restrooms. "Be better than this. I know you hate him. He wants you to. He needs you to. But don't. Alright? Be cool! Now come on. Let's get some pizza."

As we walked away, I could still hear Robert Samuel Johnson coughing in the men's room.

"Next time Motherfucker," I said under my breath. "Next time!"

As the evening moved on, I debated whether or not I was going to tell Cherrie or Olivia about my little confrontation in the men's room. Ian never mentioned it. By the time the celebration of Mark Smith's life was over, I drove Cherrie and Raven home in near silence. The radio played quietly as I drove.

"That was a beautiful ceremony. The celebration was really fun. I loved the slide show Mrs. Smith had playing on the iPad. He was a cute kid. It was a pleasure meeting Miss Colavino. I'm glad she was able to attend. She is such a sweet girl," Cherrie said.

"I agree," was all I could muster. I couldn't stop thinking about Robert Johnson.

"Are you alright?" Cherrie asked. "You really seem distracted."

"It's just been a long and difficult week," I said. I patted her thigh.

"I could give you one of my special massages when we get home. They always seem to help you relax." Cherrie raised her eyebrows a couple of times and smiled at me.

In the back seat, Raven said, "Um, excuse me. I'm kinda back here. I don't need to hear about your sexcapades."

Cherrie started to laugh. "I'm just talking about a massage, Sweetheart. Nothing more."

"Still," Raven said. "Ick!" then she laughed. "No, I'm just kidding. I'm glad you two can speak so freely about your sex life."

"It's just a massage," I said. "Just a massage!"

Then Cherrie said, "We'll see. It always starts with a massage, doesn't it Dear?" Then we all laughed. Well, everyone except Raven; she just shook her head.

The tension in my back had already began to lessen. I love my family.

Chapter Twenty-nine

One Day Before My Wedding To Cherrie

After an evening of massages from my wife to be, I slept like a rock. I woke up feeling better than I had in more than a week. I had a few errands to run to prepare for the wedding, but, for the most part, today was just going to be a relaxing day for me.

Elvis and I went for an early morning walk before breakfast. He took care of business in an empty lot along the way. As he did, I read a sign that had been posted; it read: Thank you for being a good neighbor and cleaning up after you pet. It was stapled to a telephone pole. I felt like a heal for not bringing a baggie with me. I hurried away from the area quickly, hoping none of the neighbors had seem us.

When we returned home, I showered, shaved my face and head, leaving my Ron Swanson'ish moustache where it was. "They'll get used to it," I said to myself. I dressed and went to make something for myself to eat.

Cherrie had already prepared a Belgium waffle with 7 strips of bacon for me. Boy, that woman could cook. "Not that I'm not grateful, but why only 7 strips of bacon; why not eight or six? I assumed that anytime bacon was cooked, it was always cooked in an even number. You don't go to a restaurant, order bacon and get 3 or 5 strips of bacon served. It's always an even number, isn't it?"

Cherrie walked over to the table, picked one piece of bacon up off my plate and ate it. She said, "There, now you have an even number!" The she walked to the sink to wash the dishes.

"I guess I do," I said. I preceded to eat my breakfast without saying another word. "That'll teach me," I thought.

I thanked Cherrie for breakfast, grabbed my wallet, phone, and car keys. "I'm going to go see Tara for a bit. Is there anything I can pick up or do for you before I get back?"

"No. I'm all set. I have to run to the studio this morning. I'll be gone most of the day. Just relax today. Take it easy. I'll call you later." Cherrie gave me a kiss. I left.

I stopped by the florist and picked up four pink carnations and one red rose. I drove to the cemetery, removed my little stool from the small trunk of the Jeep. I walked to her gravesite. In the warm sunlight, under a clear sky, I pulled a few tiny weeds from the dirt in front of her tombstone. I placed the fresh flowers in the hanging vase. I sat on the stool and sat in silence for a time.

Tara was always patient. She never minded waiting or sitting in silence. She always said, "You can say a lot by saying a little."

"Do you remember that one time, " I finally said, "on Saint Patrick's day when we went to Duggan's Irish Pub for breakfast? You had had a bit too much to drink and it was still pretty early in the morning. You had stated how much fun it was to celebrate the holidays with your good friends Jack, Jim, Johnny, and Evan. You asked me when the next holiday was that would allow us to hang out with them. I told you we could probably get together again for Cinco de Mayo. You asked, just exactly when is Cinco de Mayo? Is it before or after Easter? I laughed and said, 'It's probably going to be on May 5th this year.' Then you said. 'No, it's never that late in the year.' I'll remember that conversation every year on May 5th, without fail."

I sat a while longer in silence. I didn't mind. As long as I am with Tara, I'm good. I didn't need to talk. I just wanted to be with her.

After a short time, I laughed to myself. I was reminded of the first time Tara told me she loved me. "Do you remember my response when you first said, 'I love you,' to me?" I asked her. "I told you, 'I'm not quite there yet, but I'm headed in that direction.' I was such an ass. That was the only time I ever lied to you. The truth is, at that very moment, I was so head over heels madly in love with you, I almost couldn't stand myself. I wanted to tell you I loved you first, but obviously you beat me to it. I beat myself up for a week over my response. Then I realized it didn't matter. We were in love. That was the only thing that mattered to me."

I filled her in on what had happened over the last week. It took a while. I didn't leave anything out. I never do when I talk to Tara.

"I'm getting married tomorrow," I said to Tara as I stared at her tombstone. "I've told you everything I could think of about Cherrie. I know you'd love her. You'd probably be best friends. She is amazing. Do you know what she does every time I give her a kiss? No, of course you don't. But when I kiss her, whether she is sitting, standing, or laying down, and I have to lean down to give her the kiss, she smiles. As I'm bringing my lips in to meet hers, she smiles. I get to watch her smile before we kiss. It doesn't matter if I have upset her before hand or not; she smiles. Every single time. She has the most beautiful smile, too. But she smiles because she is happy that she is about to get a kiss from me. Me! Of all the people in the world, she smiles because she is going to get a kiss from me. How crazy is that?"

"I love her, Tara. I do. I'm pretty sure you are alright with me marrying her. I've never got a feeling in my gut or in my heart that you wouldn't be ok with it. So I take that as a positive sign. So tomorrow is the big day. I'm going to marry Cherrie, tomorrow."

I spent the rest of the day making sure we had what we needed for the wedding and the reception. Cherrie suggested that since it was neither of our first weddings, that we make it more a celebration and a party. Cherrie suggested that we hold it at The Coffee Cabin, that we dress in pink, and we make it a fundraiser for breast cancer research. Cherrie suggested that we invite our guests to also dress in pink and instead of receiving wedding gifts, we ask each guest to donate five dollars for the privilege of attending or ceremony. She said we could decorate the coffee shop in as much pink as possible. She wants to give out a prize for the guest that has the best or most outrageous pink outfit. I loved the idea. We went ahead and planned it accordingly.

My only task was to make a box for the donations to be dropped in. I told her I would. As usual, I procrastinated longer than I should have and with the events of the past week and a half, I didn't quite complete my only assigned task.

I made a stop at Michael's crafts store and bought a box and some wrapping paper. I already had markers and tape, glue, ribbon, and things I thought I could use to make it.

As I pulled my car into my driveway, I saw Robert Johnson standing across the street, in between the two houses that face my house. He was dressed very similar to the way I was. We both had on a Tiger's hoodie, blue Jeans, a Tiger's ball cap, and we wore matching glasses. He still had his head and face shaved, except his eyes were both black and blue from the head butt I had given him. I remembered what Ian had told me last night. I took a deep breath and let his presence not bother me. That was probably not the reaction he was hoping for. And besides, even though I didn't see them, I knew someone from Macy's crew was just around the corner keeping an eye on him.

I went into the house and decorated the donation box for the wedding reception. When I was finished, I put Lou Rawls Live from Chicago on the record player, laid down on the floor and listened to the coolest man ever to grace an album cover; well it is really a tie between Lou and ol' Satchmo himself, Louis Armstrong! I fell asleep before the first side finished playing.

Cherrie let me sleep until dinner was ready. We ate, watched the second Tiger's game of the young season. In all the confusion, I actually missed the home opener. They didn't play yesterday. When the game was over, we went to the bedroom and Cherrie gave me another massage.

Chapter Thirty

The Day Of The Wedding

Ian picked me up at 7:00 AM. We were going to the Eastern Market located on Russell Street in downtown Detroit. We were going to get fresh fruit and vegetables to serve at the reception. Cherrie wanted them brought home by 10:00 so she would have enough time to clean and carve or arrange them to her liking.

The market gets pretty busy and is fully alive by 8:00. We stopped at Motown Coney Island on Woodward for breakfast first. We were in and out in a half an hour. As we closed in on the jam packed streets around the market, Ian noticed we were being followed. He was driving and the Backstreet Boys were singing.

Ian turned the radio down. "He's behind us!"

I knew exactly who he was talking about; Robert Johnson.

"Scratch that," Ian said as I was turning around to look out the back window. Ian said, "I mean, they are both following us. Johnson is three cars back. Stonewall is behind him."

"Oh shit. Stonewall is back there?" I said. My heart started racing. I broke out into an instant sweat. "He won't even let me get married first. What the fuck? Is he going to kill me at the Eastern Market on my wedding day?"

"Relax," Ian said. "Stoney is probably just following Johnson. It's probably his turn to babysit."

"Then why is Cody Simpson behind Stonewall?" I asked. "Is it possible that none of them know that the other is part of this parade?" I was pissed. "What the fuck is going on?" I was nervous. One man wanted to haunt and stalk me, one man wanted to kill me, and the other man was probably just sent to babysit the stalker. "I don't want to go out like this. Why the hell does Mickey Royboy get to decide who gets to live and who gets to die. This is the perfect place to shank someone. Stonewall could do it too. Who would know. It's a zoo down here."

"Dalen," Ian said. "It's time you let me be Batman. Let me handle this. Alright?"

It took me a second to realize what Ian meant. When I finally did, I just looked at Ian and nodded. It was time to let Ian answer the Bat signal. I could be Robin. I was ok with it too. I knew Ian could handle this situation. I didn't know what he was going to do. I didn't want to know.

Ian said, "I'm going to pull the car over to the curb, just around the next corner. When I do, get out quickly, stay low and get lost in the crowd. Capiche? I've got this."

The light turned green. Ian maneuvered his car to the curb, just as he said he would. As I was getting out, Ian said, "Call Tommy for a ride home and don't forget to get the fruit and veggies. Now, go! Go! Go!"

I closed the car door and hurried through the crowd. When I was a block away, under the aluminum awnings, and mixed in with the festive fruit shoppers, I paused and looked around. I checked around every pillar and behind every table anywhere near me. I do not see how Roberts Johnson or Stonewall could have followed me, unless they abandoned their cars when I fled Ian's car. I didn't see Cody Simpson, though I couldn't have cared less if I had. I went about my shopping, confident that Batman was taking care of my predators.

I called Tommy and asked him to pick me up. He said he'd be there in 15 minutes seeing as he was at the studio and just a few blocks away. I filled my arms with as much fruit and veggies as I could carry. Tommy pulled his car up to the curb where Ian had dropped me off. There was still no sign of Ian, the Roberts, or Officer Cody. I tossed my purchases into the back seat and climbed into the passenger seat in the front.

I was telling Tommy, or Crash as his friends call him, all about the conversation I'd had with Stonewall two nights ago. I described the run-ins I'd had with Robert Johnson this past week. Tommy was using phrases such as, "No way dude!," "Far out man!," "So bitchin'," "Righteous Bro!," and "You are one badass cat!" when my cell phone rang.

Crash said, "Don't answer it Amigo. That's my jam." He was referring to how much he liked my ringtone, 'Play That Funky Music White Boy."

The call was from Ian. I went against Tommy's whishes and answered it anyhow.

"I'm still alive," I said instead of 'Hello.'"

"Is Crash with you?" Ian asked.

"I'm here compadre," Tommy said.

"Put me on speaker," Ian said.

I did.

"Ok. So check this out. I dropped you off, right? I drove the car for three blocks, turning at each one. All three cars followed me. I pulled into a parking lot. It was busy, man. There were a lot of people carrying shit to their cars, ya know, from the market. People were waiting in their cars for parking spots to open up. I found a spot and pulled in." Ian was speed talking. He did that when he was excited.

"Ok. So I get out of my car and waited at the trunk. I'm sitting on the trunk. I'm waiting. A few minutes pass, then I see Robert Johnson heading down the other end of the aisle. He's walking pretty fast, looking for my car, or you, or maybe both. It's like his head is on a swivel stick. Then he sees me. He stops dead in his tracks. I can tell he was expecting to see you somewhere.

"Then, I could tell, he realized you weren't going to be coming or that you weren't there with me. For a tiny moment," Ian continued, "I swore I saw fear in his black and blue eyes. Then I jumped off my trunk and started walking toward him.

"Now, this motherfucker, turns and starts to run in the opposite direction, right?" Ian was asking if Tommy and I were following his story. We were. Ian kept right on talking. "He gets maybe four cars away from where he was. And I'm chasing him now. I just start to gain momentum, right? When out from between two cars, jump two men, dressed all in black like some ninjas or some shit but without the hoods. I stop dead in my tracks. These two men get in front of Johnson. They each grab under one of his arm pits and they lift the fucker off the ground. Seriously! They step to the side, like between two cars. A black van pulls up, the sliding door opens and these guys just toss Robert Johnson into the van like he was a rag doll or something.

"Then, the van speeds down the aisle right the fuck at me. I think they were trying to run me over. I literally had to jump out of the way. Dude, they came this fucking close to hitting me." Ian was probably holding some fingers inches apart from each other. "Then the van turns out of the parking lot and disappears."

I'm shaking my head, nearly in disbelief as Ian was unwrapping this story. Tommy was sitting in the drivers seat, listening with his mouth hanging open. "That's so gnarly, Bro!" he said.

"I know, right?" Ian said in agreement. But he wasn't finished. "But wait, that's not the best part. When I turned to walk back to my car, guess who I saw standing in the middle of the aisle?" He didn't wait for us to answer. The question was rhetorical. "Robert Fucking Stonewall! This motherfucker was just standing in the middle of the aisle, with his cool-ass fedora on his head, leaning on his cane with two hands. He had on that same old gray blazer too. Dude, I just stopped and looked at him. He waited for a moment, then just like in a scene from a movie, he slipped between two parked cars and he was gone. Just like that. Is that some crazy shit, or what?"

Crash, aka Tommy, said, "Man, I wish I had that on film. Uncle Ian, you gotta add that to your book, my friend. That's how you gotta end your Searching For Frownie Mae book. That's a perfect ending for it. It just is."

"Are you going to title it Searching For Frownie Mae or Searching For Mark Smith?" I asked.

"Frownie Mae!" Ian said emphatically.

"Where do you think Stonewall went?" I asked Ian.

"Shit, knowing him, he probably went to that nasty-ass dive bar on 8 Mile," Ian said.

"Crash, you hungry?" I asked.

"Sh'ya, Baby," Tommy said, imitating Austin Powers.

"Do you want to meet us there, Ian?" I said.

"No thanks," Ian said. "I want to get a run in and a shower before the wedding."

"See ya then," I said. I ended the call. "Let's go eat!" I told Tommy where the Wicker Bar was located. He drove and we were there in 15 minutes.

Stonewall's car was in the parking lot.

The door to the bar was propped open with a wooden doorstop. A smoky haze drifted out from the inside. There is a no smoking law in Michigan that prohibits smoking inside of any public building. The patrons of The Wicker Bar and Grille must have been oblivious to the law.

Crash and I walked into the darkened room. There were probably five or six other customers inside. They were all sitting by themselves nursing their drinks. Robert Stonewall was the only patron sitting at the bar. He had one empty glass in front of him. It sat next to the full glass that Stonewall had his hand around. I sat on the barstool to Robert's right. Tommy sat to my right.

"What are you drinking?" I asked the retired detective.

"This!" he said.

The bartender overheard our exchange. He said, "He's drinking a VW. It's the house special. You want one?"

"What's in the VW, Dude?" Tommy Crashowski asked the bartender.

The bartender was stocking the refrigerator with Bud Light, Miller Lite, and Coors Light; both bottles and cans. "Vernors and whiskey. My granddad used to drink it. Some people have called it The Bug."

Tommy said, "Ah!, I get it, because of Herbie The Love Bug was a Volkswagen. I love that movie, man!"

I motioned to the bartender to pour Stonewall another VW. "What's on the menu?" I asked the bartender.

"Burgers!" he said as he slid Stonewall his next drink.

"Burgers? Just burgers?" I asked.

"It's all they make here," Stonewall said.

"Ok then. Three burgers," I said to the bartender.

He disappeared into the back room. I assumed there was a kitchen or at least a stove back there.

I looked at Tommy. He had spun around on the stool and was facing the dining room. He had his elbows propped up on the bar behind him. Smoke lingered in the air, making it difficult to see the picture on the television that hung on wall to Tommy's left.

"Are you responsible for the events that took place this morning at the Eastern Market?" I asked Mr. Stonewall.

"Maybe," he said after he finished his second of three VW drinks.

"Ian said he might have seen you in the parking lot."

"He may have," Stonewall said. He started drinking his next drink.

"So what exactly happened to Robert Johnson?" I asked.

"I honestly don't know. I think I saw him get into a black van. As to who's van it was and where they might have gone; I couldn't say."

"But you did have something to do with it, right?" I asked.

"Possibly. I may have had something to do with it, indirectly," Stonewall said. He still hadn't made eye contact with me.

"Indirectly?" I asked, hoping he would elaborate.

"I might know a guy," he said.

"What? Like a guy that kills people?" I asked.

"You didn't hear me say that," he said.

"Ok, but that's what you implied, right, that you have a guy that kills people?" I asked.

"I have a guy. That's all I said," he said.

I was shaking my head in disbelief. "I have a guy that is a mechanic. I have a guy that is an electrician. I have a guy that is a plumber; actually that's Jim, he's both my plumber and my electrician. I even have a computer guy now; that kids a wiz. But what I don't have is a guy that will kill for me. How do you actually get a guy that'll kill people for you?"

"I told you, Dalen, Mickey is not the only powerful person around these parts," Stonewall said. "You don't work for the DPD for 30 years and not make some connections. I can get things done."

"Speaking of which," I said, "between you and me; shit, I thought you were actually going down to the Eastern market to kill me."

"About that," Stonewall said, "It's no longer on the table."

"What do you mean?" I asked.

"Reese, I don't like ultimatums! I was given an ultimatum. I decided that instead of making a choice from those given with the ultimatum, I would be better off eliminating the source of the ultimatum." Stonewall just stared at his drink as he spoke.

"Getting rid of?" I asked. "What are you saying?" I pretty much understood what he said, but I wanted to hear him elaborate on this comment too.

"He asked me to choose between you and Linda. I didn't like the choice. You are my friend. I don't have many. Linda is my life. I felt it was in all of our best interests to rid our lives of the cancer that is Mickey Royboy." Stonewall was stone faced.

"Get rid of, how?" I asked.

"I just told you. I know people. I simply made a phone call. Problem solved."

The bartender brought three burgers to the bar and placed one in front of each of us. Tommy turned around to eat. The bartender leaned over the bar and whispered something in Robert Stonewall's ear.

Stonewall nodded. He took a bite of his burger. With a mouthful of food shoved to one cheek, he said, "The story will break in about an hour."

"What story?" Tommy asked with curiosity.

"It appears that one Mickey Royboy might have ended up on the wrong side of a sharp object," Stonewall said.

I swear I thought I saw Stonewall smile as he said it.

"May he rest in peace," Stonewall said.

I picked up my burger and took a bite. I was delighted to discover that it was honestly the best hamburger I had ever had, in my life. "Holy crap! This is delicious!"

Tommy had taken a bite of his. "This is out of sight!" He took another bit.

"So, we can put this whole ordeal to rest then?" I said trying to clarify the situation.

"It's as dead as a Royboy!" Robert Stonewall said. This time I did see him smile.

Without another word, we all finished our burgers. Stonewall finished his drink as well. He stood, patted my back, and using his cane, he walked out of The Wicker Bar. After I paid the bill, Tommy and I walked out into the fresh air. The sun was still shining brightly in the blue sky. The temperature was going to hit 60 degrees today. Robert Stonewall was already gone.

Tommy drove me home and helped me carry the fruit and veggies in through the back door. Cherrie was patiently waiting for me in the kitchen. She was nursing a glass of red wine.

"See you two in a few hours," Tommy said. He gave Cherrie a kiss and ten he left.

Chapter Thirty-one

Finally, My Wedding

Cherrie and I arrived at The Coffee Cabin two hours before the ceremony was set to begin. Tondalaya and Walt were placing the table cloths on the tables. Raven arrived with her date; I had already forgotten his name and she didn't imeadatly introduce us. I'm an investigator so I figured with a couple sly questions here and there, I'd probably be able to figure it out.

"Daddy," Raven said. "I'd like you to meet Gaston. Gaston, this is my father, Dalen Reese." Raven stood next to her date. I shook his hand.

"Ah, Gaston. That's right. I knew it was the name of a Disney Prince. I could only think of Aladdin, but I knew that wasn't right. It's nice to meet you,' I said, squeezing his hand firmly as we shook.

"Daddy," Raven said. "Gaston is not a Disney Prince."

Gaston jumped in saying, "Actually, Gaston is more or less the villain in Beauty and the Beast. The Beast was the prince."

I wanted to pop the kid in the mouth. Instead I just smiled. Then I said, "Yeah, I don't really keep up on my princess movies. Look, I gotta go help Cherrie."

I excused myself and went to help Cherrie bring in all the fruit and vegetables from her car. She placed them on ice and lined them up on a table we had set up for the food, in the back room.

Slowly, but gradually, our closest friends trickled in. Many lent a hand with the decorating and the organization of the tables, chairs, and the food. A lot of guests had prepared and brought a dish to pass.

It wasn't much before the start of the wedding when my mother tapped me on my shoulder. I turned around and gave her a long hug .

"Your dad is parking the car. He'll be in in a minute. I brought you some coupons," Mom said.

"You brought me some coupons?" I said sounding surprised. Though, I shouldn't have been. She is, after all, my mother.

"Yes. They are for Cheez-its. I left them in the car though. It didn't seem right to bring them to your wedding; even if it is being held at a bar."

"Mom," I said, "It's not a bar. This is a coffee shop."

"You do like Cheez-its, don't you? Because I can give them to someone else."

"No. Don't do that. I'll take them. I like Cheez-its," I said.

"Well don't let me leave without giving them to you."

I laughed. "I won't, Mom. Are they my wedding present?" I asked, joking.

My mother must not have found it funny. She said, "No. I paid the ten dollars to the pink box. Five for me and five for your dad. That's what we're supposed to do, right, donate money so we can attend our own son's wedding?" She put a hand on both of my cheeks. "You shaved off your scruffy beard. You look so much more handsome this way. You might want to shave off the mustache too. Where should we sit? I want to save my seat. I need to use the restroom before the ceremony starts."

"I love you Mom. Sit anywhere." I gave her another hug.

Cherrie and I greeted the other guests. I was surprised how many people showed up. I hope the fire Marshall doesn't show up as well. He may have to shut us down. Big came in and took a seat in the back. The church ladies, Janice and Sweet Alice were here along with Jan and Kevin. Tic-Tac showed up with a woman I had never seen. He looked happy. Victoria and Tabitha Colavino arrived. Mrs. Smith and her old neighbor friend brought a delicious looking Angel food cake. It had pink frosting. Loud mouth Kirk and his wife Nancy even graced us with their presence. Happy happy joy joy! Mr. Sanchez came stag. Feena and Anush looked nice in something other than their 7-Eleven smocks. Detective Larkin and Lieutenant Macy both looked incredible all dressed up. Hazel and Chante' were both present with their dates. Ricky and Sharona were sitting by Tommy and

Hemma. Aunt Lonnie and Uncle Bill spent a lot of time talking to the guests, as they knew almost all of them as well.

Just before I was about to walk down the aisle with Ian, my best man, I noticed a petite blonde standing outside the front door, talking to Melvin, my homeless friend. I nudged Ian with my elbow. He looked at me. I nodded at the girl outside.

"Holy shit! What is she doing here?" He said, "Can you hold off a few minutes?" He didn't wait for me to answer. Ian walked outside to greet his former fiancée, Miss Nixie Davenport. Ian stood outside the doorway, holding the door open with his back.

I heard Nixie say, "Am I too late?"

"For what, the wedding?" Ian asked her.

"No. For us?" she said.

"Well, I just finished writing the end of our story. But, I'd be happy to start a sequel. What made you come back?" Ian asked.

Nixie said, "I just don't want you to live without my love. It hurts too much. I know it's selfish."

Ian bent his tall frame down and picked his petite princess up off the ground. He gave her a kiss. "I won't let you hurt any more."

Ian found a chair for Nixie and sat her near the back. There wasn't any room any closer to the front. When I got the nod from Ian, he and I walked down the aisle and stood next to the pastor. Walt tapped the iPod that was piped through the speakers. *At Last* by Etta James started to play and Cherrie started walking down the aisle toward me. She looked amazingly beautiful; sexy even. I could not have been happier than I was at that very moment. We made eye contact. Butterflies shot up from my stomach. She smiled at me as she moved.

"I love you," I mouthed to her.

"I love you back!" she mouthed in return.

When she was standing in front of me, we held each other's hands.

Pastor Gronkowski read a few things from the Bible that had some sort of relevance to marriage. I wasn't listening. I was just staring into Cherrie's eyes, thinking about how lucky I was to have found the perfect woman, not just once, but twice.

I started hearing the pastor when he said, "Do you Cherrie, take this man with Burt Reynolds' moustache, to be your blah blah blah…when Pastor Gronkowski actually said Burt Reynolds, I stopped listening. The pastor nonchalantly held his hand out, palm up in front of Ian. As he did this, Ian slipped a ten spot into the pastor's hand. The money went directly into Pastor Gronkowski's suit coat pocket without missing a beat…he continued, "Burt, I mean Dalen, do you take this woman Cherrie to blah blah blah…" Ian couldn't hardly wipe the smile off of his face. He thought he was so funny. So did the all the guests. They laughed right along with Ian.

When the ceremony was finished, we ate. We all ate like kings and queens. We socialized. There was pink everywhere. Tara would have loved it. She would have had a blast at Cherrie's and my wedding reception. Ian and Nixie were once again inseparable. Everyone was having a great time. We moved the loose tables to the back room so we could dance. It was dark outside. The colored disco ball and lights had turned the coffee house into a discotheque.

I had danced with Cherrie to music from Louis Armstrong. After, I was standing near the fireplace, alone, watching everyone enjoy themselves, when a beautiful blonde girl in a blue dress approached me and asked me to dance. I accepted.

Strangers In The Night by ol' blue eyes was playing. The blonde stepped in a little closer to me as we stepped in circles to the rhythm of the night. She smelled nice. "With this blue dress and your blonde hair, you kinda resemble Cinderella," I said.

"That's the nicest thing anyone has ever said to me," she said. "Thank you, my fair prince."

I don't know if Cherrie was getting jealous or if she felt like she needed to save me but she politely asked the blonde if she could cut in.

"Thank you," I said to Cherrie as we slowly danced to the rest of the song by Frank Sinatra. It was then I realized something. I whispered into Cherrie's ear. We stopped dancing.

"Go. Go." She said. "Hurry back, if you can." She kissed me good bye and I snuck out the back door, undetected by our guests.

When I got out of the my Jeep, I walked up to her front door. I checked my watch. It was 9:27. Her front door was open. I stood on the porch and watched for a moment, as Mrs. O'Flannigin put the finishing touches on her dinner. She looked beautiful in her blue and white checkered dress. She wore a white apron to keep her dress clean.

I knocked on her screen door. I didn't wait for her to answer it. I let myself in.

She turned around. "Wallace, you are right on time. I just finished making dinner. You didn't need to get all dressed up. And a tie? Wow, you look handsome. Have a seat. I'll dish up your plate."

I sat at the head of the table where Mrs. O'Flannigin had one of two place settings. She had set out her best china. She placed my plate on the placemat in front of me.

"Thank you," I said.

She dragged her hand across my shoulders and she went to grab her plate.

When she turned around, she said, "Dalen, when did you get here?"

"A few minutes ago. I know how important this night is to you. By the way, happy anniversary. This meal smells amazing."

"It's so sweet of you to join me," she said. She sat down to my right.

We ate and talked and laughed and reminisced. We were having a nice evening. She made it almost an hour without thinking I was her husband Wallace.

"Wallace and I used to dance. We loved Nat King Cole. His music had such passion and flair," she said. "His cover of *For Sentimental Reasons* was our wedding song." Just as she said that, a lightbulb went on for her. "Don't you have a wedding coming up soon?" She stood and went to her refrigerator. She looked at the invitation we had sent her. "Oh. My God; Dalen, your wedding was tonight. What are you doing here? You should be with your bride." She started to cry. "You need to leave."

"I will. But first..." I removed my cell phone from my suit coat. I searched my media player for Nat King Cole. When I found him, I tapped play on the song *For Sentimental Reasons*. I held out my hand and said, "May I have this dance?"

"It would be my pleasure." She reached for my hand, I pulled her close, and we danced for sentimental reasons.

ABOUT THE AUTHOR

I am a writer from a suburb north of Detroit. I live a little further north than the characters in The McCatty Chronicles do, but I love Detroit, all the same. You have just read Searching For Frownie Mae. I hope you enjoyed reading it as much as I enjoyed writing it.

My name is Steven R. Pawley. I live in White Lake, Michigan. I am happily married, and have been for 22 years now, to one of the most amazing women in the world. I have two daughters that are currently attending college and are pursuing their dreams of teaching.

I love music, if you couldn't tell by reading the series. Music has had an enormous impact on my life. John Mellencamp, Joan Jett, and Low Rawls are at the top of my favorites list. During the winter months, football becomes my obsession, especially my hometown Detroit Lions. I also love the Detroit Tigers, Red Wings, and the Pistons. As far as collegiate sports go, I will always say, "Go Blue!"

I write as a hobby and would love to make a career out of it. It pleases me to no end to know that you have enjoyed reading about Dalen Reese, Ian Parker, and the rest of the gang in The McCatty Chronicles. I am currently hard at work on the follow-up to Searching For Frownie Mae.

Many thanks. Take it easy,

Steven R. Pawley

Made in the USA
Monee, IL
25 February 2021